"Philander"

Chapter 1

Aye, and it seems that I have been in bonds all my life; even though my master is a kindly man who treats me as one of his own. Mr. Sullivan has been a second father to me all these years, ever since my own was killed from a fall off of our barn back in Ireland.

Sean O'Leary was our lord, the owner of the land we cropped when I was but a wee lad. He was a hard man who expected more from a tenant than he could deliver, and was never pleased with anything one would do. Father worked hard, I remember from my early years. He was up before the sun and into the fields, and remained there until well after dark. I would take his lunch to him many days and set under the fine bows of an Oak while he ate his lunch and drank the flask of water I would bring.

I was but six when he fell to his end, and I was there to see it. As most children from the farms, I helped my Father from the time I could walk, and was there to tie things to a rope he may need while working on the barn. It was O'Leary's barn.

The crops had been poor for three years and Father was in debt to Sean O'Leary for the seed, so when he died, Mother had the choice of debtor's prison or servitude. She chose servitude and that was how I found myself in bonds.

I was a sickly lad after Father passed and was having trouble keeping the chores, so O'Leary put me up for auction when I was but seven. He was a cruel man, I remember, and beat me severely on occasion.

"Philander"

Mother protested when Sean O'Leary put me up for sale, yet her protests were unheard by the jackal. I was sold at auction, although the price was a far sight smaller than O'Leary wanted.

Bret Sullivan became my master and a better man I could not have chosen for my own. He was an elderly and a kind man who had aspirations for the new land of the America's, and the means to go there. Mr. Sullivan tried his best to purchase the contract of my mother, but Sean O'Leary would not consider, for she was a handsome woman and still in her early twenties.

As most Irish are sporting men, Mr. Sullivan challenged O'Leary to a horserace, with my mother as the prize against all of his own possessions. Aye, and a grand race it was for sure now.

I remember standing on an outer deck on the second story of the Pub as I watched the race. Mr. Sullivan's Red was a streak as she passed O'Leary's Black in the straight. Mr. Sullivan had held her back through most of the race, holding close O'Leary's Black but not overexerting the beast. Three times around the course was the bet, and the Red hung in there, not allowing the Black to gain a great advantage on her. It was in the last of the final lap when Mr. Sullivan gave the horse its head and allowed her to fully stretch out. The Red leaped forward at such a burst of speed you could not imagine, making the Black seem almost if it had stopped and leaving him flat toward the finish.

Sean O'Leary was a vile and foul man and was beside himself with anger at the loss. He refused to sign over my mother's contract. He hollered obscenities at Mr. Sullivan from the Pub, stating the race was not properly conducted and that

Mr. Sullivan had cheated. I listened intently from the stairwell to the second floor, frightened for the welfare of my mother. As I had said, Sean O'Leary had beaten me many times in this last year, and would surly not hesitate to take his anger out on my mother, this I knew for certain.

Although I was frightened as I listened, my respect and admiration grew for Mr. Sullivan as he stood calmly against O'Leary, seemingly not bothered by the stream of obscenities and accusations perpetrated against him. A quiet and firm man, Bret Sullivan allowed O'Leary his say and then appealed to the patrons of the Pub who had witnessed the race. All among them attested that Mr. Sullivan had won the race fare and square, and Sean O'Leary finally had to submit to the conditions of the wager and sign over the contract to my mother.

When I heard him finally agree, I ran from the stairwell down the steps and into the Pub, grasping on to Mr. Sullivan's leg and hugging it as tightly as I could. Tears of joy wetted my cheeks as I held on tightly, my breath catching from the tears.

Sean O'Leary was seated at a table. A queer sort of a man he was. He was in his early sixty's, about five foot eight and so slender it almost hurt. His eyes were set well back in his head and he had long white lamb-chop sideburns which all but covered his cheeks.

The barman had brought out a quill and ink and O'Leary was signing over the bondservant agreement to Mr. Sullivan as I ran into the room. O'Leary cursed at me as I reached Mr. Sullivan's leg and wrapped my small arms around it, and then struck out to hit me but Mr. Sullivan stopped the blow before it reached my head.

“Sean O’Leary,” he told him, “you are a coward and a braggart and I should call you out for a duel to rid the world of your black hart.”

O’Leary was in shock at the statement. His face suddenly paled in fear, for he knew that Mr. Sullivan was a man who spoke his mind and meant what he said. His eyes were as angry coals yet it was clear to see that there was fear in him. If Bret Sullivan had been a lesser man O’Leary surly would have responded. He sat there, motionless, his eyes burning a whole through my small frame and I knew right then that he would have killed me if he could.

Mr. Sullivan reached down to the table and took the contract from in front of O’Leary, waving it in the air to dry the fresh ink. He then asked the barman to witness and to date the signature and laid a half a crown next to the contract for payment. The Patrick Tally hurried over and grasped the quill and signed the contract as witness. He picked up the money laid there for him and stood there a moment with his hands on his hips and an angry look in his face.

“I have witnessed the signing, and now I must ask you to leave. Both of you,” he said forcefully.

“I’ll not have my pub turned into a setting for a dual.”

O’Leary’s eyes cut from me to the barman and his face flushed red in anger. He was a lord and a bully and the owner of much land and property. To be expelled from the pub was far below his stature and his believed dignity.

“And is it necessary to remind you just who you are talking too, Mr. Tally?” O’Leary said angrily. “Remember your position.”

“Aye, and I remember my station Mr. O’Leary, and that is proprietor of this establishment,” Tally said, a firm and determined look on his face. “You may own the country-side around me, but you don’t own me, nor this pub. If you don’t leave now, I will call the constable and have you thrown out!”

O’Leary face reddened even more and a stream of obscenities came from his vile mouth, cursing Mr. Tally, Mr. Sullivan, the pub, and finally me. When Mr. Tally started toward him to bodily eject him from the premises, O’Leary suddenly stood up and walked to the door, cursing loudly with every step.

He stopped when at the door and turned toward Mr. Tally.

“You’ll rue the day you crossed with me Tally,” O’Leary said loudly. “I’ll stop my tenants from coming here, all of them and immediately.”

O’Leary stomped through the door and there was silence in the pub. Several of the people at the bar and at tables stood and started to leave. They were tenants of O’Leary, men working the land and with no other existence or future and knowing that they must submit to O’Leary’s furry or be ejected from their lands to see their children starve.

Mr. Tally sat down at the table and placed his head in his hands. He had signed his own doom by ejecting Sean O’Leary from the pub even though he had a perfect right too.

I stood and felt sorry for him. I knew the cruelty of the man too well and knew that he would not stop until Mr. Tally was ruined completely.

Sullivan put a hand on Tally's shoulder. "Sure and I am sorry for all of this Mr. Tally. It was not my intent to cause you any trouble now."

"Aye, and it was no trouble I was looking for. I wanted to stop the trouble before it went too far Mr. Sullivan," he responded. "What ever will I do now?"

The room then was completely empty except for three of us and the sudden silence was almost deafening. Mr. Sullivan stood still over Patrick Tally trying to think of a way to save his business, yet there was nothing that he could do. Sean O'Leary had too firm of a hand in the small shadow of a village. The people of the community would comply with his wishes, for they knew the lives of their families would be at stake if they were to defy him.

I still stood next to Mr. Sullivan, my arms wrapped tightly around his leg. He was a kindly man, a man who had heart and true feelings, and it had been nearly a year since anyone showed me they cared if I lived or died. Mr. O'Leary had kept my mother away from me, my father lay cold in a grave and I had faced the world entirely alone, which was hard for a then six year old. It was just recently that I had turned seven, and a sad birthday it was for I had been beaten again by O'Leary for not doing my chores fast enough. A sudden thought came into my mind and I spoke it without thinking;

"Mr. Sullivan sir," I said loosening my grip on his leg and looking up at him.

"Yes Philander, and what is it son?" he said kindly.

"Why don't we take Mr. Tally to the America's with us?" I stated in a boyish tone.

Again there was silence as his eyes immediately shot over to those of Patrick Tally. A slow smile started to come into his face, replacing the lines of concern.

"Of course Patrick," he said to him. "You must come to the America's with us. I will hire you on, and you will come with us. We'll need all of the good men we can muster."

"The America's?" Patrick responded in a question. "I've never considered leaving Ireland before. What will we do in this new land?"

"Aye, and it's a wonderful land indeed Patrick Tally. A land of opportunity and of freedom, where the O'Leary's of this world do not exist and are not welcome," he said beaming. "You must come with us Patrick, there's nothing left for you here, and there's a new world filled with opportunity to discover."

Patrick Tally sat in awe for a moment or two as the thought penetrated through his being. He was not an adventurous man. He was born in this very county, and had been here all of his life. The new thought was frightening to him, yet intriguing as well, and it was something he would have to try to digest in his mind and in his heart.

"And I thank you for the offer Mr. Sullivan," Tally said to him. "I will think of it and let you know in a few days."

"Yes Patrick Tally you do that. But don't be too long about it, for we leave in less than a week. I have all of my stock together and the boat is hired and our date to depart is on the 22nd," he responded.

A strange and worried look then came into Patrick's face, as if it were something he had forgotten yet was critical.

"Mr. Sullivan, you had best go and fetch Molly Sherman from out of O'Leary's grasp. He's a hard and a cruel man for sure, and I'm afraid of what he will do to her if you wait too long."

"Aye, and I must go," Mr. Sullivan said as he turned quickly forgetting that I was holding his leg. He stopped abruptly and looked down at me, a look of urgency upon him.

"Leave the lad with me," Patrick said. "It's time for his supper and I've a good stew made. When you retrieve Mrs. Sherman, bring her back here for I've plenty of empty rooms which her and the boy can stay the night."

"And it's thankful that I am to you Patrick Tally. It's a kind and sensitive man you are now," he said as he began again to walk toward the door.

I ran to the door after him. I didn't want to stay and felt like I wanted to cry, to run after him and plead with him not to leave me. As I watched Bret Sullivan mount the cart, I saw him check the load of a pistol he had tucked away there and freight came over me. Mr. Sullivan had been kind and caring to me these past few weeks, the first caring I had experienced since my fathers death a year ago. I feared for his safety and feared for that of my own, for I was a dry sponge that would soak up as much love and kindness that could be shown to me, and still have a desire for all the more.

Patrick Tally came behind me, placing a kind hand on my shoulder.

"Come now son, we'll get you a bowl of this stew and a glass of milk. Come now, he'll be all right and return with your mother soon," he said gently.

I looked up at the man, tears swelling in my eyes and my lower lip quivering for the fear of being alone again, and the fear of what might happen to Mr. Sullivan and to my mother. Patrick Tally knelt down beside me, placing his big burley arms around me, and my head against his shoulder and then stood up gently cradling me in his arms, and the dam burst loose. I had held in my emotion for an entire year. I had been afraid to cry, afraid to vent the despair and the hurt I had within, and now in the arms of this gentle man it all came like a geyser from within.

"There, there lad," he said gently as he cradled me in his arms and patted me on my back. "It's all right lad. You just let it out now, no one else is going to hurt you."

■■

Chapter 2

I huddled there in his arms a long time, the tears flowing and at times uncontrollable spasms in my breath. It's hard for a youngster to hold his emotions and I was not free with mine for the last year. I cried for the beatings, for fear over my mother and Mr. Sullivan, and for the loss of my father. The vision of his fall had never left me, and I would awake at night sometimes reliving the horror of that moment of his death.

When I look back on it now, I can truly appreciate the kindness and gentleness of Patrick Tally, for it took patients and a true heart to deal with the terror I was feeling, and with the uncontrollable tears. He patiently held me close to him, patting me on the back gently and whispering encouragement to me. This lasted for an hour and then the tears dried up as I fell into a sobbing sleep in his arms, completely drained by the burst of emotions I had expended.

It was morning and bright daylight when I awoke between two clean white sheets. I was lying on a bed I knew, but the place was strange to me and a fear came over my being. I shuddered inside as I realized that I had not seen Mr. Sullivan and my mother safely back to the pub. I started to arise from the bed when I was held back by an arm around my middle that I had not noticed until now. The weight of the arm was dainty on my small frame, and I quickly turned my head to see the sleeping face of my lovely mother lying next to me.

My heart nearly burst with joy as I saw her, and I rolled toward her, my small arms flinging around her neck as I cuddled against her. Her warmth was divine and I pressed my cheek as tightly to hers as I possibly could, feeling her soft skin and the love only a mother can give for a child.

Her eyes fluttered open and took a moment to focus on me, and then her arms were around me as well and I could feel the sweet nectar of her joyous tears as they started rolling down her cheek and onto that of my own. For the first time in months I felt complete, for I had all of my security, everyone who ever showed love or a kindness to me stripped away and thrown aside as one would toss a ruined garment.

"Aye now Philander. Sure and I thought I'd never get to hold you again my son," she said as softly to me she tenderly cuddled me.

"Oh mother," I cried as I held her tightly to me. "I was so afraid that Mr. O'Leary had hurt you. I was afraid that I would never see you again."

"There, there lad," she said tenderly, "the pain is all in the past now.

There's no scars on the future Philander and we're together again. Sure and I'll never let anyone hurt you again my son, never."

A knock came to the door then and the gentle voice of Patrick Tally.

"Mrs. Sherman, we have your breakfast ready, and Mr. Sullivan would like to talk to you and the lad."

"We'll be right down Mr. Tally, and I thank you," she responded.

I hated to hear the knock even though I was quite hungry, for I had missed my supper the night before. It was not unusual to me to be hungry this last year, for Mr. O'Leary had at times withheld my food in either an effort to train me in his ways, or for just pure meanness. At this moment, with the joyous reunion between me and my mother, all I wanted was to continue to lie next to her and to cuddle.

"Come now Philander," mother said. "Mr. Sullivan has called us and we must go."

"Yes mother," I responded and let go of the hug I had on her. "He's a fine man mother, and I'll not disappoint him."

When I had gotten from the bed, I waited for mother to get ready, for I was already dressed from the day before, and we walked down the stairs of the pub together, hand in hand.

When we reached the bottom of the stairs we were greeted by Mr. Sullivan and he walked with us to the table, and seated my mother there. Patrick was already seated and arose from his chair as my mother was seated, and then he reached over and lifted me to my own chair.

We ate in silence with only a few words passed between the adults. I was about my food for I was hungry and did not pay attention to the conversation. When we finished eating Patrick filled our cups with tea again, and we sat around the table sipping our tea and just enjoying the morning.

“Mr. Sullivan,” Patrick said. “I have made up my mind, and I shall go with you.”

“Aye Patrick, and I’m glad you have decided so,” he responded. “We’ll be leaving Castlebar day after tomorrow. Our ship will leave from Galway harbor on the 22nd, and we’ve much to do before then.”

“Day after tomorrow you say?” Patrick responded. “I’ll have to get busy my own self for sure. There’s a man over at ‘Carrick on Shannon’ that has been after my pub for some time. I’ll need to go there and close the deal with him.”

“That will take a day, for ‘Carrick on Shannon’ is forty miles,” Mr. Sullivan said. “Take my Red Patrick. She’s a fine and strong horse with an easy gate, and should save you a couple of hours on your trip.”

“I’ll leave today, and be back in the morrow,” Patrick said in response. He looked over at me and gave a wink, and I grinned back at him. Somehow, a bond had formed between Patrick Tally and me from the night before. It was a bond formed by him sharing my pain, and a bond that would last my whole life through.

“And can you spare me the lad for the journey now Mr. Sullivan?” Patrick Tally said as he continued his smile toward me.

My heart leapt at the question for I wanted to be with my mother. Yet I had never been on a journey before, and I wanted to spend some time with Patrick as well.

"And you're welcome to him if he'll be a help to you now, Patrick," Mr. Sullivan responded, and then looked over at me.

"Sure and you do as Mr. Tally tells you now Philander," he stated.

"I will sir," I responded.

"Sure and I knew you would now Philander. You're a fine strong lad, and you've never given me reason to believe otherwise," he answered, a smile on his cheeks.

Patrick stood from the table and looked over at me, "and are you going to dottily there at the table all day now lad? We've miles to go before we rest."

I stood on the deck of the Dutch ship three days later, and looked out across the water of Galway bay, excitement filling my breast. I had never before been on any kind of a boat, and the ship was magnificent to me. It had sleek lines to her, and looked fast and sturdy. The Captain was a Dutchman and the crew was from all over. There was a man in the crew, small and almost yellow of skin color, with slanted eyes and a long thin pigtail of hair that came down his back. He spoke a gibberish, or so it seemed to me, and wore strange cloths. Patrick told me that he was from China where there were millions more just like him.

I had no idea the ship would be so large, and could not know how small it actually was to the Atlantic Ocean we would soon be journeying upon.

It was two days before we would make sale, and I was anxious to be off.

“Philander”

My short journey with Patrick three days earlier had wetted my appetite for seeing things that were new and different.

It was an exciting time and I dearly loved seeing the stock Mr. Sullivan was taking to the America’s. Big Irish draft horses they were and a more handsome lot you could not find anywhere. They were mostly rich beige in color with their mane and tails and the long hair around their tremendous hooves blond. They were so large that I would barely come up past the first joint in their legs. It was amazing to me to see such stock, creatures so large and yet so gentle. I would walk among them and they would reach down with their muzzles for me to pet and talk to.

The chores Mr. Sullivan had given me were the daily care and feeding of the stock, and not alone. He would help me out with their care, and he had other servants in his employ assigned to the stock as well.

Mother had her duties. She was to act as cook for Mr. Sullivan’s party and it would be no easy chore on the ship, but she was grateful for being here and out of the evil clutches of Sean O’Leary. In all, Mr. Sullivan had purchased the contracts of twelve bondservants, and had included two men who he had hired, including Patrick.

It took us only a day to reach Galway, a small hamlet next to the bay yet an important stop for the passing ships. Mr. Sullivan had hired the whole ship at a great cost to him. He wanted plenty of room for his stock, wanting to keep them healthy on their journey to the new land. Mr. Sullivan had also purchased a great deal of supplies, not knowing just what we would face when we arrived, and making sure it would be no great hardship for us to be fed.

There was much work to be done in these next two days. The stalls for the stock had to be made before we could board them and the loading and securing of the supplies. We all worked hard this day preparing the craft for the journey, and I did my part and then some. It was only after supper that I had the time to stand here on the deck of the craft and look across the water at the setting sun.

Aye, and I loved the smell of the sea. It was a tonic to me and peaked the excitement that I was feeling and the desire to see and experience the new land. The old life was over now, Father was gone and could not be brought back to us, and mother and I felt lucky to be in bonds to such a man as Bret Sullivan. He was a quiet and gentle man who was in his early fifty's, tall and strong he was, and black Irish as was my mother.

As I stood dreaming and watching the setting sun across the water of the bay, I felt a truly gentle hand touch my shoulder and turned to see my mother had come up behind me.

"And are you going to dream your life away now Philander?" she asked with a smile. "Your supper's getting cold now."

"I was just thinking of the new land mother. And I was wondering about what strange things we would see and what we will do when we get there," I responded.

"Yes my child, and Mr. Sullivan has told me he has inherited some ground in the Virginia's. He intends to settle there and to raise these fine horses and some crops," she responded.

“Philander”

I looked back across the water and the sun was almost half down, the sky had turned a brilliant red around the sun, and the few clouds that were in the sky had turned pink and gold. It was a wonderful sight, unobstructed by hills and trees and free for all to see. I heard mother gasp at its beauty when she looked and she cuddled up close to my side, her arm hanging on my shoulder.

“Aye, and it’s a lovely sight now Philander, and a good omen to see,” she said dreamily as she looked across the water at the sky. “We’ll have good fortune now my son, of this I am sure.”

We stood there side by side and watched the sky explode into brilliant colors, the red, pink and gold against the blue, until it was nearly full dark.

“Come now Philander,” mother said. “I’ll warm your supper for you and you must get to bed. Mr. Sullivan deserves a good day’s work from you and you’ll need your rest and your nourishment.”

“Yes mother,” I said as I turned to go with her. We had moved on board the vessel and I was looking forward anxiously to sleeping on the ship. It seemed that everything was new and exciting to me, as it would be to any seven year old, and I wanted to take my fill of the new experiences that awaited.

We walked from the ship across a wide plank that had been placed there for boarding and to the fire where mother had prepared the meal. I sat as she poured me a cup of tea. A couple was setting there with their baby girl, a lovely little lass by the name of Caroline, and I played with her a moment until mother brought over a dish of cabbage stew she had prepared.

Caroline was a little over a year old, and had a constant and quick smile for all. Her parents, the Shaw's, were bondservants as well in the employ of Mr. Sullivan. The Shaw's were from the same village we were, and had been purchased from O'Leary as well. I had not known them while under O'Leary's employ, for we were separated on different area's of his estate. The Shaw's knew my father for he had helped them out a time or two with their crops before he passed.

Mr. Sullivan and the Dutch Captain came down the ramp to the fire, and Mr. Sullivan took little Caroline from her mother. Caroline seemed pleased enough to be with him, and he played with her, teasing and tickling her as she laughed.

The Captain was a young man in his early thirties. He was big and broad with long blond hair and a gold ring in his left ear. His face was broad and his nose was flat, as if it had been broken in a fight some time in the past. There was a scar that ran over his left eye and onto his cheek, yet he talked gentle enough and made good sense.

He told us we'd leave on the tide the morning after next, which would be just before daylight, and that we all must be on board. He said the currents were treacherous beyond Galway harbor, and we must catch the tide early on to pull us far enough out to see.

That night my dreams were filled with adventure and it seemed that the pain of the past was gone from me. O'Leary's evil hand would no longer box my ears and his foul breath would fall on someone else as he cursed at them. Though I felt badly for the next victim of his tyranny, I was equally glad that it would no longer be my mother or I.

I had made my bed aboard the vessel in the storage compartment on the tarpaulin atop a stack of flower sacks. It was a good choice as the flower sacks provided some comfort underneath me, and when I had eaten, mother summoned me off to bed.

I was awakened early the next morning as it was the last day of preparation and there was much to do. Mr. Sullivan and the Captain had worked out the chores and it took all day and well up into the night before they were completed. All hands aboard the schooner as well as all of those working for Mr. Sullivan had a full day of it, and it was nearly midnight before things started to settle down and I made my way to my pallet.

The horses nickered and snorted at their strange assignment, not liking being cooped up in the center stalls of the ship, and as tired as I was it took some time for me to get used to the noises and to find a rest.

▪▪▪

Chapter 3

I awoke to a soft rolling of the ship. I wanted to be awake when we left the harbor, but the late night’s work to get everything done had caused me to sleep and soundly when I did.

Hurrying to the deck I ran over to the side of the ship and looked, and all I could see was water and sky. I ran over to the other side with the same results, and then stopped to think. We were leaving the harbor, so the land would be behind us, so I ran aft to look over the rail. Again, there was nothing to be seen but water and sky. In the distance I could make out some clouds, just over the horizon.

Disappointed that I had missed the sight of my country as we left, I kicked my foot in boyish frustration and walked away from the railing, my head down and my lower lip extended. It was that moment that the strange man, the one with the slanted eyes and yellow skin came to the deck with two buckets of slop from the cooking. I watched as he walked to the rail and set one of the wooden buckets on the deck, and threw the contents of the other over the side.

Following the slop in it’s trail to the water, ‘twas then I noticed huge fishes that were swimming with the schooner. There were quite a number of them and they had bottled noses and their tails turned sideways instead of up and down as every other fish I had ever seen.

I ran to the rail to watch them as they kept in time with the ship. They would dive into the water, and then break the surface in a sleek motion as they dove from the water into the air and back again.

These fish were huge, the largest that I had ever seen in my short years. I was transfixed by them as they portrayed their comedy before me. There seemed to be no end to these fish. It seemed to me that if one were to step off of the ship they could walk across the water on the backs of them.

A long time I stood there and watched, and suddenly it struck me. I had responsibilities that I must do. The horses would be in need of water and food and I had been neglecting them completely. Their stalls would need cleaned out and fresh straw spread for them, and then there was the grooming to take care of. Sure, and I could not do much grooming, for their size and that of my own, but I could be a comfort to them. I could talk to them and pet their muzzles, which would help them to keep calm and happy.

Leaving the railing I ran to the doorway leading to their chamber and went through it. When I had reached the bottom of the stairs I saw that Mr. Sullivan had Mr. Shaw and mother with him tending to my job. Fear as an electric shock overtook me, for I remembered too well the beatings I had received from O'Leary's hand. Suddenly, I ran over and grasped the bucket of corn in Mr. Sullivan's hand by the strap.

"Please sir," I said as I pulled at the bucket. "Please sir, I will do this. I am very sorry for not being at it sooner sir, and I'll do better from now on."

"And of course you will lad," he said looking down at me with a smile.

"Sure and your doing a fine job of it now for a wee lad of your age."

I looked up into his smiling face and the fear left me. I found myself smiling back at him, tentatively at first, and then broadening across my freckled face.

Mr. Sullivan let loose of the bucket and then reached over and rubbed the hair on my head.

"Aye, and it's supposed to be good luck to rub the hair of a redhead I'm told," he said. "And good luck we'll be needing now, with the ocean voyage ahead of us and all."

We worked hard to tending the stock this day, and it was quite a job just keeping their stalls clean. I could not count the number of buckets of dung that I carried up onto the deck and threw over the side. Although I wished to stare and watch the magnificent fish that were escorting our craft in it's journey, I dared not, for there was more work to be done than I could do.

Evening came on too soon and with it a time of relaxation from the work of the day. Mr. Sullivan said it was enough done this day, and had us all assemble for our evening meal. Mother and Mrs. Shaw served the meal to us as we sat around the deck of the ship in the waning daylight. The ships crew walked around us as they performed their duties about the ship while we sat to eat.

When all had their plates before them, Mr. Sullivan led us in a prayer of thanks for the food and the safety thus far, a beautiful prayer that inspired us all and made me glad again I was in his employ.

Mother got her plate and sat down next to me on the coil of rope I was setting. We were silent while we ate, looking across the endless expanse of the ocean, and the gold in the water from the setting sun. Mr. Sullivan came to us when we were just finishing up our meal.

"Mrs. Sherman," he addressed. "And I would like to know if the lad's education has been started as yet?"

"Aye, Mr. Sullivan," she responded. "He's a bright lad and my late husband had spent many an evening teaching him his letters and his numbers. But there has been none such since his death."

"Sure, and with your permission, Mrs. Sherman, I'd like to start instructing him in reading and math then," he stated.

"And I'd sure be thankful to you sir if you would sir. I'm not much in these area's myself, and a very little I could teach him indeed now."

"Fine then, it's agreed," Mr. Sullivan said happily. "We'll get him started without further delay then."

"Philander, you will report to my cabin after supper, and each night after supper thereafter," he told me. "We'll get a proper education into you lad, and it's something that will help you all of your life through."

Mr. Sullivan reached over and rubbed my hair again briskly and then turned and walked off toward the Captains cabin.

"Sure and he's a fine man now Philander," mother told me. "We're lucky to be with him. Sure and I want you to be polite to him and study hard now."

"Yes mother," I said. "I'll do the best I can."

Mother smiled at me, and then reached over and gave me a big hug. "I know you will now Philander. You're a good lad."

I smiled at her as she withdrew her hug, although I was a bit scared at having to study. Father had taught me much before he passed. We'd sit in front of the fire in our house of an evening, and he would read to me from the Bible, showing me the different letters and having me sound out words and all. Still, it had been a long time, and I was worried about how much I had forgotten

I finished eating my supper and mother took my plate from me, and then told me it was time to go see Mr. Sullivan.

I stood in the gangway of the ship, feeling the mild roll of it as I hesitated before knocking on the door of Mr. Sullivan's cabin. I was uneasy from not knowing how well I'd do, and not wanting to disappoint him. Mr. Sullivan was not just a fine man to me, he was a hero, the savior of my small family and the one who had reunited my mother to me. Sure and he deserved my best effort, and even more than that now.

Tentatively, I lifted my hand and wrapped on the door face. I heard a scraping of wood against wood as if a chair were drug across the floor heavily, and the footsteps from the other side. A moment only and the door sprung open and Mr. Sullivan's smiling face was in the doorway.

"Aye lad, and you have not forgotten," he said gladly. "Come in lad, come in."

"Yes sir," I said as I walked through the door into the small cabin.

I looked around briefly to see a small cot tucked away neatly in the corner of the room. In the center of the room there was a table and two chairs, and on the table was a Bible, a bowl full of apples, two glasses and a pitcher of water.

"Sure, and I'm glad you took me up on my offer now lad. It's something you'll never regret your whole life through now," he told me as he walked to the table. "Education, learning how to read and write and cipher will give you a better and richer life lad. You can never have too much of it, and it will help you in every aspect of your life, no matter what you decide to be."

"You'll not be in my service forever lad, and you'll need to be prepared to meet the world and to conquer it when the time is right. Now come, come here to your future lad, let us study and learn."

Encouraged by his words and fascinated by his intentness to the subject, my fears left me and I moved to the chair beside him.

"Sure and that's a fine eager lad now," he told me. "Take an apple lad, it's much easier to concentrate on the subject at hand when anticipation is set aside. Take an apple, fill your mouth with the fruit and look here at the Bible."

My mouth had been watering ever since I saw the red delicious fruit in the bowl, and I was convinced he had noticed it. I picked a ripe and red apple from the bowl and took a large bite from it and then leaned my elbows on the table and looked intently at the letters above his finger.

"And can you recognize any of these letters now lad?" he questioned.

"Yes sir," I said around the mouth full of apple, and some juice escaped my mouth and started running down my chin. I reached up with the sleeve of my shirt and ran my arm across my mouth to dry it.

"Good lad, good. And can you tell me which letters I am pointing to?"

I swallowed the half-chewed apple in my mouth and responded.

"Yes sir, there's a P, and an A, and a U and a L."

"Very good lad," he said. "And can you tell me what those letters spell when they are together in a word?"

"I think so sir. My father taught me to sound out some words."

I studied the word for a moment, my mouth sounding out each letter, and then putting them together slowly at first, and then faster and with more confidence. Finally I responded audibly, "Paul. The word is Paul sir."

Mr. Sullivan laughed loudly and then slapped his knee and reached over and rubbed the hair on my head briskly.

"Excellent lad, truly excellent," he said joyfully. "And I'm glad to see your father had spent much time with you in your study."

"You're a fine and smart lad now," he continued as he laughed loudly.

"Thank you sir," I said to him. "May we do some more sir?"

This pleased him even more, and he gave me an approving look.

"Sure, and we'll do this over and over again until you can read every word in this book lad," he responded smiling and picking an apple from the bowl. He took a big bite of it, and then pointed toward another word.

▪▪

Chapter 4

We had been at sea now for six weeks, and in all that time it had been a pleasant voyage. Oh, there was plenty of work to be done and my days were filled with the endless task of cleaning the stalls of the horses, and of their feeding and care.

The sea had lost much of its charm to me and I was anxious to be on land again, as were the horses, which were getting extremely restless and moody. Oh, they still loved the attention they were getting but were starting to get cross at times with one another and would stomp and snort.

This morning, however was different. The horses were much more tense than normal and the sea had a much more exaggerated and choppy roll to it than I had felt before. It was at times even difficult to stand, for the ship was tossing sharply, and the roll of it would pull you to one side of it and then to the other.

When I had taken my first load of manure and straw to the deck to dump over the side I was amazed to see that the waves of the sea were almost higher than the ship itself. I set down the buckets on the rolling deck of the vessel and looked in shock at the endless sea. It was beautiful, and yet frightening at the same time. I looked up into the overcast sky and noticed that much of the sails had been lowered. The wind was gusting something fierce and there was a thick spray of salt water that would rise into the wind when the bow of the ship plunged to the bottom in the valley between the waves, crashing audibly into the water.

A hand touched my shoulder and surprised me, causing me to jump when I felt it. Looking around quickly, I saw Mr. Sullivan standing beside me.

"Aye lad, sure and the good weather could not last the whole trip through now."

"And I don't want you near the railing today lad. Just clean out the stalls and pile the dung and the straw in an open space for today. Stay below deck now, and be a good lad for me," he told me with the most serious look on his face I had seen from him since I had known him.

"Yes sir," I said obediently as I started to lift the buckets.

"Sure, and I'll take that for you," he told me as he took the buckets from my hand.

"You stand fast lad, and I'll be right back."

Mr. Sullivan walked to the railing and dumped the two buckets over the side. As he did so, the ship bottomed out in one of the great waves and he was soaked from the spray of the water. He walked back to me unsteadily, blowing water from his mouth that was dripping from his hair and down his face.

"Aye, and that wave would have carried you over the side lad, and would have made shark food from you now."

He handed me the buckets and added, "And be a good lad now Philander. Go below and do as I have told you."

I nodded my head and immediately went down the stairs into the belly of the ship, with some difficulty. The ship was tossing much more exaggerated now, and the wind was a whistling sound as it went through the sails and the ropes and over the deck of the ship.

To say that I was frightened would have been an underestimate of what I really felt as the ship rocked in all four directions sharply. I was glad that Mr. Sullivan had told me to pile the dung for the day, for I didn't want to approach the side of the ship, fearing that I would be swept overboard. I put my mind and back into my work to try to forget the terrible sounds that emanated from the deck. And yet as hard as I worked, I could not drown out the creaking of the vessel, nor the constant careening from side to side and front to back.

The day drug on, even though there was aplenty of work to be done. Mr.

Shaw was there to help with the chores, or rather, for me to help him, yet it was little comfort in my young mind. I could not see how the ship could take much more of the constant punishment it had been receiving.

At noon, mother came to me with Mrs. Shaw and little Caroline with our noon meal. We all sat down in the straw that was everywhere on the floor of the vessel to eat our lunch. Mother had a worried look on her face even though she tried to cover it up with pleasant conversation and jesting.

As we ate, little Caroline played in the straw beside us, climbing up on the pile, or trying to as small children will. I had become one of her favorites over these past weeks, and I took it personally to keep an eye on her and to keep her out of danger.

I ate a little of the bread and cheese mother had brought and it seemed to sour on my stomach immediately. The constant rocking of the ship had me feeling sleepy and had caused me some dizziness. I fought it off through my work, yet now, of a sudden, from setting still on the deck; my stomach started to turn with the rolling of the ship and I felt as if the contents in it would soon spill on the deck.

Mr. Sullivan had come to join us, checking on our progress and to report on the condition of the vessel.

"Aye, and it's a fine ship. Captain Hanson has told me that it has weathered much worse storms than this, and we'll come through it well enough," he told them.

"Sure and that's a comfort to hear Mr. Sullivan," mother responded. "And

Philander, you must eat your meal and back about your business," she continued as she looked at the napkin she had laid my food on and seen there had been little of it eaten.

"I don't feel so good mother," I responded.

"Aye there lad," Mr. Shaw said. "Sure and you do look a little green around the gills now."

Mother moved quickly beside me and placed her cool hand on my brow. "And what's wrong with you now Philander?"

"My stomach mother, and I feel dizzy," I said.

Mr. Sullivan smiled, saying; "It's a fearsome thing Mrs. Sherman. The lad is seasick I'm afraid."

Mother looked relieved, although I felt no better from the news.

"Sure, and you'd best go and lay down now lad. I'll not make you do the chores this afternoon," Mr. Sullivan stated. "And Mr. Shaw, what would you have me to do now?"

Mr. Shaw looked a little shocked from his request, and then responded, "Aye, and we have most half of the stalls cleaned, and we have to feed and water them again."

"And if you'll lead the way sir," he said.

Mr. Shaw kissed his wife then reached over and picked up Caroline, tossing her high into the air before he hugged her firmly. He gave Caroline to his wife and stood with Mr. Sullivan and they were off.

"Come now Philander," mother told me, and helped me to my feet. My knees were buckling underneath me as I stood and mother helped me to my bed.

When she had me tucked in she sat beside me, softly humming a tune and petting my hair. It was a comfort to have her there with me and I closed my eyes as the room spun around me. I thought of all the times I had needed my mother like this over the last year. It was hard loosing father as I had, and witnessing his death and all, and it angered me that O'Leary had kept her from me when I needed her most of all.

Something else that bothered me was that I was having trouble remembering father's face. Oh, it may seem silly, but to me it was devastating. I had the constant picture of his fall in my mind and of his broken body afterward, but I just could not picture his face anymore.

I remembered vividly the events of that day. O'Leary had come to our cottage the night before beside himself with anger. It seems that a leak had developed in one of his barns and had ruined some of his stores, and he demanded that father fix the roof the following day. Father had told O'Leary that it was the wrong time to repair the roof because of the storm that was upon us, but O'Leary reminded father that he was indebted to him and that he had no choice.

The morning we went to the barn was cold, bitterly cold and the wind was whipping from the north. There was rain falling, sometimes just a little, and then the bottom would fall out and it would come in torrents.

We had been there only a few minutes when a strong gust of wind hit my father as he was standing on the wet roof in a torrent of rain. The roof being slick as it was, there was no place for father to grab and he slid to the side of the roof and then over the edge.

I could still picture his eyes as he fell, but not his face.

When he fell I ran for help as fast as my legs would move but when we returned, there was no hope for father, for he had expired when he hit the ground.

"There, there Philander," mother told me gently as she continued to pet my hair. "Close your eyes and get some rest. You're my strong, brave lad now. Sure and I'm proud of you, son. Your father would be proud to see how hard you work and how attentive you are to your tasks. Get some rest laddy, for a new day is on the horizon and a new experience to be had."

Mother continued to set next to me, petting my hair and humming a tune to me as the storm worsened and the ship was tossed on the angered seas. I closed my eyes and enjoyed her attention and when they opened again, it was the morning of the next day, well into the morning.

I hurried to dress and to get to my responsibilities. It was well past time for breakfast and I knew not to take the time to try to eat. One thing that I had learned while under Mr. O'Leary's charge was not to be late, nor to neglect your chores. I had neglected my duties the previous afternoon and was late to them this morning, and the old fear came over me that I'd felt time and again while under O'Leary.

When I reached the stalls, Mr. Sullivan was there and working with Mr. Shaw. Stark fear arose in my breast as I just knew I was in trouble, and I ran and grabbed the shovel away from Mr. Sullivan and hurriedly began to clean the stall he was working.

"Aye now lad, slow down now" he said as he placed his hand on my shoulder. "I've been expecting to much from you, and for that I apologize."

"Apologize, sir?" I responded as I stopped my hurried effort to escape the beating I had expected to receive at his hand.

"Aye lad, apologize it is," he responded looking into my small and bewildered eyes.

"You've taken on a man's share lad, and you've held up to it for all these weeks now. Sure and I should be beaten myself for placing it on you. And I'll not place such a pressure on you again now lad."

"But sir, I want to work," I responded in a confused expression.

Mr. Sullivan was taken aback by my response, and for a moment just looked at me, and then broke into a broad smile, then a laugh.

"And did you hear that Mr. Shaw," he said through his laugh. "This lad here is more of a man then any who ride aboard this ship now. Go lad. Go and get some breakfast and the work will still be here when you return. There's plenty to do, and the beasts with which we work add more to it by the minute," he said as he took the shovel from my hand.

I released the shovel tentatively at first, and then realized that I was not in trouble for my sloth and there would be no beatings. Confused, a moment I looked into his gentle gray eyes and then I turned and ran toward where my mother's station would be.

There was still quite a roll to the ship but much less than the day before. I ran to the makeshift kitchen Mr. Sullivan had prepared for the trip, and there was my mother, looking lovely as ever, as I ran to her and placed my arms around her middle.

"And there's my strong lad," she said to me. "Set down to the table and a bowl of porridge will be yours soon enough."

Setting at the table during the rolling of the ship turned into a challenge, and it took me a moment to mount the chair. My legs were not long enough to reach the floor and brace myself, and so I slid from side to side on the chair with each roll of the waves.

"Mother," I said enquiringly as a child would.

"Yes Philander," she said as she turned from the stove, a steaming bowl of porridge in her hand.

"Mr. Sullivan's a kind man, isn't he mother?"

"Sure and he is that," she said. "And a thoughtful man who can not stand the sufferings of others now."

Her answer seemed to satisfy me. Either that or I was so hungry that I suspended further conversation to eat from the steaming bowl she had set before me.

Chapter 5

The days seemed to run together after that for the sea calmed and the winds died down and we settled into our work. Mr. Sullivan was beginning to worry, for the feed stores he had brought on board for the stock were dwindling quickly. He cautioned Mr. Shaw and me to waist nothing for he felt we would need everything we had to complete the journey.

"Philander"

These were hot and sullen days, and all of us reddened and then browned from the constant reflection from the sun on the waters. It was nearly three weeks that there was little wind, and our ship was carried aimlessly by the currents of the sea.

One evening after my studies, I overheard Mr. Sullivan, the Captain and Mr. Lindquist discussing the dilemma. Our ship had been carried much farther south than expected, and they were concerned for the welfare of the ship and it's cargo, should the wind not rise to fill the sails.

Mr. Lindquist was a merchant, a trader, and had hired a small portion of the ship to carry his cargo of goods to trade with the Indians and those colonists living in the America's. He had told me once that there was great wealth available by trading merchandise to the Indians, for valuables such as fur skins and even gold. He also said it was a dangerous business, for there were Pirates sailing off the coasts just waiting for ships loaded down with treasures from the new land.

It was a wonderful thought for my youthful mind, a thought of adventure, of challenge and of heroism, and I played different scenes of battles with the pirates and trading with the Indians over and over again in my mind's eye.

It was just short of four weeks that I arose one morning to excitement on the deck. I ran up the stairwell to see what was going on, and felt a lovely cooling breeze hit me as I entered the ship's deck. Aye, and it was something to see. The crewmen were running around, their sullen faces lit-up with excitement as they worked to get canvas in the wind and as the ship lurched forward at a lofty speed.

There was once again hope on the ship, for the crew began to laugh and to sing to themselves once more. Excitement seemed to build and to climax on everyone on board as their hopes arose that we would soon be on shore.

It was a grand day, and we worked with a renewed hope and strength as the day quickly passed. That evening after supper, as had become our ritual over these past three months, I went to Mr. Sullivan's room for my lessons. He greeted me with a smile on his lips as the door opened at my knock.

"Aye Philander, it's a good day we've had," he said to me. "Come in lad, come in."

When I entered the room, I noticed that the table was spread differently than before. Instead of the Bible, paper and quill, there was spread upon it a large piece of paper, one with strange markings to me and one as I had not seen before.

"Come and set down lad," he said in a jovial tone. "Come now, I've something to show you now."

When I had seated next to him, he pointed to the paper on the table. "And do you know what this is now Philander?"

"No sir" I responded.

"Sure, and this is a map lad. A map of the new lands we are approaching, and of our new home."

I studied the paper yet as hard as I tried I could make little out of the symbols and marks it contained. I had come a long way with my reading and Mr. Sullivan told that my reading skills were greater than most full-grown men and that I had a natural gift for mathematics, which pleased my mother greatly.

He went on and on as he pointed to one symbol and then another, discussing the land and how it was lain. For hours he went on and by the time he was through, I understood every symbol, but could put it to no practical use. Unless you've seen land associated with a map, it's hard to see it. What I knew was little but what he told me and that was little indeed.

He pointed out the savannas that we must cross after we port the ship in a place he called Cherry Point. We would travel for weeks upon them until we reached the mountains, and then cross them to the flats on the other side. The town we would settle in was in Virginia, he told me. Abingdon is one of the earlier and oldest colonies in the new land. The property he inherited was half in Tennessee and half in Virginia and near Abingdon and Johnson city.

Mr. Sullivan had an uncle that left Ireland over thirty years before and settled this land. He had been successful in his ventures, a man who had started off as a trader before settling. He had become a man of property and of wealth, saving his hard-earned money and thriftily utilization of his assets, until his death a year earlier.

An attorney from Boston contacted Mr. Sullivan with the news and included a draft for the money he had inherited almost six months ago. The Sullivan clan, although a proud group, had never had wealth for they were sharecroppers as were my own family.

He told me of his earlier years, and of how he served in the British Military in an attempt to change his fate. Recognition was hard to gain and royal influence impossible for one of his background, so when his enlistment was up he resigned himself to a life of working for the other man. Years had past yet his dreams never faltered, and when the news of his uncle's demise came with the draft for the fortune, he eagerly grasped the chance to move to the new land.

Bret Sullivan was a tender man, a man of sensitivity and of wisdom. His dream had always been to raise the big Irish draft horses and yet his whole life's work would not even allow the purchase of one of the animals. His first action after receiving the inheritance was to purchase the heard now upon this ship, and his second was to hire those he would need to help him in his endeavor. He found out quickly that hiring those to come with him was not possible, and so, he started looking for bondservants such as my mother and myself to purchase their contracts and to take along with him.

This explained his tender compassion toward those under his servitude, for he was not a man borne to position. He was however, a man who could have been on the other side of the contract with just one more failed crop.

This answered the questions that were in my own mind, even at the young age I was. I remembered father telling me about how men came by their sir-names; how that King James of England in 1600 had ordered every man to adopt their sir-names, either as the province in which they were living, or by the trade they practiced. He ordered that lords were to place an O' in front of their names, and that nobles were to place a Mc in front of theirs, thus they would be recognized by their stature. Father told me that it was all by birth, the only way to change ones stature in the land would be to be recognized for a noble or brave work by the royalty, and be given property along with the title of sir. I had wondered how Mr. Sullivan had come to his position with none of the titles which father had told me of.

That night my mind was filled with the visions of the new land we were about to see. I had heard them talk of the Indians, and the thought of these natives frightened me, yet intrigued me as well. I wanted to see some of them, to see the primitive way that they lived.

Every time I closed my eyes in my bed this night, I could picture the land as he described it. His property was bordered by a large lake to the east, I think he called the name of it Holston Lake.

I don't remember when I finally went to sleep, but I certainly remember awakening the next morning. I awoke to loud voices, many of them coming from the deck above me. The voices were distressed it seemed, and there were commands given sharply.

I stumbled out of my bed and pulled on my pants as I climbed the stairs to the main deck. When I reached the deck, men were running everywhere, the Captain and the first mate were hollering out instructions to the men loudly. I looked around to see what the excitement was about and could not discern it. The sky was a rich blue without a storm cloud to be seen. The sails were filled with a good wind and as I looked over the side of the ship, all that I could see was water, no land in sight.

Bewildered, I stood there in a boyish fashion and watched as the men moved quickly from one task to another. The man in the crows nest at the top of the main sail I noticed was pointing off to our starboard and calling something down to the captain when I felt a gentle hand touch my small shoulder.

"Philander"

"And you will go below now Philander," mothers soft voice told me. "You've work to do and you must not bother the crew now."

"Aye mother," I responded as I turned and looked at her worried face. "And what is happening?"

"They've spotted a ship just off the horizon there. They're fearful it may be of pirates now. We must not bother the crew Philander. Go below and tend to your watering and feeding of the stock. I will help you this morning now, for Mr. Sullivan, Mr. Shaw and the others have been compelled to the deck to help out."

"Yes mother," I said in disappointment. I wanted to be on deck to watch as the drama unfolded before us and to help out if I could, yet being a small lad, I knew I would just be in the way.

As I turned to leave, I noticed two crewmembers at the bow of the ship removing a tarp from something I had been curious about ever since I boarded. I stopped to watch for a moment and as the tarp was removed, there appeared a cannon. It was a small weapon, but nonetheless a weapon of war. My boyish enthusiasm compelled me to stare in wonder at the weapon and desire to touch it, but mother had spoken, and I watched for just a few seconds before I went below to tend to my chores.

Nervous excitement filled my breast as I worked at watering and feeding the horses below. I dearly wanted to be up on the deck and see what was happening, but I knew I would just be in the way, and we were facing a possible desperate situation.

After the horses were fed and watered hurriedly, I crept back up the stairwell, just high enough so that I could see what was taking place. Standing with my back to the wall so as not to be noticed, I watched as the crew worked. I wanted to be up there, to see what was happening, but knew I had best be content with this much.

As I watched, I noticed that the Captain had moved in front of the opening of the stairwell just a few feet away from me. The first mate came to him a minute later.

"She's a pirate ship indeed Captain," he told him.

"Yes, and a speedy craft they have. They've picked up a lot of distance on us since we saw her," the Captain responded. "It's clear we can not outrun her, we'll just have to pray for a miracle."

I could see the worried look on his face as he turned to speak to the first mate, and for the first time, I realized that we might be in danger. A panic ran through my body as the realization struck me.

I continued to watch for a few more moments, and then from the crows nest came the call.

"Land ho, Captain. Land ho off the port bow."

Eagerly, the Captain ran toward the bow of the ship and looked off into the horizon. He turned and walked briskly to the aft of the ship and out of my view.

The crew seemed excited by the news and worked even more feverishly as the Captain and the first mate shouted their commands. I could see Mr. Sullivan and Mr. Shaw working feverishly with the rest of the crew, and I eased a little closer to the opening of the stairwell so I could get a better view. It was at that moment that the Captain resumed his position in front of the stairwell, standing not more than four feet from me.

Mr. Sullivan came to stand beside him, and it was easy to overhear their conversation.

"Is there hope Captain?"

"Aye, Mr. Sullivan, aye indeed. That's the Barrier Island yonder of Pimlico Sound, if we can make it inside the sound around Cape Lookout, we'll escape their evil grasp, I'm sure. It will be close Mr. Sullivan. Aye, very close indeed."

It was then that Mr. Sullivan spotted me from the corner of his eye. He smiled, a knowing and understanding smile, and held out his hand for me.

"Philander, lad," he said to me. "Come here to me now."

I slowly stood from my position in the stairwell, guilt flooding me. I took the steps tentatively as I walked to him, knowing I had disobeyed and was looking for his chastisement. Bravely I fought back tears, which filled my eyes as I stepped beside of him.

"What's this Mr. Sullivan?" the Captain said. "Send him below, I'll not have him on deck and interfering with the crew, we have enough to worry about this day."

The Captains face was stern as he spoke to Mr. Sullivan.

"Aye, and he's a good lad Captain. He just wants to see what's going on up here, and I'll take responsibility for him."

"Aye, and I'll be there to help him," said a voice that came from behind me. I turned to look and saw Patrick Talley standing there. "I've been watching the lad for the last ten minutes as he stood in the stairwell, and he means no trouble Captain."

He looked at me with his stern eyes for a moment silently before he again spoke.

"All right, he can stay, but he's in your charge Mr. Sullivan. If he gets hurt it'll be on you, and the first time he gets in the way, I'll tie him up and have him thrown in the locker and you with him. Is that clear Mr. Sullivan?"

"Aye, and it's clear enough Captain," Mr. Sullivan said. "He'll be safe and out of the way with me now."

Bret Sullivan reached a hand over on my shoulder, which encouraged me as he gently patted it.

"Come now Philander, we'll go up top with Patrick and see better what's happening now."

"Yes sir, thank you sir," I said to him. "I'll be no trouble to you now, no trouble at all."

He smiled at me and guided me to the steps that lead up to the deck above the cabin on the stern of the ship. Patrick sat on the deck, his legs hanging over the side of the cabin when we got up top. I had never been up here before and was surprised at the view that one could see from this height.

I looked around and could see the ship approaching from the aft. It was still a goodly distance away, but seemed to be traveling faster than our vessel.

"Cape ho, Captain," came a loud voice from above us. "Cape ho, three points to starboard sir."

"Helmsman," the Captain ordered. "Three points to starboard now, look alive man."

"Aye, aye Captain," the helmsman answered.

I turned and looked toward the bow and just a little to the starboard, and there in the distance was a break in the long Barrier Island. As I looked intently, there was a loud splash in the water behind me that was followed by a thunderous sound, and I jumped at it.

"They're firing on us Captain," the helmsman shouted.

"Aye, and I can see that helmsman, I'm not deaf," he retorted loudly. "Just steer the boat now and let me worry about the putrid scum aft I say."

I turned to look at the craft behind us, and as I did, I could see smoke billow from it's bow, a narrow white puff that came in a sudden stream ahead of the ship. Then I saw the water erupt in a huge splash some hundred yards behind us, and then the thunder from the cannon at their bow.

I put my arm around Mr. Sullivan's leg and stepped closer to him when the sound came to my ears.

"And it'll be all right now lad," he said. "They're just testing for range now. We've a good chance of getting away, for the opening to the Cape is not far."

I watched as time and time again the scene repeated itself. The white puff of smoke followed by a splash and then the sound of thunder as the ship came nearer and nearer to us. Each time the cannon fired, the shell landed in the water, yet each time it was closer to our ship.

The channel to the cape came into our view, and it was close. At the speed we were traveling we would make it in about ten minutes I thought. Mr. Sullivan had his hand on my head and would rub it gently from time to time as we helplessly attempted to beat the pirate vessel to the gap between the two Islands.

It was then that a shell landed parallel to the center of the ship, wide to the port and harmlessly in the water. The splash sent out a spray that wetted some of the crewmembers on that side of the ship, and then there was the shock that they had gained range upon us.

"Look alive now" the Captain shouted to the crew. "She'll turn to broadside us with her big guns if I don't miss my bet. First mate, stand ready to drop sail on my command."

"Aye Captain" the first mate responded, and then proceeded to issue his own commands to the crewmembers as they frantically worked. Some of the crew started climbing the masts to the sails, and I watched them with boyish interest.

"Why will we drop sail Mr. Sullivan?" I asked. "Won't that slow our speed?"

"Aye, and that's a bright lad you are now. Sure and we've too much sail on to maneuver the channel lad, we'll have to slow the ship to stay off the rocks and the sandbars."

"Ho Captain," the shout came from the crow's nest. "She's coming around, She's coming around."

I looked back at the ship and was surprised to see how close it had come to us. It had started a sudden turn to the starboard, which would in a few seconds bring her broadside guns to bare upon us.

"Mr. Sullivan" I cried out. "Look!"

He turned to look and Patrick stood from his seated position as the ship came into baring range. It was at that moment that their cannons blossomed into a show of fire and smoke. Eight of them in all, and the sound reached us before the cannon balls this time, a deafening sound, sharp and thunderous.

All but two of the shells landed in the water, some to starboard and some to port. One of the shells hit our mainsail high up toward the top where the crow's nest set, and broke it in two.

There was a blood-curdling scream from the crewman in the crow's nest as the section in which he sat started to fall, throwing him from the nest to fly into the air between the ship and the water to our port.

The last shell from the volley hit the ship solidly toward our bow on the starboard side, with such a force that it knocked us from our feet and sent us sprawling to the deck. The shell that hit was well above waterline, and although it was a solid hit, it was not a fatal hit for the ship. The sound of the shell as it tore through the ship is something that I can never forget. It was the sound of splintering wood mixed with the screams of the crew and of a woman.

Seeing that their last desperate effort to stop us with the broadside had failed, the pirate ship broke off, for we had entered the channel now, and the safety of Pimlico sound lay but a few feet away.

"Damage report Mr. Smith," the Captain shouted to the first mate. "I want a damage report on the double now."

"Aye Captain," he answered and disappeared through a hatch forward as he waived to a couple of the crewmembers to follow.

The Captain ordered some sail in and joined us on the upper deck. A man was forward by the bow, a rope with a wait on the end, and threw it off of the bow and then retrieved it.

"Mark fourteen sir," he shouted back to the Captain as he took over the weal from the helmsman.

Another man was stationed at the bow, just center of the ship.

"Rocks eight points off port sir," he called.

"Mark eleven sir," the other man reported.

I looked up questioningly to Mr. Sullivan and before I had a chance to ask, Patrick answered for him.

"Aye, and the men are reporting the conditions of the water forward to the Captain to steer us safely through the channel now Philander. The one with the rope is reporting the depth of the water, while the other lookout is reporting obstacles that we could hit now," he told me.

The first mate had appeared through the stairwell before us, the one I had been hiding in earlier. His face was white as he turned to mount the stairs to the upper deck and he looked at me and then averted his eyes almost immediately, a sickened look on his hard and weathered face. He continued to the Captain who was but ten feet or so behind us at the wheel.

"Damage report Mr. Smith," the Captain commanded.

"Aye sir, we've a whole in our starboard bow, well above water. We've lost our top sail from our mainsail sir."

"Aye, and that of our crew?" he asked.

"One man lost sir, two men injured, one seriously, two crewmen and one of the women from Mr. Sullivan's party killed sir."

I heard the words but they did not register with me when they were spoken. The one man lost must have been the poor devil in the crows' nest I was thinking, and than Mr. Sullivan's hand was upon my shoulder firmly. The words had registered with him, and he knew that our makeshift kitchen had been forward, and realized it was probably my mother that had been taken from us through death.

▪▪▪

Chapter 6

We buried my mother in New Bern where we landed instead of Cherry Point. New Bern was a small settlement much farther up the inlet than Cherry Point off of the Pimlico sound.

As I stood over her grave, the story of Mosses came to my mind. He had led the children of Israel from their servitude in Egypt, through the deserts and a forty year march only to see the Promised Land from a distance, and was not allowed to enter.

Mother was like that, for she had seen the Promised Land and had desired to be there, yet was denied access to this haven for the refuge's of the world, the America's.

I stood over her grave a long time after the services. The Captain had conducted them, and a good job he had done as well. My eyes were filled with tears for my mother and a little for myself too. I was truly alone now, no family that I could claim as my own. Father was gone for a year and a half now, and mother had joined him in their rest in the Lord.

It wasn't fair, I thought. So many are able to keep their parents so long, even into their old age, and yet never desire to be with them, to draw from their strength and their love. I however had needed my parents. I had admiration and respect for them both. Strong people they were, and loving toward each other and toward me. Why had this happened? Why was mother torn from my arms and my life after so shortly ago being reunited with me? How could I make it on my own?

I lay down on the soft warm earthen mound that now covered her and sought comfort, yet none came as the tears swelled from my small eyes. It's hard to face death at any age, but a youngster as I made it even more tragic.

For hours I lay there with no comfort being given, and I finally fell asleep in the midst of my tears and grieving. I never knew when it was that Mr. Sullivan came back to the grave plot. I never felt him take me in his arms and carry me into the comfort of a bed. I never heard his consoling remarks, nor did I see the tears in his own eyes, yet years later Patrick told me of what happened.

When I awoke from my long and grief filled sleep, we were far away from New Bern and entering a settlement known as Washington. It too was small as settlements go, yet it would not have mattered to me if it were the city of Boston or New York. My grief had eaten me up. I could find no happiness, no place of peace and my life had become a desperate existence without my parents.

Aye, and even this land, the land that I had so desired to see and experience held nothing for me now, for I was truly alone and unloved in this cold and dark world. I was frightened over my future, and I wanted things back the way they were. The way it had been before the famine back home and the failed crops. Oh, we were in no wise rich. We had little as compared to others, but what we had was real. The work had been brutally hard, and long days of work had beset us, but our evenings beside the fire and after our evening meals were filled with love, of acceptance and contentment.

Mother would always do something special. We could afford little, yet she always found a way to provide some special surprising treat as father taught me from the Bible next to the fire.

This feeling lasted for days and I was reclusive from the others. My work went undone or was conducted by others. Every time Patrick, Mr. Shaw or Mr. Sullivan attempted to talk to me I shut them out. I would turn my head stubbornly and not allow them into my thoughts and memories. I rode in the cart, not eating when food was presented to me and completely closing everyone out, even little Caroline as she would chatter and try to play with me.

This lasted for most of a week. I overheard Patrick and Bret Sullivan talking one evening of how worried they were about me, yet the words did not register in my mind.

One evening after a long day of travel through the savanna's and swamps, we made a camp. All were about their business and occupied by their task at hand, when I saw little Caroline playing next to the water of the camp. She had a pinecone she had picked from the ground and was tossing it as one would a ball. On one of her tosses, the pinecone rolled into the water and I saw her start after it. The current of the stream grasped the cone and pulled it farther into the water. With a lung I came from my pallet on the back of the cart as I saw her reach over the water for the cone, and fall head first into the stream.

Diving into the water, I laid hold of her and pulled her into my arms. The shock of the cold water had frightened her, for she was far too young to know the danger, and she started balling loudly. The water here was only about waist deep to me, but I knew we were both still in grave danger, for I was a small framed boy and the current here was strong.

"Mr. Sullivan, Patrick, Mr. Shaw! Someone help us, please" I shouted as loudly as I could.

Mr. Shaw was the first to the bank. He came from the darkness at a run and didn't slow down as he reached the waters edge. His lunge sent a spray of water as he ran in to retrieve us. He grasped me around the middle and wrapped his other arm around Caroline who was in my arms, and lifted us from the water and on to the bank he strode.

"Say, and how did you two get in such a mess now Philander?" he asked as he sat me down on my feet on the bank.

"Caroline fell into the stream," I said, "and there wasn't time to call for help sir."

He looked down at little Caroline who was still sobbing in his arms. She was soaked through and through, her long dark hair matted against the sides of her face.

"Aye lad, and it's indebted to you that I am then," Brody Shaw said. "You'll never be in need as long as I'm alive now Philander, you've saved my little lass now."

The others had come up around us and had heard the conversation. Mrs. Shaw came to me and hugged me thoroughly.

"Aye, and that's my thought too Philander, you're a brave lad now. Come, let's get some dry clothing on you two before you catch your death."

From that moment on I knew I still had a purpose in life. Oh, I still missed mother. I still had an empty whole in my breast that would never be filled, and a lonesomeness that would stay with me, but I had a purpose.

The next morning I reported to Mr. Sullivan after eating a hearty breakfast.

"And what will you have me to do then Mr. Sullivan?" I asked.

"Aye lad, you'll help with the stock now," he said smiling at me. "And mind that we lose none of them now lad, for they are our future."

Slowly, the country started to gain my interest. It was so different from my native Ireland in just about every way. The first thing that I learned was about snakes, for there are none that are poisonous in my homeland, and yet in this new land, there were a variety of vipers that could kill with a single bite.

My first experience was with a huge rattlesnake that Patrick Talley had come across and killed. It's body was twice around the size of my arm, and it had a rattle section that was over two inches long. None of us new much about the viper, yet all knew it was dangerous and sure death to be bitten by it. We studied the viper intently, learning its features and the patterns on its back. One of the things that amazed me was that the patterns blended in perfectly with the droppings of the scrub pines in the area we were traveling. It would have been too easy to miss the viper for what it is, and think it was a fallen branch, unless it sounded off.

Patrick cut off the rattle section from the vermin before he buried it, and when it was dried, he gave it to Mr. Shaw as a toy for Caroline.

We traveled slowly day after day. Brett Sullivan had us move from early morning until just after noon each day. A wise man, he did not wish to stress the stock, even though they could have handled much more than they were given, and he wanted the time for us to learn the land.

I walked with him almost every afternoon, sometimes miles from our camp, exploring the country and learning from him. One thing we learned quickly is that this land was diverse and full of surprises. There was much game to be had, and no lords around to have you imprisoned for poaching either. There were an abundance of dear, bear, ducks and geese, and one day we came upon an awesome beast, like a huge cow except covered with thick long fur, especially around it's neck and front forelegs area of it's body. Mr. Sullivan told me that this must be the Buffalo that he had heard so much about. He said that they were plentiful over the distant mountains, or so he had been told, but were getting rare on this side of them.

I could imagine why, for there would be enough meat on one of these beasts to last a family a month or more. They would be prized by the settlers, and hunted constantly for their stores. Their hide would also be useful as a mattress for their pallets, I thought, and would be warm on a cold night.

It was on our forth outing that Brett Sullivan brought a rifle with him, and told me that we would do some hunting while we were on our adventure. That night, we ate venison. Thick slices from the haunch that was roasted over the fire, and we all enjoyed the meat after such a long time at sea.

Little Caroline had become the community child. She was as content with one of us as another, but preferred me it seemed. We played together of the evenings and before my studies began with Brett Sullivan. I surely missed being able to be with my real family, yet these had all become a second family to me, and I dare say if I would have made it without their constant support and affection.

Mr. Sullivan had become a father figure to me, and I admired and respected him with all of my heart. Patrick Tally was more like a rogue uncle, the kind that you admired and had fun around, and yet knew he could lead you into trouble. Mr. and Mrs. Shaw were the homogenizing members of the family. Their deeply seated love for each other and for the rest of us was the catalyst that bound us together as a family unit. Always gentle, always supportive and loving they were, and their happiness spread amongst us as a fever would spread through a community.

There were times, especially at night, when I would have despair set on me. Sometimes I would wake up scared and alone, trembling and crying in my bed. It had been an awful lot for a wee lad to go through. Witnessing the death of my own father, then the year of servitude and beatings at O'Leary's hand, and then the tragic loss of mother at the hands of pirates. Mrs. Shaw would always be there to comfort me and to cuddle me up until it passed.

The year my father passed was 1820, and now it was just one year later, and I had lost both of them. In the seven years of my life, I had experienced love and acceptance from my family, bitter cruelty, slavery, hunger, cold, and physical beatings at the hands of Mr. O'Leary, and abstract grief at the loss of both of my parents. I would rather have stayed in the service of Mr. O'Leary than to have lost my mother, for those were easier burdens to bare.

▪▪▪

Chapter 7

Aye, and that was all many years ago now. It is now 1835, and tomorrow on my twenty-first birthday, I will have my freedom. As I said earlier, it seems though I have been in bonds all of my life long, and sure it has been mostly so.

I've grown tall, strong and healthy under the gentle watch care of Bret Sullivan and the Shaw's. Patrick Talley left us many years back under the paws of a bear. He had been out hunting and had made a kill. It was a big buck and while he was dressing it, a she bear decided that the kill was her own, and challenged Patrick for it. Patrick got lead into the bear, but not enough, for the bear attacked and he was left with but a knife to fend her off. Aye, and fend her off he did indeed, for he killed the bear, but suffered mortal wounds himself in the process.

The land that we came to could not have been better, and Mr. Sullivan's heard has grown fat and rich on the good grass. After we had settled, a traveler came through and admired the stock greatly. Lem Malone was a breeder of mules, and was taken with the notion of breeding our Irish Draft's with a donkey stud to make mules for the building of the Eire Canal. Mr. Sullivan hired the man, and we started to breed the strongest and largest mule stock that one could imagine. It took two years to build a heard of the beasts, and when they were ready, Mr. Sullivan took them up north and sold them to make his fortune.

Aye, and lovely animals they are too. Lem has taken me under wing and has taught me the techniques to breed the stock rightly.

I have watched Caroline Shaw grow and blossom into womanhood. She is still young, only just fifteen now, but a fine and a lovely lass she is. We have always been close, ever since my mother died so many years ago, and we have grown closer as the years have past. I have pledged my love toward Caroline, and she her troth to me.

Tomorrow, on my twenty-first birthday, I shall have my freedom. The debt my father left will be paid, and I shall be a free man. I have thought long about this freedom, for I am a man with nothing. I have no family, no home to go to, no possessions and no money. All that I posses is here with Mr. Sullivan, the only home that I have known for these past fourteen years.

Tonight I shall talk to Mr. Sullivan. I shall ask for a job and wish my pay to be in stock. Aye, I have thought it through thoroughly, and that is what to do. There are open lands out to the West and to the South. Lands that are not settled, lands that are crying out for one to work with the promise of a good living and happiness. I've my heart set toward this. I shall ask for a dozen breading mares and a stud, and a donkey stud as well, for I have learned a trade, and learned it well indeed.

Mr. Sullivan has taught me well. My education, although not a formal one, is better than most in the new land. I have been an avid reader, for Mr. Sullivan instilled a love of literature in me early and has kept a good library all of these years. My favorite book has always been the Bible and I have been teaching classes and holding devotions at the Methodist Church in Abingdon for some years.

Aye, and September is beautiful here with the change of seasons and the added color to the hardwood leaves. It was coming of evening and I had spent the day of it cutting hay in a field for the stock to winter on. I stopped to sharpen my blade and while sharpening, witnessed a brilliant sunset to the west. There were a few clouds in the sky, billowing high in the west, and the sun was working her magic on them turning parts of them gold, and parts pink changing to red against the bright blue background of the sky. Lem was working with me in the field, and we had cut a good thirty acres this day. He came over to where I stood, my rock moving against the blade of the sickle and my eyes and mind upon the majestic beauty of God's creation.

"And is it that you've had enough of work this day now Phil?" he asked in his usual cynical tone. "We've still an hour of light left."

"Aye now Lem. I just had to look at the sunset but a moment Lem. Look at all of those wonderful colors now," I responded.

He leaned against his sickle and looked off into the west with me. "Aye, and it is lovely. I miss my home in Ireland now Phil, but this country is something special, very special indeed."

"Lem," I said almost dreamily. "Have you ever wondered, that if the sky is so beautiful from this side, how much more beautiful it will be from the other? I can't help but dream at times about God's creation, and have a longing to see it all and to experience it all as well."

"Aye Phil, we've all felt that way a time or two. That's how I wound up in this land you know. I had a natural curiosity to see what I haven't, and to taste and smell those things I have never seen. And it's a happier man that I am for it now, Phil, for I've left the home of my birth and traveled across the sea's and into lands far away."

"Aye," I said. "Aye indeed."

We stood still, feeling the moment and looking at the sky, a simple quietness between us. When I looked at the blade it was sharp and ready, and I went to work again, as did Lem.

"And what are you going to do after tomorrow now Phil?" Lem asked. "Are you going to taste and smell the new lands? Maybe travel to the west now and chase that setting sun?"

I was working on the grass with long and powerful strokes against the grass. "No Lem," I responded. "I've a plan for my life. A dream that I will see through now."

"Aye", he said. "Follow your dream now Phil. Follow your heart to the majestic places that you've dreamed of."

He stopped his broad swing with the sickle for a moment. "And what is this dream that you have now Phil?"

"Aye, and it's my dream Lem. You're a good friend, but I'll share it with only one other now," I responded.

"And I know who'll that be for sure Phil," he said with a chuckle. "Caroline is a lucky girl that you love her so now."

My face flushed red as he said this. Surely I do love Caroline, with all of my being. I have had the dream for a few years now, a dream that changes little. A dream that provides peace and happiness whenever I enter its boundaries. I guess that it is obvious to all that Caroline is the biggest part of my dream, the greatest hope in my meager life, although I have tried hard not to show my feelings to much to the others.

We worked until the sun had completely set and the first twilight had past. Darkness was besetting the land when we walked from the field toward the barns to place our sickles.

After I had put up my sickle, I went to my small cabin and washed the dust and sweet of the day and then put on some fresh clothes before going to the main house for supper.

When I stepped on the porch, Mr. Sullivan was there to greet me.

“Philander,” he said as he placed his hand on my shoulder. “And it’s hard to believe that so many years have passed now. Aye, and I remember the small timid lad that first came to my house so many years ago. You’ve grown well Philander; you’ve grown well indeed. Come in now, come in and have a birthday supper with those who love you.”

“Thank you Mr. Sullivan, and I’d like to have a word with you after supper now, if you don’t mind,” I responded.

“Absolutely Philander, you’re a free man now, and full grown as well. You‘ll address me as Bret from now on, and I’ll have no backtalk on that now,” he said as he slapped me on the shoulder.

We walked into the cottage, and a fine one it was now indeed. Patrick, Mr. Shaw, Mr. Sullivan and I had crafted it well from the hardwood of the area. The logs were all smoothed and notched and fit together as tightly as a glove. Aye, and it would weather any storm that might come upon us too.

As I entered the room, I saw the preparations. The table was set with Mr. Sullivan’s best china, and filled with steaming bowls of food. Mr. And Mrs. Shaw were standing off to the side with Lem, and smiled at me as I entered. And then Caroline came in through the kitchen door. Aye, and lovely she was, dressed in a flower printed gingham dress, a little faded and worn, but still lovely. Her hair was shiny black and hung over her shoulders and to the center of her back in pure contrast to the print dress. Small she was, and small she would always be, standing no more than five feet one, and weighing only about 90 pounds.

"Happy birthday Phil," she said to me with a broad smile on her red lips.

"Aye, and a happy birthday it 'tis indeed," I said smiling back at her. "And to see you dressed so lovely is all of the present I need now."

She flushed red with embarrassment, and yet her eyes were still in contact with my own, burning into my very soul, and the smile never left her lovely lips. "Go on with you now," she answered in reply, and then set the bowl on the table.

"Aye, and you've the golden tongue of the Irish now, Phil," Lem told me as he walked to the table and pulled a chair out to set.

"Aye," she said with a pout, "a golden tongue that will be his undoing one day," Caroline stated with a wink as she turned to the kitchen again and disappeared.

"Enough now, enough," Mr. Sullivan said. "Come Philander, you'll set at the head of the table now, as an honored guest. This is you're day now, and the last command I'll ever give you."

Caroline came back from the kitchen, a Turkey all golden brown on a large platter. My mouth watered as I looked at the golden beast and the smell of it was pure ambrosia. She set it before me and took a chair at my right side, and then

Bret Sullivan carved the lovely bird in thick slices while he stood at the left side of me.

Our meal was perfect, and I thoroughly enjoyed every bite, and made an utter glutton of myself in the process. There were mashed potatoes and turkey gravy, corn bread and hominy, and green beans that had been canned from our summer crop.

When we had eaten our fill, there was not much left on the table, except for empty dishes and bowls, and a few bones. Mrs. Shaw got up and poured coffee for all, and Caroline went back to the kitchen. She came back a moment later with a large cake she had baked for the occasion, and as full as I was, I made quite a dent in her handy work indeed.

While we were yet eating the cake, Bret Sullivan pulled from his coat a rolled paper, and tied in the middle with a red ribbon.

"Aye Philander," he said with a tear in his eye. "And this is a special gift I give you now. This is your freedom lad, you may come and go as you please."

"You've been more a son to me, and you're always welcome in my house and on my land."

I reached over tentatively and took the paper from him, a sense of loss looming in my breast as I took it from him. Aye, these had been hard times, and a hard life I had lived until now, and Bret Sullivan was more a father to me than a master.

"Sir," I said quickly as I looked into his tearful eyes. "I'd like to stay on sir, and I'd like to ask you for a job."

He broke into a broad smile, "Aye lad, Aye indeed. A job you will have now and always if you wish."

"It is my wish sir, and I'd like to ask you sir, what will it take to purchase Miss Caroline's freedom as well?" I asked boldly.

There was a gasp from the chair to my right as Caroline sucked wind at my question.

"Caroline is it?" he said with a laugh. "She is fifteen now with six years on her tally. You stay and work for me for three years and I will call the debt paid."

"Aye, and a contract I will sign with you Mr. Sullivan," I said gleefully. "And of her hand in marriage now, will you agree?"

Bret's eyebrows furrowed as a serious look came across his face. "And you're asking the wrong person now lad, 'tis Brody Shaw you should be asking and not me now. And have you considered Caroline's feelings in this matter at all now lad. Have you bothered to ask her?"

Before I could respond Caroline eagerly answered.

"Yes, and it's what I want too," she said. Embarrassing herself with her sudden outburst, she sat quietly back in her chair, a slight pout on her lovely lips.

Turning, I looked at Brody Shaw.

"Mr. Shaw, and may I wed your daughter?" I said boldly to him.

Brody Shaw had light his pipe and was puffing it after the fine meal. He took the pipe from his mouth, looking stern and powerful as he pondered the question for a moment.

"You're a fine lad now Philander, and I'd be proud to have you as a son-in-law now, but Caroline is a young lass, and too young to know her own mind."

"Papa!" Caroline said in shock.

"Shush now daughter, you're only proving my point," he said sharply to her.

"I'll grant my permission only on one condition now," he continued. "That condition is that you wait until the summer after her sixteenth birthday. If she still wants you then Philander, you'll have my blessing."

"And mine as well," Bret Sullivan put in.

I sat back in my chair, satisfied with the answer and with myself.

"Aye, and it's a deal then."

"A deal?" Caroline said loudly. She stood from her chair, anger flushing her lovely face.

"You all act like you are bartering over one of your precious mules, or a horse, or a barrel of fish for that matter now."

She suddenly burst into tears and ran from the room, slamming the door to her bedroom as she entered. Mrs. Shaw stood from the table and excused herself. She then walked through the door after her.

"Aye, and there's my point," Brody Shaw said. "She's still too young to know her emotions yet."

Lem Malone pushed back from the table and stood up, "And it's to bed with me now. I thank you for the fine meal now Bret. And congratulations to you Philander, on your birthday, your lovely betrothed and on your freedom. I'm sure all things will work out for you, and good night I say to all."

Brody Shaw went back to puffing his pipe, and briskly, filling the room with the thin blue smoke from it as we sat in silence for a few moments.

Finally, I spoke again, although a lot of my heart was not in further conversation.

"Mr. Sullivan."

"That's Bret lad," he responded.

"Aye, Bret then. I'd also like to purchase some breading stock and a fine Donkey stud. I've learned a good craft here, and I intends to earn my living by it."

Bret Sullivan sat thoughtful for a moment before he spoke in response of my question. He was a careful man in all of his endeavors, and not one to make rash decisions.

"That will take some consideration now lad. I've a fine heard, and much of it you're responsible for. I'd not want you competing with me."

"And that I would not do sir. When I've bought Caroline's freedom and the stock as well, I'll move on to the west and out of your market now."

"Aye lad. Aye indeed I say. Sure and I'll consider the matter now Philander, and consider the price you'd pay for them as well."

We shook hands then, and I arose from the chair. "Thank you for the fine birthday meal sir, and all the years before it as well. Good night then," I said as I turned and walked to the door.

"And good night lad," he responded. "And don't you worry about Caroline now, she'll be as right as rain by the morning then."

Chapter 8

The next morning found me in the field again, with Lem working as the day before. There was much to do in preparation for the winter and feed for the stock was our primary purpose this day. The morning was cool with a bite of frost in the air and a hint of the forthcoming winter. Lem and I worked hard, barely speaking as we dedicated ourselves to the task of cutting the field.

“Philander”

It was coming to noontime when I looked up and saw Caroline coming over the crest of the low rise of the land. Here in the valley, there was rolling land. None of it could be considered flat, yet all of it was fertile and lovely. Most of the lands surrounding us were pretty much on its side. The mountains jutting striate up from the rolling hills of the valley, and rolling slowly to the lake to the east of us, with the sharp contrast of mountains again past the lake. It is a beautiful land, unlike our native Ireland, and yet similar at times. The winters here were hard both on men and on stock. We had learned to respect the winters upon experiencing our first here, and now, with the experience of fourteen winters behind us we had learned to take nothing for granted.

Game was generally plentiful here. Spring and summer were good times to hunt and generally the winters too. Many dear and buffalo were run from the mountains with the advent of cold, yet we had seen the times where even in our valley the winter would be so severe that the game would move on farther south, leaving little for us to hunt.

Mr. Sullivan had added cows to his heard and had a fine mess of them indeed. They had become our salvation a few winters when game was not so plentiful, and they bread on their own, leaving little for us to do with them other than assure they had feed and water.

I worked steady, working the blade in my hand with an easy fluid motion that continued methodically. I had learned early on to pace myself, to find a motion that would be constant and provide as little stress as possible. Along with that, I always occupied my mind with some thought or some problem. Working the problem through in my mind would take it off of the drudgery of the work, and allow me to continue at an even pace without feeling. I would dream continuously as I worked. I dreamed of having a home and land of my own, of Caroline and of raising a family.

Aye, and Bret Sullivan had not allowed my education to lag either. He had worked with me every evening as I grew, working mathematics, the studying of books and on my reading too. This had lasted until I had become as good as he, and then it changed some. We still had our nightly classes, but they changed into more of a competition between us. We would see who could solve a problem first, or would debate a Biblical point or the value of one of the books. He had taught me a game too. A game that was called chess, and it was one that would make you think a problem through, and to plan a strategy.

I thought on these things as I worked, and when I looked up again, I saw that Caroline had spread a blanket on the ground under a big Chestnut tree. Lem had already stopped his work and was walking to the blanket as Caroline set food on it from a basket she had brought.

"And Phil now," she said. "Are you not going to stop long enough to eat your meal".

I leaned on the shaft of the blade and smiled at her. "Aye Caroline, and it's appreciative that I am you've come with the food, although I don't know which looks better to me right now. You're a lovely lass always, but so much more when you have a meal with you."

She stopped her work and stood straight up, placing her hands on her hips and fire in her lovely eyes. "And if it's the food that you're interested in more than myself Philander Sherman, you can pack your own lunch from now on and eat it without me now!"

"Aye, and that's what I like to see in a good meal," I said. "A little fire and spice always makes it more palatable now."

She smiled at me then, a smile that would shame the Angels in heaven for sure. Her smile would light up a darkened room, and replace the cold with warmth too. I lifted the blade by the shaft and walked over to the blanket, leaning the blade against the tree, and sat down on the corner of the cloth.

The air still had a chill to it and I had not noticed the temperature in hours do to the work, yet as I sat down, I could feel it again.

"And did you bring a shall for yourself now Caroline?" I asked.

"Aye and a coat for you as well. I knew you would be without one and I'd not have you die of the lung fever before we could wed now," she responded in a gentle voice.

She reached into the basket and pulled out a thin dear skin coat she had made for me, one I had not seen before, and then passed it over the blanket to me.

"Aye, and what's this now?"

"For your birthday Phil," she said modestly. "I've been working on this in my spare time for a few weeks."

I held the jacket up and looked at it, and a fine one it was too. Made from finely tanned dear skin, and sowed well with strips of leather. There were fringes on the arms and at the bottom to help it dry faster if it were to get wet, and the leather was so finely tanned that it was almost white.

"The Cherokee woman that visits with me now and again taught me how to do it Phil, I hope you like it," she said.

"Aye, and a finer coat I've never seen Caroline," I responded. "And it is a grateful man that I am now."

My pleasure seemed to thrill her, as she looked almost giddy with a smile she could not subdue even though she tried.

"And you'd best eat your lunch now," she said. "Bret Sullivan asked me to tell you to come in early now. He'd like to move one of the herds before nightfall he said, and he has something he wants to discuss with you."

"Aye," I said acknowledging her statement, and reached for the plate of cold venison, cheese and bread she had prepared for me.

As we ate our lunch, there was a flirtation in her eyes. Aye, and those eyes now, deep and blue and sparking a promise of the fire that lay behind them. No wards were spoken as we ate for none were needed. Our eyes spoke all things to each other. I could set all day and look into the depth of those eyes and it would thrill me all the while.

Lem was completely silent during our meal. I was sure he didn't want to interrupt the flirtation between Caroline and I, for we did not try to hide our feelings but sat boldly and looked at each other.

When we were through with the food, Lem lit his pipe and lay back on the blanket, puffing blue billows of smoke that dissipated quickly in the clear crisp air. My coat was warm and fit like a glove, yet I believe it was the warmth of

Caroline's eyes and smile that held the cold from me.

"That was a fine lunch now Caroline, and I thank you," I said when I was through eating. "We'll walk back with you and see what Mr. Sullivan's about."

She stood from the blanket in one easy fluid motion, as graceful as an angle and even lovelier, her eyes flashing and a hint of a smile on her lips as she moved, and my heart fluttered in response. Lem was already up and gathered the tools. I helped Caroline pack up the basket, shaking the blanket before I folded it to place in the basket.

Grasping the basket in my left hand, and Caroline's soft small hand in my right, we started off. It was a little over a mile to the house across the rolling hills, most of which had been cut close by Lem and I, and the hay gathered in stacks reaching sometimes over ten feet tall.

We walked hand in hand, the birds singing in the background, and the lovely land showing it's brilliant fall colors before us. Aye, and it was a lovely thing, and a scene I would hold in my memory forever. The small beauty at my side, her eyes still flashing and her hand giving me a gentle reminder of the depths of her love as we strolled through the countryside.

But it lasted all too shortly, for we were at the barn of the house before we knew it.

"And I'll get Mr. Sullivan for you now," Caroline said as she gently squeezed my hand before she let it go. She took the basket from my left hand, crossing in front of me and so closely I could feel her warmth, as she flashed a bit of a smile and turned to leave.

"And we'd best clean these blades before they rust up on us now Phil," Lem told me as I watched Caroline walk away. "That is, if you are through courting for the moment now."

"Aye, and it's a black heart you have indeed now Lem," I responded, still watching Caroline as she approached the steps of the house. "A black heart for sure, if you'd deny a man the look at an angel."

"Sure and there's a poet within you now Phil, but its time for work. A free man you are today, and a free man must please the one for whom he works to obtain his payment."

"Aye." I responded. "Aye indeed now Lem Malone."

We both took a blade and a stone and went to work, cleaning and sharpening the tools before we hung them in the barn. A farmer's livelihood is dependant upon his tools and his stock. If they are ignored, then he can look to failure for sure, and most times, failure meant death.

"Lem now, saddle us four horses if you would please," Mr. Sullivan said as he walked into the barn. "I'd have a word with Philander while you get the horses ready."

"Aye Bret," he responded as he hung the blade from the rafter in the corner of the barn.

"Phil, I have a job I'd like for you to do," Bret said.

"Sure, and anything you'd want now Mr. Sullivan."

"We've a team to deliver down to Knoxville as you know," he started, "and I'd like for you to deliver them. We also need supplies so you'll need to take a wagon with you then."

This was a surprise to me. Oh, I'd been with Mr. Sullivan quite a few times to deliver stock and to get supplies, but I had never gone by myself before.

"It's a long trip there and back Phil, and I want you back before snow flies. I've a notion the snow will come early this year, and we'll need those supplies," he continued.

"Aye, but the fields," I started to say.

"And you and Lem have cut most of the hay we'll need," he continued. "Lem can finish up with the cutting of what's left now. I'd go myself but my gout is acting up, and I feel the ride would be too hard on it."

I looked at Bret Sullivan and for the first time realized that he was getting on in years. He was not a young man when I entered his service, and many years had past since then, and my heart went out to him.

Such a man he was. Such a man to take a rag-tag lad like myself to raise, and raise with kindness and love as one of his own, even though he had no obligation too. There were many nights I still thought of Sean O'Leary and his cruelty. Many nights indeed I awoke with a start and the sweat of cold fear covering my brow. If had stayed in his service I surely would have been broken or dead by now, with no one to care the less about me.

"Sure, and you'll not have to worry now Bret," I said to him. "I'll deliver the stock and return in short order with all that you asked."

"There's a good lad now," he said as he slapped my shoulder, a gentle and loving slap of approval.

"Brody and I will finish the hunting and the jerking of the meat while you are gone. It should not take you more than three weeks to return," he said.

"Three weeks" I said to myself. That's a long time not to see my darling Caroline. Truly it seemed a long time to be separated from her tenderness and her fire, and the gentle support of her love. It seemed an eternity to me as my eyebrows furrowed unconsciously.

Firming his grip on my shoulder, Bret said gently," and she'll still be here when you return now Phil. And no worse for the wear I'm sure."

It had always been that Bret Sullivan seemed to read my thoughts, seemed to know what was in my heart.

"Aye, and I'd have you to leave tomorrow Phil," he continued. "Come to supper tonight and we'll plan the trip now."

"Sir, and I appreciate you're trust in me," I said. "I'll not fail you."

"That's exactly why I'm sending you now Phil. A finer lad I've never known."

▪▪

Chapter 9

It was an hour before dawn the next morning when I drove the buckboard from the ranch heading south. The morning was frosty and brisk, stars shown above me in all of their brilliance, and the kiss from my darling Caroline before I left kept me warm from the chill of the air.

“Philander”

It was a long trip that I was starting, and especially since I had never gone by myself before. Mr. Sullivan had trusted me, and I took that quite seriously. In all of my short years on this earth, Bret Sullivan had shown me trust, kindness and love, and this made me determined to succeed.

By the time that the sun was in the sky and burning off some of the frost, I was five miles from the farm and beginning to enter the long rolling flat lands. There were possibly sixty miles of these flats before I reached the mountains that held Knoxville, and I knew that these days would be the easiest part of my journey. I also knew from experience that this day I would make more ground than those to follow, for the stock were fresh and well rested. The following days we would make less progress and I would have to spell them more often.

A lot of game had moved from the mountains into these flat-rolling hills that I now rode, and it was in my mind to load the wagon with them upon my return journey. There were still some buffalo in this country at the time, although their numbers had dwindled considerably since we moved here some year’s back, and I saw a small herd of them in the early hours of the morning. Dear were plentiful and I could see them moving off from me every few moments.

I had been raised these last years with the Cherokee as my friends. They were a good and a gentlepeople that lived off of the land. There was some resentment in them for the white man, but not a great amount. We had been there to help them when the Seneca attacked from the North, and had formed an allegiance of sorts, each warning the other when danger was present, and each helping the other to defeat their raids.

We had lost a few horses to them, but not many. Ours were workhorses mostly and were not the speedy horses of endurance that they sought.

Horses were not a species that were indigenous to the America's. The Spaniards introduced them when they sought for the riches from the new lands, and the Indians were quick to steal what they could. Most of the Spanish left their stock when they returned from the America's, and their stock turned wild, breading in the richness of the American landscape, and adapting quickly to the mostly fair environments here. The Indians were quick to pick up on the value of the beast, and they bread them and learned to ride better than most white man.

As I would usually do, my mind would occupy itself with thoughts and plans as I traveled. It was a way with me, to absorb my mind in working problems or working out dreams, for this was the way Bret Sullivan had taught me.

"An idle mind is the Devil's playground Philander. Never let your mind be idle and learn to use it while being sensitive to the elements around you. Work out problems that we have discussed, plan your future, debate points of contention and always stay in constant prayer," was what he taught me. I found him to be right about this, for it made the work easier and the drudgery of the day pass quickly. It also nurtured my faith and I found myself teaching lessons from the Bible, or preaching sermons in my mind as I completed my day's work.

By nightfall, I was camped near a branch, and had a good forty miles behind me. I was pleased with the day's travel as I sat at coffee after my evening meal. The stock was ground hitched to their tethers, cropping the rich tall grass and resting from their forced march of the day. Tomorrow, we would be lucky to make thirty miles I knew, for I had pushed the stock this day, and they were tired. We would lounge around in the morning for a while, allowing them to fill their bellies with the grass and water from the branch when the sun arose.

I made my pallet that night under the low bows of a huge old cedar tree knowing that it would keep the frost from settling on me, and I slept well and secure knowing that the horses and mules would let me know if something were to intrude.

I was up before sunrise and took each of the beasts to the branch allowing them to drink long and deep from the fresh clean water, and then staked them out on fresh grass for their morning feeding. This I did before tending to myself.

When I had fixed myself a breakfast of bacon, some loaf bread and coffee, I ate it enjoying every bite. There's something about a brisk morning that makes the food taste better, something about an open fire that flavors the coffee differently, warming a body to their very soul.

After eating, I cleaned up and packed up and then sat with my back to a tree and dozed in the morning sun until the stock had eaten their fill, and then I hooked up the team ad once again was on the trail

It was the third day out when I came upon them. Three men on horseback they were, all three filthy and looking run down at there heals, truly a rawhide outfit if I ever saw one. They saw me from the knoll of the hill before me and came right on. It was nervous I was as the men approached, yet I did not let them think I was rattled by their sudden appearance. While they were still a good distance from me, I got my rifle and placed it in the seat beside me close at hand.

"Philander"

The shotgun I had brought was a short one, double-barreled it was and it lay across my lap and covered by a blanket I had placed over my legs, as the morning was chilly and damp.

I was sure they had seen me stand the rifle next to the seat, for when I first saw them they were tightly bunched together. Immediately, they spread across the road. One to the right side, one to the left and the biggest of the three rode right down the center.

As I came closer they slowed their horses to almost a stop and it was then that I knew they were up to no good. There were bandits in the area, this I knew and Bret Sullivan had warned me to be careful.

I kept the team at an even steady pace and as I came up to them I slowed to a stop some fifty yards off.

"What's wrong boy," the fat greasy one in the center called out to me. "We ain't a'goin' ta' hurt you none."

I looked at the man and could see that he had not been in a barber's chair in many a year. His hair was a gray and hung past his shoulders from under his battered black hat. He wore a greasy homespun coat and a vest that showed the residue of many meals, a shirt that at some time would have been white, but was stained with dirt and sweat and looked more brown and gray. He wore a long gray beard that was stained brown around his mouth from the tobacco he chewed, and eyes that were black and close set and reminded me more of a weasel than a man.

Cautiously I started the team moving forward slowly, for they had made room for me to pass. As I approached them, the fat greasy one kicked his heals in his horses flanks and he jumped into the road, causing my team to rear up on their hind legs in surprise.

"What's the hurry there boy?" he said as he spit tobacco juice through the side of his filthy mouth.

"No hurry sir," I responded. "Just need to get past and about my business."

"Say Blake," the man on the left said, "get a look at that there teem will you."

"Yea, them's some more horse flesh," he answered. "Where'd you get a team like them boy? And them big mules you got on tether there."

"I'm afraid that's my business sir. I really don't mean to offend you now, but I must be on my way," I responded.

"Now would you hear that Blake," the one on the left said again. "He's a bloody Mick."

I looked over at the man. He had a square jaw covered with a week or two of whiskers and dirt, and as equally skinny as the one he called Blake was fat. He wore a sheepskin coat that was worn out completely, a checkered shirt underneath and homespun pants that were tucked in sat the top of his worn down boots.

"If you mean that I am Irish sir, you are right now," I said. "Right for sure, and proud of my heritage now sir."

This brought a laugh from all three of them. It seemed they could see no good in the Irish.

While they were still laughing, I started the teem moving again and a hand the size of a ham grabbed the rigging on the horse nearest him.

"Say boy," Blake started, "you ain't a bein' too friendly now. We jus' want to talk to you some."

I had one hand under the blanket and I pulled the hammers back on that shotgun. The sound was loud and ominous in the stillness of the morning air, and it immediately brought caution to the three.

"And I'll be on my way now sir," I said sternly as I could. I had never faced a situation like this before and was a bit unsure of myself. My insides were turning and shaky, but I presented an air of confidence as best I could.

"Say now boy," Blake said, "there ain't no call for you getting' all riled up an' such. This here ain't your stock an' they sure ain't worth no dyin' over."

"And I sure don't plan on dying sir," I responded. "But you'll not take my stock now, and I'll be on my way."

The ham like hand still held leather on one of my team, and a mean look came into the black eyes that were looking through me.

"Listen son," he said in a low and angry tone. "We got three guns to your one. You may get lucky and get lead into one of us, but you'll surely be dead. You ever shoot a man before son."

"Aye, and I'll thank you not to call me son," I said coldly. I dropped the blanket and revealed the shotgun. "Even poor Irish trash know what a shotgun will do at this range now. And I've two barrels, and that means that two of you will be blown nearly in half if you try anything. The third I will surely get lead into as well."

The small black eyes of the big man grew to almost twice their size when he saw the shotgun, and he knew what I said was true, for he released his grip on the rigging of my team immediately.

"Now, we don't mean no harm boy," he stuttered, "we was jus' havin' a little fun 's all."

"Aye, and at the expense of my stock and my life as well now," I responded. "Throw down your weapons in the back of my wagon now."

"That ain't human," Blake protested. "A man can't live out here without a gun."

"Aye, and it seems that other men can't live around you three when you have them. Sure and I've told you all that I'm of a mind to, put your weapons in my wagon. I'll drop them off a few miles down the road for you when I'm safely away."

They didn't like it much, but they shucked their rifles out of their boots and lay them in the back of the wagon, and then their pistols as well.

Taking a rope from under the seat of the buckboard, I tossed it to Blake. He wasn't ready to receive it and it slapped him sharply in the face.

"Now sir, if you will get off of your horses and tie them to the back of the buckboard."

"Say now," he started to protest.

"Do it now," I said threateningly as I raised the shotgun and pointed at his middle.

Blake cursed violently for a moment, and then reluctantly dismounted the poor animal he had been riding. When he had tied his horse to the rope, he looked at the other two and angrily motioned them to do the same.

When their horses were securely tied, I looked at Blake one more time. "Aye, and there's one thing more I forgot to mention to you sir. I'll need your boots as well."

"Now see here...." he started, but I cut him off sharply by issuing a surprisingly loud "NOW".

The three of them sat in the grass at the side of the road, all cursing angrily as they pulled off their boots and threw them one at a time into the back of the buckboard.

Un-cocking the shotgun, I said, "and I'm a man of my word sir. Sure and I'll leave your belongings a few miles down the road now. Just far enough so that you can not follow and murder me when my back is turned."

Blake's face was red with angry blood and the skinny one was whining like a puppy at being stripped of his boots.

"You hear this and you hear it good Mick," he said threateningly. "You ain't seen the last o' me for sure, an' I'll be there to make my water on you're your grave boy, you kin count on it."

"Aye, and it's a pleasant day that I wish for you and yours too now," I said as I shook out the reigns and the team started to move out. I smiled at him as I passed and he cursed even more violently than before. The skinny one bent over and picked up a rock, throwing it at the wagon as I topped the hill, and I could hear loud cursing and arguing for nearly half a mile further on.

As I had told them, I left their stock, guns and boots for them, picketing the horses in some rich grazing and close to water, but it was many miles down the road. I figured it would take them nearly a day and a half to reach their belongings, maybe a little more since their feet would be sore from the walk without boots. I carefully unloaded each of their weapons, and although I left them their ball for their weapons, I took every bit of powder that I could find in their belongings.

That night, I camped by a stream, cold and crisp running down from the Clinch. I figured that tomorrow I would make Knoxville, and as was my custom, I bathed myself thoroughly in the icy waters of the creek before retiring.

As I rolled into my pallet, I could not help but to chuckle at the three I had left behind and their predicament, even if they had brought it on themselves. Surely, if I had been less prepared the scoundrels would have slit my throat and made off with the stock and wagon to sell for whisky and loose women. I was sure that no bath would see a penny of the money they would have made, nor would a church offering plate either.

It took half the next day to make it to Knoxville. Aye, and what a sight it was to me now. The city was bustling and much larger than my only previous visit.

I placed the stock and the wagon at the livery stable and then began a walk from one end of the town to the other, looking at the people in their different dress and the items in the storefront windows.

At noon, I entered a Tavern and ordered coffee and a lunch. The Tavern was crowded, yet I was able to find a table to myself and enjoyed watching the variety of people passing in and out of the establishment

When my food came, I dug in with relish, for I wasn't used to eating my own cooking for such an extended time. It was a venison stew with carrots and potatoes, and a loaf of bread that was just right for sopping the gravy.

Busy at my meal, I was surprised to hear the chair opposite me at my table scruff against the floor, and when I looked up, a big man was setting down in it. I looked at him with a question mark in my face I was sure, and the big man smiled.

He was maybe forty and neatly cut with a handlebar mustache, piercing gray eyes, and white temples contrasting the black hair of his head. I also noticed a shiny silver badge that was clipped to the pocket on the front of his shirtfront.

"Hope you don't mind some company friend," he said casually.

"And sure you are welcome to set with me at my table sheriff if you've a mind to," I responded around a mouthful of stew. "And would you care to join me in some lunch now?"

"No, thank you," he responded, "but I might drink a cup of coffee with you."

I waived to the fair maid who had been serving me and she brought over a cup that he filled from the pot set on the table.

"Saw you come into town earlier. That's some mighty fine stock you have there," he said casually.

"Aye sir, and they truly are. I'm making a delivery of the mules for my mas.., my employer," I responded.

He shook his head knowingly at my comment, for it wasn't unusual to meet a man freed from bond service with an accent like that of my own.

"You have any trouble coming over the trail?" he asked. "There's been a number of gangs working these hills of late."

"Not much," I responded as I swallowed the mouthful I had been working on, and then took a long drink from the cup of coffee.

"Met a bunch yesterday, but there wasn't much too them. I had a shotgun under the blanket over my lap and they got friendly when they heard the hammers cocked," I stated.

He chuckled for a moment and then took a drink from his cup.

"Don't take many chances do you friend?"

"Aye, and Bret Sullivan raised me to be a careful man now," I responded, a coy smile on my face.

"Did you know those who tried to stop you?"

"No," I answered shaking my head a little. "There was a big man, with long gray hair, and two smaller men. None of them looked like they knew what water was for, and one of the smaller men called the big one Blake."

The smile left the sheriff's face immediately and he sat at attention at the table.

"Son, you were lucky indeed. If I don't miss my guess, that was Blake Thompson and his bunch. They'd murder you sure, just to steal the penny's off a dead man's eyes if that's all there was. Heard they were workin' the hills around here again, but wasn't sure 'till now. "

"Aye, and I must have been lucky, or the Lord was with me then," I responded.

"Hard to figure though," he said with a question on his face. "Blake Thompson wouldn't a' give up on you. He'd a' just tracked you down, or got ahead of you again and shot you from cover, especially with those animals you had. They're worth a lot of money."

I grinned at him then, a big wide grin that would have brought a question to anyone's mind.

"Aye, and that's what I figured sir. I had him throw his guns in the back of the buckboard, and then took their horses and boots and set them afoot."

He was taking a drink of coffee when I told him that and it choked him something awful. Coffee sprayed over half of the room, and when he caught his breath, he just sort of looked at me all confused and in wonder.

"Son, if you done that to Blake Thompson, you'd best be back on the next boat to Ireland. He's a known killer and doesn't need no reason," he said seriously.

"Why, there's a two hundred dollar price on his head, dead or alive. You'd of been better off shootin' him and bringing the bodies in with you."

He again tried to drink from the coffee suddenly stopping when the cup reached his lips.

"Say, were 'bouts did all this take place?"

"Days ride north," I said.

"What did you do with his guns and his horses?" he asked anxiously.

"Staked them out on good grass about four or five hours ride from town, next to Clinch creek off of the road," I said smiling at him. "Left him ball for his guns, but I took every bit of his powder and I unloaded all of them. Aye, and I'm sure now it'll be late evening today before they come up to them, walking as they are in their sock feet."

He suddenly stood up. "Son, if I can beat him back to those horses, there's a reward in it for you. That's a dangerous man, a thief and a murderer, and he's a wanted man in six States and a few territories."

As he turned to leave, I asked, "say sheriff, can you tell me where the Swede runs his freighting business? I have to deliver those mules to him."

He didn't turn but started in a fast walk to the door, saying over his shoulder, "'bout a half a mile down the west road. You can't miss him, only place out yonder."

■■■

Chapter 10

I continued to lounge around the town that day, visiting some of the general stores and placing orders for the supplies that Bret Sullivan had requested.

Tomorrow would be soon enough to deliver the stock to the Swede, and I knew it would take some time for the merchants to gather the orders for loading. Most had back doors, raised up to the height of the wagon bed to ease somewhat the burden of loading and packing the supplies. Although it had taken me less than a week to make it here to Knoxville, I knew it would take almost twice as long to return, for the wagon would be loaded heavily and the team would tire easily in these hills and mountains.

I took a room finally at the local Hotel. Bret Sullivan had given me the money for it, and for my meals, and insisted that I stay in the hotel during my visit. The room was small but clean, and sparsely furnished, as was the custom in those days. It included a bed that was freshly made, a wooden chair to set in while dressing or undressing, a commode on a pedestal and a pitcher filled with fresh water. Truly, this was all that a man needed for a night's stay.

I lay on the bed and dozed for a while after taking care of the placing orders, and to kill some time before supper. Bret Sullivan had taught me to rest when you can, eat when it is available, and stimulate the mind continuously. This way a man would be ready for whatever he may have to face, in mind, body and soul.

It was coming up to four o'clock when I decided to walk the short distance to the Swede's place and make arrangements to transfer the stock to him in the morning. Eight fine big mules of mixed Irish Draft blood they were, beautiful animals all with rich brown hair and tan main's and ankles, and muscular beyond belief.

"Philander"

As I walked into the yard of the freighting company, a man in a run-down hat and homespun pants held up with leather suspenders over a checkered shirt approached me.

"If'n you're lookin' for a job boy, we ain't doin' no hirein' today," he said.

"Aye, and a job I have sir," I responded pleasantly. "And could you direct me to the Swede now, for I've business to conduct with him this day."

He looked at me a bit confused through his blonde eyelashes and blue eyes. He was a man about forty, maybe six foot tall, and slender yet muscular.

"I'm the Swede," he responded tentatively, "what kin I do for you."

"Aye, and I'm Philander Sherman," I stated proudly, "and sure if I'm not making a delivery of Mules to you from Mr. Bret Sullivan now."

He grinned and bent to the side a might as if looking down the road behind me. "Don't see no mules boy," he said and then spat to the side, wiping his mouth with the back of his hand. "And if'n they's small 'nough to fit in your pocket, you'd best jus' head on back home for they won't do me no good."

His comment was one that surprised and humored me and I chuckled at it. Bret Sullivan had told me that the Swede was one of quick wit, and one who enjoyed making fun with a situation, but he also warned me that he was a man as quick with his fists as he was at cracking a joke, and I could see that now as he smiled at me, for he was missing the whole top row of his front teeth.

"Aye, and they're at the livery in town. I thought we could meet in the morning and look them over before we made our deal," I said.

"Good Philander, good," he said as he slapped me on the shoulder. "I start my day early 'cause there's a lot of work to be done. How 'bout we meet at the livery at first light, and then you can buy me some breakfast while we seal the deal."

"Agreed," I told him as I turned from the yard. "And I'll see you at first light then."

By the time I had got back to town the evening chill had set on. It seemed at this time of year that the air would chill the moment the sun started to set and I was wishing I had worn the fine leather coat that Caroline had made me.

I was headed for the hotel to retrieve my coat before going to the Tavern for some supper, when I heard horses coming up the street of the hard packed earth. Turning, I saw the sheriff, and three deputies, and they were leading three horses. Two of the horses had bodies lain across their saddles, hands and feet tied underneath the bellies of the horses. A crowd was beginning to assemble and follow the men down the street as they approached the sheriff's office.

The sheriff reigned in at the hitching rail and the deputies followed, and all four of them dismounted. A deputy took a long skinning knife from the sheath on his belt and cut the ropes tying the hands of one and then the other of those tied in the horse's saddles, and one man spilled to the ground, cursing violently as he hit the hard packed earth. It was the skinny fellow I had encountered the day before. The other man gingerly removed himself from the posture he had been forced to ride in, a scared look on his face as his feet touched the ground, and one of the deputies placed a cocked revolving pistol in his back.

I stood a few feet from the sheriff's office and watched as they hustled the two inside, and the sheriff turned and looked at me, a hint of a smile on his face, and then turned to a deputy.

"Get Doc over here to tend to that one that's got a hole in his shoulder, and get 'em both locked up in a cell", he said commandingly. "I'm goin' to get me some supper."

He then turned to me and said, "join me young feller?"

"And it was supper that I had on my mind when I saw you come down the street," I responded.

He smiled at me then and slapped me on the shoulder, starting to walk across the street, and I followed like an obedient puppy.

He slowed a bit for me to catch up to him and we walked side by side. "You know them feller's?"

"Aye, and they were two of the three who tried to rob me, that I'm sure," I said.

He chuckled again. "Boy, you sure served 'em up to us. We found where you'd staked out their horses an' jus' set an' waited for 'em to come on. When they come, we road from cover an' caught 'em flat footed for sure. That one had a hide out gun he didn't turn over to you, an old muzzle loaded derringer. He fired but the powder didn't ignite an' one of my deputies shot that there pistol from his hand when he fired into his shoulder."

It was just then that we reached the door to the tavern, and the sheriff lifted the latch and opened the door for me to enter. I went to the nearest table that wasn’t occupied and sat down, the sheriff taking the seat opposite to me.

“Aye sir, that was two of them, but what of Blake Thompson?” I asked.

“Reckon he got tired of walkin’,” he told me, “for he sent those two to get their gear an’ told ‘em to come back an’ pick him up. We went to the place they were supposed to meet, up on a hill like, no trees or nothin’ to block his view none. That Blake Thompson’s a careful man. When we worked our way to the top of that there hill, he weren’t no where to be found.”

I shook my head in response, a little disappointed in his answer. I had not made a friend of Blake Thompson and if a murderer as I was told, he would not soon forget me, and may even decide to come hunting me.

The waitress came over and took our orders, bringing a pot of fresh hot coffee and two cups.

“By the way young feller, what did you say your name was?” the sheriff asked.

“Philander Sherman sir, from Abingdon,” I said.

“Well, this here supper’s on you tonight,” he said smiling at me. “Seems how those two we caught were Newt Pearce and Bully Bone. Both got a hundred dollar bounty on their heads, an’ that goes to you son.”

His words set me back for a moment. In all of my life, the most I had ever had to my name was a few pennies to rub together, and this seemed as the riches of the entire world to me.

“I…I appreciate the offer sheriff, but sure and I did nothing,” I finally responded to him. “You and the deputies now, you were the ones who took the risk to catch them. Sure, and I wouldn't know what to do with such a sum if it were mine now."

"We took the risk, but we get paid by the county to do that young man," he answered. "We never would have had the opportunity to catch them if you hadn't done what you did an' told me about it. No, the money id yours Philander, and I'm proud that it goes to you. Drop by my office around seven in the morning and we'll do a draft and get your money for you."

I sat long and looked into my coffee cup. This was a Kings ransom to me, the start on my new life and my life with Caroline that we would need when the time came. Sure, and there were years ahead of us still before we would be totally free and have the stock to support ourselves, but this was more than a year's salary for a farm hand or a cattleman. It was just a little under half of what the eight mules would bring from the Swede for Mr. Sullivan, and those mules took a lot of hard work to keep alive and to nourish to their full growth. And then even more work to get them to act as a team, almost a year of training that started even before they reached maturity.

"Aye, Caroline" I said to myself under my breath, "and this is the start to our future, to our farm."

"That's right son, this could be your big start if you use it wisely," the sheriff said.

I had not realized that I had spoken my thoughts aloud, and my face flushed red with embarrassment.

"And what will happen to these two sheriff, this Newt Pearce and Bully

Bone now?" I asked in genuine concern.

"They'll be tried by the courts son. If found guilty, they could go to prison, or they could be hanged," he responded. "Personally, I vote for hangin', for they're cut-throats who've sent more than one man to an early grave." He took a pipe from his vest pocket and a sack of Bull Durham tobacco from his shirt pocket to load it with. When he lit the pipe and a billow of white smoke hung low over his head, he continued; "there's been a lot of robbin' an' killin' in these here hills these last months, an' I'm sure these two and Blake Thompson were responsible. Found a gold watch that belonged to Matt White in Bully's pocket. Matt was killed last week on the road to Decatur where he was headed to tend to some business."

He puffed again from the pipe, filling the air with the smoke, "Matt was a good man, left a son an' three daughters an' twelve gran' chillin' behind. Rich man too, done a lot for the community. I'm sure the judge will take this into account before he sentences 'em."

The waitress had returned with two heaping plates of food and a pan of corn bread. She sat the cornbread in the center of the table and slid a plate in front of both of us. I smiled at her and gave her a little nod and a wink of appreciation as she set the food down, and her cheeks flushed red.

"Aye sheriff," I said to him. "Sure and I'd not have brought any man to his death if I could help it, but it sounds like these two are deserving of justice."

"That they are son," he said around a mouth full of food. "That they are indeed. They sure ain't worth you frettin' over none, let the law deal with 'em. It's on their shoulders now, and the weight of the decision will weigh heavily on their minds, not ours."

We ate the rest of our meal in silence, paying strict attention to the good food that was placed before us. It had been a long time since I had such a verity of vegetables in front of me, and the roast pork had always been a favorite of mine. The cornbread too was high and light, hot and tasty, and made with bacon fat in it, such as I had never experienced before.

When we were through eating, the sheriff again reminded me to report to his office around seven the next morning to work out the details for the reward. I nodded, threw two quarters in the center of the table and started back to my room.

It was full dark out now and the evening chill had set on heavy. Already there was frost beginning to appear on the hitch rails and the boarded side walks. The dull glow of lamps through windows I passed exposed a thin layer of frost circling the window pains, and I was really wishing for my jacket.

It was but a short walk to the hotel I was staying, and a good thing for sure it was, for my teeth were chattering and my steps quickened by the time my hand touched the outside handle to that door. When I opened the door, there was a gush of warmth, mingled with the smell of tobacco that hit me square in the face, which beckoned me to move a little faster inside the room and get that door closed behind me. I worked my way to my room, and placing a chair under the latch of the door from the inside, so that no one could disturb me, undressed and went to bed.

The next morning before first light, I was dressed and waiting outside of the livery for the Swede, who came as he said, and with two men in tow. They walked up the road and I watched them as they came nearer, and when they were just about to the livery, I stepped from the shadows into the light of the lamp hung from the front of the building and over the doors.

The Swede stopped for a moment, surprised at my sudden appearance. "Well now, you surprised me young feller," he said as he spit tobacco juice from the side of his mouth. "Thought we'd have to pull you out'a that there warm bed of your'n an' drag you out in the cold ta' get this here deal done."

"Aye, and a fine brisk morning it is to you too sir," I responded with a smile.

I was sure he didn't know how to take me, a young lad with a lot of responsibility placed on my shoulders, but I could see a bit of respect coming into those hard eyes of his as he passed by me into the stable.

Taking a lantern from the inside hook by the door, he struck a match to it and lighted the area of the barn where we stood.

"Now where's them mules you brought for me young feller?" he asked.

"Aye, and if you'll follow me now sir, you'll see the finest mules you've ever seen and only dreamed of owning," I responded as I started off toward the back of the barn.

There were around thirty stalls in the livery, and I had chosen the back eight stalls for the mules I had brought, keeping them out of view as best I could. When the light surrounded the stalls that kept the big beasts, they snorted a greeting to us, their eyes rolling as we came upon them.

A quick smile came on the Swede's face as he viewed the beasts for the first time. All were seventeen hands tall, strong and muscular, young and in good shape.

"Well now young feller," he said rubbing his chin, "this here looks like some right fine stock."

"Aye, and trained to boot," I responded. "Molly here," I said slapping one of the mules on the rump, "she's trained to lead the team. We always harnessed her to the left front position and a fine and steady girl she is for sure now."

The three went amongst the stalls, leading one and then another out of the stall and inspecting them closely. Finally, when satisfied that the deal was right, the Swede came over to me and grinned. "We'll hook 'em up, see if they pull as good as they look. If they do, I'll be back 'afore noon to sign the deal."

"Sure, and if you need more time to proof them it will be fine now sir," I said in response, and the three led the team out of the doors and down the street, talking lowly and briskly as they made their way down the road.

Light had appeared in the sky and the first twilight of dawn was upon the land before we came from the livery. I looked over in the direction of the tavern to see light in the windows and knew they were open for breakfast, so I turned and walked toward my morning meal.

If all went right, I would be able to finish my business today, load the supplies and by this time tomorrow, be on my way home, and to my love, my darling Caroline.

▪▪

“Philander”

“Philander”

Chapter 11

Blake Thompson walked, or rather, stumbled into the little cul-de-sac that held their camp. His feet were bloody from walking so many miles on the shark rocks; pinecones and whatever else could cut or splinter. He had stopped and wrapped his feet with the kerchief from his neck and a piece of shirt he had torn off after his socks gave out, but they did little good. He was tired; he was hurt, he was mad clean through when he stumbled into camp, alone.

Setting around the fire was his other two cohorts. Bill and Melvin Long had stayed behind on Blake’s last forage through the countryside in search of a victim. Melvin had taken a bullet in a previous outing when they made off with some stock from a farmhouse near the Severe River. It wasn’t much of a wound, but enough for him to cry over and the Long brothers were not exactly Blake’s favorites, so he gladly left them behind.

He came up to the camp, stepping down on a sharp rock that caused him to squall out a blurting stream of curse words. This caught the Longs by surprise. Diving for cover, the Long boys pulled Iron, ready to cut down the interloper, when they recognized it to be Blake.

Bill stood in a quandary, his left hand rising to scratch his filthy dark hair in wonderment. In all of the years he had known and ridden with Blake, he had never known him to walk anywhere, or to exert any kind of an effort that actually required work.

“What the Sam-Hill you doin’ sneakin’ up on us like that there Blake?” Melvin said suddenly. “We done ‘bout blown yer foolish head plumb off.”

Blake was in no mood for explanations, nor was he ready for any of Melvin's antics this day. He was poison mean and just wanted to find a place to set and get off his hurt and bleeding feet.

He cursed violently, and then said, "Bill, get your fat butt over hear an' hep' me into camp."

Bill set the rifle down gingerly and ran to assist Blake's final few steps to the fire. By the time he had taken him by the shoulder and helped him to a filthy pallet, Melvin had come over to meet them.

"Where's yer boots Blake? What happened to your horse and where's Bully an' Newt?" he asked like the half crazed idiot his father had always accused him of being, that is, until the day Melvin hung him from the rafters of their barn and unloaded a revolving pistol into his belly.

Blake looked at him with blood in his eyes. Most men were afraid of Melvin. He was big, ugly and mean, and had the calculating mind of a criminal. On some men, these characteristics are hidden and unseen, yet one look at Melvin and one knew not to turn their back on him.

"Done told you to shut-up boy, now do it!" he responded angrily.

Bill had always tried to protect Melvin from himself and from others. His whole life had been dedicated to his brother, to keep him safe and to not allow him to go too far with things.

"Melvin, heat a bucket of water over the fire there. We got to bath his feet an' get the dirt off'n these cuts," he said sincerely.

Melvin didn't like to be told to shut-up. Another man would have seen his wrath at that moment, but he listened to Bill and walked over to a bucket, and then the spring.

"You don't keep that brother of your'n in line Bill, an' I will," Blake said as Melvin disappeared into the brush surrounding the camp.

"Awe he's harmless Blake," Bill interceded. "Just curious is all."

"Don't matter to me Bill," Blake told him. "I'd jus' as soon put a bullet in that small brain of his as not."

Bill continued to work, allowing Blake to cool off. He unwrapped Blake's feet one by one, and was horrified by what he saw. Some of the cuts had already begun to fester, they were ugly and torn.

When Melvin returned from the spring, Bill told him to bring over some water and the bottle of whiskey that was in his saddlebag. Dipping a rag in the water, he bathed the feet gently, cleaning off some of the blood and dirt while the rest of the water was getting hot.

"Don't look any none to good," he said to Blake.

"Feel worse than they look," Blake responded.

Bill offered the whiskey to Blake, and he took a long swig from the bottle, turning it up and swallowing a number of times before he let it drop from his lips.

"I'll kill that kid if'n it's the last thing I ever do," he said under his breath.

"Melvin don't mean no harm Blake," Bill responded. "He's jus' a little addled."

Blake looked down at Bill who was trying to provide some relief to his sore and battered feet.

"I ain't talkin' bout Melvin, I'm talkin' bout that Irish trash who set me afoot," he responded belligerently.

Bill knew Blake well. He knew that the story would come out in due time and when his rage had cooled some, so he didn't respond to Blake's comments.

"Melvin," he turned toward his brother. "That water ready yet?"

"I'll bring it right over," he said taking a rag and lifting the bucket by it's strap from the cooking rock on the fire.

When he sat the bucket down in front of them, Bill took the whiskey bottle and poured a generous amount into the water.

"Put your feet in this bucket Blake. It's gonna hurt some, but they'll feel better soon."

Blake put a foot in the bucket slowly, and cursed violently as he did so. The pain was intense, yet he knew what Bill was asking him to do was right. When the pain eased up a little from the first foot, he eased in the second, and again a stream of cursing came from his lips.

Bill handed the whiskey bottle again to Blake and he immediately drew deeply from it, and then again.

He brought the bottle back down with a slosh to see that Bill was no longer at his feet. Bill wasn't such a bad sort, weaker than Blake liked his men, but not a bad sort. He was always obedient, followed his orders to the letter, and kept the camp better than any man he had ridden with. It was that perverted Melvin he couldn't stand. Melvin, who was addle minded and could always rub him the wrong way.

Night was setting on and it was cold already, and yet Blake was sweating profusely. His forehead was beaded with huge drops of sweet from the pain his feet were causing him, and possibly from the anger he felt. Never, in all his fifty-three years had anyone ever gotten the drop on him before. He had always been the victor, the one who rode away with the booty. Oh, he had met better men than himself, yet he could always recognize the situation before it developed and take counter measures. There was a whole string of graves left in his path, some whom he had taken head on, but most without giving them the slightest chance at all. To think that a youngster, not much more than a rag-tag boy had gotten the drop on him was more than he could bare.

He looked up from his thoughts to see Bill standing before him, a plate of steaming food in his hand.

"Thanks Bill," he said in an almost defeated tone as he reached for the plate.

Bill got his own plate and two cups of coffee and returned to where Blake was setting. They ate in utter silence. By the time they had finished, Blake was feeling much better. He wasn't sure if it was the grub, the soothing warm water on his feet or the whiskey, but the blood had left his eye and he was beginning to relax.

Bill called Melvin over, and immediately Blake started to tense up again.

"Gather up the dishes and go to the spring and wash 'em," he told Melvin. Obediently, Melvin gathered up the dishes and the pot and started through the woods.

Bill had brought over some hide that they had tanned, and went to work on it, skillfully cutting out pieces of the hide to make a pair of moccasins for Blake.

Blake continued to nurse the bottle, and when Melvin had left them, began to talk some.

"Gonna' kill me an Irish boy, Bill," he said as he moved the bottle up to take another draw from it's contents. "Gonna' do it slow like, put him through some o' the Hell he done to me for sure."

Bill continued to work, not responding to Blake, but listening to every word. He knew the way to get Blake to tell all was just to listen, not to ask questions, and to agree with whatever he said, and he was right. Blake continued to talk, telling of the young man they had met and were set-up to rob when he pulled a greener from under his blanket, and then set them afoot, taking their guns, horses and their boots.

He learned how Blake had sent Bully and Newt to fetch the horses after they had walked a few miles. Blake was a big and heavy man, and it was harder for him to walk than for the other two. And then when he had heard horses coming up the hill where he was waiting, he saw the sheriff and a posse, along with Newt and Bully tied belly down to their saddles. There was a whole between some rocks there, and he took cover in that whole until they gave up looking for him, and then started the walk back to home camp.

By the time Blake had finished telling the story, Bill had the moccasins cut out and was beginning to sow them together. Melvin had re-entered the camp and had set down quietly off to the side and out of Blake's view and had listened intently to the story.

"What you reckon on doin' now Blake?" Melvin asked when he had finished.

Blake's head whipped around and he saw Melvin setting on a log by the fire. Melvin could anger him as no other, and the only reason he put up with him was for Bill.

He cursed as his face flushed red with angry blood. "We're goin' to get us a Mick," he responded sharply. "We're goin' to make him wish his Ma and Pa had never met for sure."

■■

Chapter 12

There was frost in the air when I walked out of the hotel the next morning, and I felt good about things. Tucked behind my belt was Bret Sullivan's money for the mules, and one hundred and eighty four dollars of my very own. Things had gone well yesterday, without a hitch. The Swede didn't wait until noon like he said. After he hooked up that team and saw how they pulled, he came right back into town and hunted me up, taking me to the bank for the money he owed.

The supplies were all ready, and were loaded quickly into the buckboard, and then lashed securely. One thing I had learned when aboard the ship on our journey from Ireland was to tie a descent knot, and to lash cargo securely.

By one o'clock yesterday, everything had been loaded and all of my business had been taken care of, so I spent the rest of the day lounging around town, taking in the sights and eating.

By seven o'clock last night I had paid the bill at the hotel and was settling in the night. I had made a few purchases of my own this day, gifts for those back home and a few new cloths for myself. I found a lovely bolt of material at the general store, and some real silk ribbon and had purchased that for my darling Caroline. How surprised she will be, I thought to myself as I looked over the goods before retiring.

It was now almost first light and I wanted to make an early start of things, anxious to be home. This was quite a trip and successful as well, and I knew Bret Sullivan would be pleased. I almost left when the goods were packed away in the wagon yesterday. The team was hitched, all business had been transacted, and my gifts secured, and it was still early in the day, yet I decided to stay on for one more night. The tavern served a good meal, and I wanted one more supper there before I left.

By the time I had the team hitched and pulled into the street, there was the slightest hint of lemon yellow in the eastern sky. I noticed that the lamps had been lit in the tavern, so I ground hitched the teem in front of the tavern and went in for my breakfast before my journey. When I entered the tavern, there was not a soul there as yet except the cook and the waitress who had been waiting on me the past few days.

"Out awful early this morning Mr. Sherman, " she commented as I took a seat at a table.

"Aye ma'am. And it's off for home with me I am," I responded back to her with a smile.

She had learned me well, this one, and ordered me some eggs and meat while bringing over a cup and a pot of scalding hot coffee.

"We'll miss you around here Mr. Sherman," she said as she set the coffeepot on the table. "Sure does my heart good to see a man enjoy his food like you do."

"Sure, and if a man does not enjoy the food you prepare here, he doesn't know what good food is," I said smiling back at her.

About the time she sat the plate in front of me, the door opened and in walked the sheriff. He saw me setting at the table and came over to join me.

"Mornin' Philander," he said as he sat across from me. "I see you've got your gear packed up and you're ready to leave us."

"Aye sheriff," I said around a mouth full of potatoes. "Sure and it's a nice town you have here, but I must get home."

"Mary, bring me some coffee will you?" he said over his shoulder. "Listen Philander, I want you to ride easy when you go. Remember now, we didn't get Thompson, and he's not the kind of a man who forgets easy."

Nodding my head up and down in response to his statement, I finished chewing the piece of ham I had in my mouth, and then washed it down with the coffee. "Sure, and I'll be ready for him if he comes sheriff, I've my rifle and shotgun loaded, and I'll hold them close at hand now."

"That's what I'm tellin' you boy," he said in genuine concern. "Blake Thompson won't fall for the same trick twice. You ride easy and be alert. If'n anything seems wrong to you, be wary of it and pass it by. He's an old he-coon from way back an' he knows every trick in the book, and some that haven't been writ down yet."

I stopped eating and looked at the sheriff, and could see the genuine concern on his face. He was worried, and that I could see, but I felt in my heart that Blake Thompson had probably had enough of my trouble and would go harassing someone else.

"Aye sir," I responded. "Sure and I'll be careful now."

By the time we had finished eating there were a half dozen others in the tavern, all getting their morning coffee and their breakfasts. It was a nice and cozy place this one, and I would miss the conversation with my newfound friends, yet it was time to leave.

Calling Mary over, I passed her a quarter to pay for my meal, and then handed her a sliver dollar for her own.

"What's this?" she asked in surprise.

"Aye, and this is for the service you have done for me these past days now Mary. You've made a lonely backwoods boy feel at home now, and provided me with the nourishment that I have needed. Spend it in good health now, and good luck to you," I said as I stood and placed my hat on my head.

The sheriff reached his hand over the table to me and I took it gladly. "Remember what I said Philander! Be on your guard at all times, even after you get home. Blake Thompson a bloodthirsty and grudging man."

"Aye, and I thank you sheriff. Sure and its good luck to you and yours now," I said as I turned and walked to the door.

The sun was just breaking over the horizon as I pulled out of town. It was a cold morning, one of those mornings that seems colder as the sun rises. The team felt good this morning and liked to pull together. They had a couple of days of feeding and lazing around and were ready for the road, or so it seemed to me.

Knoxville was built in the midst of the foothills. As I topped over a hill, I looked back on the bustling city that was already busy even at this hour. It was a long ride I had, and carrying the load, it we would make slow progress.

It was as hard on the team going down a hill as up one, for the weight of the wagon was on them both ways. They would have to pull hard, straining their harnessing as they went up, and then it was reversed, holding the load back as the gravity tried to pull the weight of the load down.

I had to stop the team often and allow them to blow. One thing Bret Sullivan had given me was a deep love for life, all life, and an abiding respect for the animals that we raised. Good animals all, strong and with bottom and could work from dawn to dusk with strength and endurance, yet it was a long way home and I wanted to save them as much as possible.

At noon, we had made about ten miles, and I pulled off the road next to the creek where I had staked out the horses of the men who had tried to rob me. The day had warmed quickly after the sun arose in the crystal clear skies and it was now in the mid fifties. The sun was warm and after I had eaten some jerked meat and bread, I sat with my back to a tree and allowed the team to graze some.

The sun was warm on my face, and before I knew it, I had dozed in its warmth and the serene peacefulness of the setting. I must have slept for near an hour, and when I awoke I was shocked to see the big filthy man I had defeated only a few days ago squatting on his heals not three feet in front of me.

When I recognized him I reached for the shotgun I had braced against the tree and it was gone. It was then I saw another man, as big and as filthy as the first but much younger, a broad smile on his face and exposing teeth that were brown and green from his uncleanness.

"Well there Mick," Blake Thompson said to me in a cruel tone. "Time to get some o' my own back boy," and then he cursed at me violently.

I looked back to him and there was a ghastly cruel look in his eyes. Not a look of anger, but one evil such as I had never seen in any man before. I started to rise and was bludgeoned on the top of my head by a man I had not seen, standing on my left. There was a loud crack as the rifle butt came down on my head, and I thought for a moment that I would loose consciousness.

"You done played hob with the wrong gent boy," a voice was heard saying. My vision was blurred from the crack on the head, and the pain was something awful.

"Philander"

The next moment, I was pulled from my seat at the base of the tree, and was looking eye to eye with Blake Thompson who had ahold of my shirtfront. His breath was as foul as his appearance, and I could see through the blur that there was a smile on his cruel lips. The smile was one of conquest, of achievement and of revenge.

With a ham like hand, he rang my jaws with a backhanded blow, and an evil laugh came from his demented throat. "That there's jus' the start of things Mick," he said. "I'm goin' ta' beat you boy, beat you 'till you wished I'd kill ya."

A fist came to my middle and the air was pushed from my lungs, leaving an incredible pain, and then there was another fist to my side that doubled me over.

"Melvin," I heard Blake Thompson say. "Get over here an' hold this boy up so's I kin beat him proper."

A demented laugh was what I heard behind me as a man grabbed my arms securely.

"Now Mick, we'll see what you're made of," he said as a ham like fist hit me like the kick of a mule, and lights exploded in my brain. There was the taste of blood in my mouth as another punch landed in my ribs. I could hear a crack as that punch landed and then there was nothing else.

I awoke some hours later. It must have been for it was pitch black outside. There was a weight on me, one that made it impossible to move. My vision was blurred still and I hurt all over, and I was cold.

It took me some time to figure out that I was covered with dirt. My arms and my legs were immobilized by the heavy weight of it, and I worked my sore and throbbing arms making slow progress against the weight. It took me nearly a half an hour, some because of the pain, to get a hand free and work an arm out of the dirt that covered me. My eyes and mouth were clear of the dirt, although I could feel that my ears were full, and that there was weight pressing on my head.

Continuing to work, resting at intervals when the pain was too much, I finally wiggled free of the would be grave.

There was a stream next to me, and when I finally did work free, I rolled into the icy water. It took me a number of attempts to get to my feet, and I was unsteady and unable to stand upright. There was a terrible pain in my side, and it hurt to breath. If I tried to breath in deeply, the pain was excruciating, and would cause me to drop to my knees holding my right side from the pain.

The moon was up full, and by judging the position of the stars I could tell it was approaching midnight. I attempted to brush the dirt from my face and out of my ears. Looking back at the place where I had been buried, I could see that it was nothing more than a ledge in the turn of the stream that they had placed me under, and then broke down the ledge on top of me.

My cloths were gone and I stood only in my long handles. My boots and socks had been removed as well, and it was cold, so cold.

I must get help I thought. I must somehow get back to town and to a Doctor. With that thought in mind, I slowly made my way to the road, stumbling often and falling completely at least three times.

When dawn broke, I had traveled less than two miles, and was in such pain that I could hardly stand. Feeling my face, I could find where my left eye was swollen nearly closed up completely from the beating.

The warmth of the sun was beginning to melt off the frost and it was welcomed to me, for I had never been so cold in my entire life. As long as I could move I refused to be beaten by my injuries. I would walk and continue to walk until I reached Knoxville and the help I knew was waiting there for me.

Evidently, Blake Thompson and his men had thought me dead, or close enough to being dead to bury me. I was just grateful that they had not done a better job of it. Bret Sullivan had told me on many occasions that criminals were lazy and that is why they turn to crime. They always look for the easiest way, whether it was to get out of work, or for the pursuit of money.

I was wounded seriously, this I knew, but what hurt me the most was the knowledge that I had failed Bret Sullivan. He had entrusted me with completing a job, and now I walked not only with empty pockets, but no pockets at all. The cash, the supplies, the wagon and team and all of my clothing were gone. I had failed, and failed miserably.

I stumbled and went down, unable to stop my fall or lesson the severity of it on my battered body. My feet were becoming a bloody mess and it was harder now to walk and to keep my balance than before. I lie there in the middle of the road, face down with the sun warming my back for a few minutes, trying to muster the strength, no, the will over the pain to regain an upright position. My side hurt me terribly and I had to take short shallow breaths, for the pain was too great when I attempted to breath deeply.

“Philander”

I lay there, engrossed in my pain and attempting to gain the strength of will, and when I finally did try, I must have passed out from the pain of it.

It was some time later that I awoke, coming out of the deep sleep of pain and shock slowly. I blinked my eyes at the light, and my vision was still blurred when I came too in strange surroundings. It took a moment for it to seep in through the pain that was overloading my mind, but when it did sink in, it was a shock and I jumped, immediately causing more pain and almost causing me to blackout again.

“Best just lay still there Philander,” a voice said gently. “Doc said you got two broke ribs, an’ you’re lucky that they didn’t puncture a lung. Got you a pretty good bump on the head too, and he’s a might worried ‘bout that left eye.”

Obediently, I lay back against the pillow under my head. I was throbbing all over, and it even hurt to think. I tried to place myself, tried to place the voice, but my vision was too unclear at the moment, and then the gent that spoke to me came over to the cot with a cup of water.

“Here Philander. Take some of this here water, it’ll he’p you to feel better,” he said.

Obediently, I raised my head from the pillow and this time, with his close proximity, was able to make out the sheriff.

“Come now boy, drink it slow, but drink it. You can’t let ‘em beat you like this son, you can’t let ‘em kill you,” he said.

“Aye” I replied hoarsely. “Aye now sheriff, I’ll not let them beet me at all now,” I said as I took the cup to my lips and drank slowly from it. The first mouthful hurt and strangled me, but I continued to drink of the liquid knowing it would bring me strength.

I lay back on the pillow, the water had made me feel some better. I didn't realize how parched and dry I was until I had drank that water, and it eased some of the pain in my mouth. Before I knew it, I was either asleep or had passed out again.

When I awoke the second time my vision was much more cleared. I looked around the room where I lay and could see that I was in the sheriff's office, laying on his cot. Looking around, I could see that I was alone and it was twilight.

Slowly and painfully I sat up in the cot, and then tried to move my legs to hang over the side. It hurt me terribly when I did this, but I was determined to get to my feet. It took a few minutes to adjust to the pain before I attempted to stand, and when I did, I felt the pain from my feet. They must have been in bad shape, but I never was one to coddle an injury, feeling it better to exercise it and allow the muscles to move instead of setting up and stiffening.

I was thirsty and stumbled with some difficulty over to the olla of water hanging by the open window. I walked hunched over, my left arm held closely to my side for it pained me greatly. When I reached the olla, I took a tin cup from the windowsill and filled it with water and began to drink. Just then the door opened and the sheriff came in carrying a tray of food, behind him was the waitress, Mary from the tavern with a similar load.

Surprised to see me up, he said; "Philander boy, you shouldn't be out'a bed. You been beat pretty fiercely now and you shouldn't rush things too fast.

Come and get back down now, for I've brought you some supper. Should he'p to make you feel some better."

The waitress from the tavern's face was turning a pink color, and it was then that I remembered that I was wearing nothing but my long underwear.

"Aye, and it is sorry that I am now ma'am," I said with sincere embarrassment as started back to the bed to cover-up.

She raised her chin, "I was raised the only girl in a house with eight brothers Mr. Sherman," she responded. "I've seen more and don't think a thing of it."

She sat the tray she was carrying at the table and then came over to help me, placing her arm around my middle and lifting my right arm around her shoulders. She gently set me on the bed, and then lifted my feet up to the bed as I turned to lay down with some difficulty.

The sheriff continued through the room and opened a door to the back of the room where I supposed the cells were located. It was but a moment and he was back, the tray empty of its dishes, and he closed the door behind him.

Mary adjusted the pillows at my head and propped me up in the bed into more of a setting position, and then she took the empty tray from the sheriff and set in my lap. Taking a dish covered with a tin pie plate from the table, she sat it on the tray in front of me and then got the pot of coffee and a cup and poured me a cup.

"Sure, and I thank you now," I responded to her. She smiled at me with her eyes, a lovely smile that lit the room.

"And you eat every morsel on that plate Mr. Sherman," she said. "You'll need it to rebuild your strength."

The sheriff had sat at the table and had started on his own plate of food. He looked over at Mary saying; "Thank you Miss Mary. I'll bring the trays and dishes back when were through. If you will, put this here on the county's bill."

She nodded knowingly at the sheriff, gave me a brief smile, and then left us alone.

I looked at the food before me, I was hungry, but the thought of eating sort of turned my stomach at the moment.

"You heard the lady Philander," the sheriff said. "You need to eat."

"Aye" I said in response. "But the food they prepare is too good to spill on the floor because it won't stay down now."

"Most likely it'll stay down Philander," he said. "You'll never know 'till you try it."

Sure, and he had a point now. I lifted the lid from the plate, and the smell of it was pure ambrosia. One small bite and I didn't care if it came back up or not, for it tasted excellent and I was hungrier than I imagined.

The sheriff got up and refilled my coffee cup twice while I was eating, and again when I was through.

"Smoke?", he asked while I was drinking my coffee.

"No, and I thank you for the offer there sheriff," I responded. "It's something I have never had the desire to do."

"Can I get you something else?" he asked.

"Aye, that you can if you will sir," I responded. "I'd like a set of clothing, a good horse and a shotgun to borrow for a few days."

He looked at me with surprise. "You'd best forget that Philander. They done took your gear, best keep your life. Leave it be son"

"Aye, and that I can not sir," I answered seriously. "Bret Sullivan trusted me to do a job. He's counting on those supplies for the winter and the cash to tide us over and I'll not disappoint him now."

"Well now," he said, "I appreciate your feelin's son, but you just ain't in no shape. Give it a few days, and if you still feel this way, I'll arrange a posse to go with ya'."

"Aye, but I must go now sir, and I must go alone," I responded. "A posse would never get near them, and in a few days they will be impossible to track now. Please sir, allow me these few things and I will bring them back as soon as I get through recovering our property now."

■■■

Chapter 13

"It's again' my better judgment Philander," he responded to me the next morning, "but I got a horse packed up with some grub and gear, an' the things you asked. These here cloths aught to fit you, an' I got you a pair of moccasins fer your feet. You'll need to wear somethin' soft on 'em 'till they heal up."

"Aye, and it is thankful that I am for this now sheriff," I said rising from the bed. "I won't disappoint you now sir, for I'll be back to return your kindness."

He shook his head at me like I was daft. "Get dressed, an' I'll buy you some breakfast 'afore you take out. Sure do wish you'd change your mind though."

"You go ahead and I'll meet you there in a moment," I replied. "It's a proper bath I need and shall have before I dawn these cloths."

He smiled, and then nodded his approval. The sheriff liked me this I knew, from the very start, and yet I had never stopped surprising him. Sure he thought me daft for going while my injuries were unhealed, yet he respected my feelings and understood that the trail may be lost to a gusty wind or a storm. Every moment of delay could pause the possibility that the trail would be lost.

Sure he wanted me not to go alone and felt that I was jeopardizing my life by doing so, but it made sense that a posse would attract attention, and he respected my decision to do it alone. Against Thompson and his gang, a posse would have little chance, yet one man alone could possibly get close enough to surprise the bandits. It was a risk, but the same risk and the same logic that the sheriff would have used if faced with the same situation.

As he left the room, I fixed a bowl of water and taking a washrag gave myself a good bath. Bret Sullivan had always taught me to keep myself well groomed and clean no matter what situation I was faced with. The seeds he had planted in my mind, my heart and my character took root deeply, and of these rules I had built my life.

When I had thoroughly bathed, I unwrapped the package that the sheriff had brought me. There was a complete outfit including a new set of long handles, a pair of denim pants, belt and moccasins, three pair of socks, and two new shirts, both a tan in color to blend into the background of the woods. There was also a hat and a sheepskin coat, and a pair of leather riding gloves. I sure owed this man a lot I knew, for all of the supplies had come from the general store, and were brand spanking new.

When I walked through the tavern doors, Mary greeted me with a cup of coffee, and I sat down across from the sheriff. He was half way through his breakfast and smiled at me when I sat down.

“Boy, you look a sight,” he said. “Can you see out’a that there eye at all?”

“Aye sheriff,” I responded, “that I can. What hurts me the most are my ribs.”

“And that they should son,” he said around a mouthful of food. “Doc said two was busted. Wrapped ‘em up tight like that till they heal.”

Mary brought me a plate of steak, potatoes and three fried eggs, along with a platter filled with fresh biscuits. It was coming of sunrise and folks were coming in the tavern for their coffee and breakfasts. Most of them looked me over real close, so I must have looked a sight. I still had no idea of how I got to town.

When we had finished eating, and were drinking our coffee, I asked the sheriff how I had gotten to his office, and when the doctor looked at me.

“One of the local farmers found you layin’ in the middle of the road, ‘bout four miles north of town yesterday. Threw you on the back of his rig an’ brought you to my office. The Doc saw him bring you in an’ come over to the office while we were tottin’ you in. Fixed you up the best he could an’ told me to keep you there for a week,” he responded.

“And if you wouldn’t mind,” I responded, “please tell the farmer that it is thankful to him that I am now," I said. "And thank the Doctor for me as well. It is a grateful man that I am indeed now."

He laughed a short spurt, "I'll not tell Doc a thing. That man will eat my lunch for sure once he finds that you've gone and not stayed in bed like he told you to."

"Well sheriff, I've miles to go before I can rest now," I said as I stood, a little uneasily from the chair. "If you will point out the horse you have prepared for me, sure and I'll be on my way now."

"Over at the hostler's," he said. "Big bay, he's loaded with supplies. There's a double barrel shotgun in one boot, and a .50 caliber in the other. Be careful lad," he said sincerely as he held out his hand for me to shake. "Blake Thompson ain't no one to mess with. Sure wish you'd change your mind."

I grasped his hand securely and gave him a wink. "I'll be back sheriff, and with my outfit too."

Three hours later found me tracking the wagon from where I had been attacked. There was blood in the grass where I had been beaten, my own blood. I followed the wagon tracks as they pointed to the northeast until I reached the Clinch Creek. There the tracks seemed to end, or so they had hoped. Most men believe they could enter water and go either up or down the creek without leaving a sign, but they are wrong. Bret Sullivan had taught me to work out problems in my mind, and when those wagon tracks seemed to disappear, I rode the bay into the water and studied the bottom carefully. If I had been a day or two later, I would not have been able to work it out for the water would have replaced the sand moved by the wagon wheals, but the tracks were there.

Thinking that they had killed me and buried me, I was sure they were not thinking of pursuit, and would not take much care in covering their trail. The place they had buried me was well hidden, and if ever found, it would have been some time.

They followed the creak for almost two miles before they exited, and I found where they had made camp last night. They must have had to stop early, as I am sure they would have worn the team down by making them pull that load through the uneven bottom of the creak, and then over the sharp crest of the foothill where they exited. It was mid afternoon when I came upon the old campsite, and they weren't too much on cleaning up after themselves. They had allowed the fire to burn itself out instead of making sure it was suffocated, and there was bits of bone and other trash lain around on the ground and next to a fallen log I am sure they had used for their seating.

It was a fine and strong horse that the sheriff had lent me, and smart too. I could tell he was used to tracking and enjoyed it, for as much as anything else, he helped me to work out the trail.

Unsaddling the bay, I rubbed him down with some dry grass and let him roll, and then staked him out on some good grass. It was early, but I was tired, and the constant jarring from the horse as he moved hurt my side something awful. I made my camp where they had the night before, and built my fire over their old one. Tomorrow would be soon enough, I thought. They cannot travel as fast as I, for the wagon and the team were a burden.

I ate hard tack and jerked meat that night, washing it down with coffee, and before the sun set, was rolled up in my blanket and ready for sleep. I moved the bay in closer to camp, knowing it was a trail horse, and would warn me should someone intrude the camp.

The sky had turned a lemon yellow in the east before I awoke the next morning. The ground was whit with frost, and the trees covered so heavily that it almost seemed as if it had snowed. The morning was cold, and the coffee tasted good and warmed the depths of my being as I huddled over the fire. When the sun hit the sky, it was over the Clinch Mountain.

Saddling the horse was difficult for me for the wrap on my ribs was tight, and raising my arms that high with the weight of the saddle hurt terribly. The trail they had taken was still visible, most of the grass that had been knocked down from the horses and the wagon wheels was undisturbed by the elements as yet, and one could ride at a fast trot and still see it plainly. I rode for a few hours and then took off to the side of the trail, up higher so I could see it easily. I was sure that I was getting close, and I didn't want to be seen, especially tracking them. If seen, I wanted it to seem that I was a man at his own purpose and not a man in pursuit of them. Two hours later brought me to their camp of the night before.

Their trail was clear, and their direction had not varied a mite. They were heading for the Clinch I was sure, and now we were only a few hours apart.

Allowing the bay to stretch out, we traveled quickly, and I no longer paid any mind to the trail. I wanted to get ahead of them, to set a trap of sorts and allow them to come upon me. If they did change directions, it would be easy enough to pick up their trail again, and so for the rest of the morning we traveled hard, that bay and I.

When I finally stopped, it was dusk and about half way up the Clinch. I had chosen a spot that would give me a look at a large area, and I could see anything that would be coming up the mountain. Settling down, I made a cold camp. There would be no coffee tonight, no warmth from a fire. The spot I had chosen was obscure indeed, but a fire of any variety could be seen for ten miles or more.

All night and the next day I waited, watching the side of the mountain for movement. There was a number of times that there was movement, but it was from animals and not of the human kind.

The second morning in this location brought me to the realization that my tactic hadn't worked. I would have to go back down the mountain and work out the trail, which was something I didn't want to do, but now had no choice.

That day of setting up there had done me a lot of good. The swelling was almost gone from my left eye, and when I saddled the bay, it didn't hurt near as bad.

I rode off the mountain the same way that I had come up, and when I reached the bottom, I started casting back and forth to try and locate their trail, which I found without any problem.

It was there, as plain as the nose on my face and as easy to recognize, and moving in a direction that would surely have put them in my view should they have come up the mountain. It made no sense to me that I could have missed seeing them, so I came to the conclusion that they must have stopped somewhere short of that mountainside.

We rode easy, that bay and me, and rode well to the side of that trail so we would be harder to be seen. It continued to the bottom of the mountain and started up, and then turned suddenly to the east. It was there that I decided to scout the trail afoot, for they must have held up somewhere close at hand.

The Cherokee children I had played with while growing up had taught me much. Bret Sullivan had given me an enquiring mind, and the games we played taught me how to travel through the woods without making a sound, and how to navigate my way through unfamiliar surroundings.

There were deep woods surrounding this area, of pine, oak, mulberry, cedar, chestnut, cherry and hickory. All were old trees, untouched by the civilization of man, and taking the shotgun from the boot, I moved like a ghost through them.

As I said, the trail continued up the foot of the mountain and then suddenly turned to the east. I followed that trail now afoot, and keeping to the cover of the woods. About two hundred yards after they had made the turn, the country suddenly dipped down into a hidden cove, or cul-de-sac in the side of the mountain, and I could see signs of human life. There were trees whose lower limbs showed evidence of axe marks, and the ground in places showed where a log or heavy limb had been pulled through the woods for fuel.

I slowed my pace, and looked carefully about before I moved, for I could come up on them at any time, and I wanted to be on my terms, not on theirs.

As I started down, I saw that the trees started to thin, and there was a clearing at the bottom, and in the clearing stood my wagon and the stock staked out on grass, and two men lazing around the fire, two big men, one of the Blake, and the other the man he had called Melvin. The third man was nowhere to be seen, and I studied the area and the terrain for some time trying to work out a plan.

■■

Chapter 14

Working out the trail was no problem. Finding them was one thing, now recovering my property and capturing them without having a shootout was quite another. I had a deep and abiding respect for life, all life, and never shot an animal without need. My deeply seated Christianity would not allow me to take another man's life, and this I would not do. I must bluff them, must figure a plan that would give them no option for escape, or means to carry on a fight.

That third man bothered me. Where was he? What was he doing? Was he setting guard duty somewhere unseen? Had he already seen me?

Lying there, I started looking over all of the possible places a man might stand guard. Looking long and hard at each place. A man was not easy to see in cover as long as he remained perfectly still, and I looked at each spot, dwelling for a long time at each to assure myself that no one was hidden there.

Noon came and passed, and I ate jerked meat and drank from my canteen to wash it down, continuing to study the layout and to try and locate the third man. By late evening, I was no closer in locating the third man. I noticed that one of the men in the camp, Melvin, had been working around the fire, and I presumed was about cooking their supper. This may be my chance to locate the hide out, the lookout post that had evaded me the whole day.

As the sunset, a plan had begun to develop in my mind. Although careful in the daylight hours, these may not be so careful during the night and this may be my chance to capture them, all of them without having a shoot-out. The men I was facing were no strangers to gunplay, and as the sheriff warned me, they had little regard for human life. All were wanton killers, none would hesitate to put a bullet through my brain, and they had already tried to kill me once.

When the sun had set, and the twilight had settled into the cul-de-sac, Melvin stood suddenly next to the fore, and taking a metal plate and a spoon, looked up the side of the hill in back of them, and hit the plate with the spoon five or six times. From the side of the hill and a fallen log, a man arose from the nothingness and started down the hillside toward his supper.

I looked back at that fallen tree he had been hiding behind and tried to see something different than I had seen before, but I could see nothing that had changed. They must have a hole dug out from behind the log, or a natural depression that he had been hiding in.

When I looked again at the camp, all three were at the fire, dishing up something from a pot into tin plates. The wagon I could see was still loaded with my belongings and Bret Sullivan's supplies. Looking again around the fire, for the last stage of twilight was upon us, I could see them eating and passing around a bottle amongst themselves, a whisky bottle I assumed, which could work for my good.

I rolled over right there and then, deciding to get a little sleep, for I was sure it would be needed before this night was over. I would nap until around midnight and then make my move.

My eyes opened to the brilliance of the stars in an unnaturally clear sky overhead. The wind had picked up, it was a bit warmer and then I heard the distant roll of thunder. The wind was gusting sometimes, rattling the leaves that remained on the trees and making the natural sounds as it passed over the landscape. This could work in my favor and it could help me indeed.

Looking at the camp, I could see that the fire had burned down. There was still a glimmer of flames, enough to light the camp area, and I could see three men lay rolled up in their blankets next to it and to the same side of the fire.

Taking the shotgun, I moved with utmost care, not wanting to make any noise that may sound unnatural. I waited for a gust of wind and then I would move with it; covering whatever sounds I would have made in the natural rustling sounds of nature. When the wind stopped, so did I and patiently waited for another gust before moving again.

I went around to the backside of their camp, and watched for a moment, making sure that they were asleep. During the breaks in the wind, I could hear the deep breathing that accompanied sleep, and knew the three were out.

Moving cautiously, I walked right into their camp and sat down on a log that was across and to one side of the fire. I reached over with my left hand, the shotgun being held as one would a pistol in my right, and picked up the coffeepot. It was still almost half full, so I sat it down and reached in my pack for my cup. When I had poured myself a cup of the coffee, I sipped it while I watched the men sleep, assuring myself that I had gone unnoticed.

Thunder rolled in the distance to the west, and I could see lightening far off as it lighted the clouds in uneven streaks that ran through them, giving an uneasy feeling to the night and to the situation at hand.

The men didn't move any, their breathing steady and relaxed. I was sure that I had gone unnoticed so far, and felt good about it for I wanted this to be on my terms and my terms only.

When I had drunk my coffee, I threw the dregs into the coals of the fire and then looked around for some means of getting their attention that hopefully would not startle them. Off from the fire and within reach of my position was a large clump of moss, evidently used to start their fires. Reaching over, I grasped the clump and threw it on the coals of the old fire.

Immediately the flame caught hold and lighted the camp brilliantly, and I could see that the bright light was suddenly bothering Blake Thompson. His eyelids fluttered while not opening, and then opened slowly to the light. He lay flat on his back, his massive stomach rising sharply from the filthy blanket in which he was wrapped. He blinked his eyes a time or two, and then started looking over to the fire. The blaze was bright and no man should look directly in a fire when it is night, for it will affect their overall vision for a bit when they look away again.

His eyes moved slowly inspecting the camp and then he saw me. His eyes grew in size as he saw me, and he suddenly reached over his body with his right hand to a rifle that he'd been leaned against a tree.

As he reached, I pulled the hammers back on that shotgun. The cocking of that gun sounded loudly in the silence of the night and he hesitated, his hand only about six inches from his own weapon.

'I wouldn't," I said in quiet tone, and his hand slowly retreated back across his chest and to his side. His face was turning red with angry blood and as he started to speak, I quickly took my left hand and raised a finger to my lips.

"Aye, and lets not disturb the others rest quite yet now," I said softly.

Melvin rolled over a bit, being disturbed by the conversation and the light, but did not awaken and was quickly snoring lightly again.

Coming from his deep sleep, it took a moment for Blake to realize who I was, and when he did, his eyes enlarged again and a slight smile came on his lips.

"Mick," he said softly. "Done thought we'd seen the last of you for sure boy."

"Aye, and that you did," I said. "Dead and buried is the way you left me."

He chuckled deeply and softly, "guess I misjudged you boy," he said. "Must be more of a man in that skinny body than I thought there were."

"Aye, and there's man enough to take back what you stole from me now," I said softly. "Set up Blake, and lean against that tree at your head now," I continued. "But do it gently, for this shotgun has a hair trigger and I'd hate to blow you in half."

He looked at me with pure hate. This was the second time I had bested him and it was something he was unused to.

When he was fully sat, I said; " now take your hands and latch your fingers behind your head."

He moved his arms slowly and cautiously following my orders. When he was taken care of, I took the muzzle of the shotgun and gently nudged the one that is called Bill. Of the three I figured him the least danger. His eyes opened immediately and he was looking down the business end of that shotgun. The third man was snoring some harder now, so I figured to be relatively safe.

"And good morning to you sir," I said in a whisper. "And I'd be quite pleased if you would tie your friends hands behind his back for me now."

There was no argument in him as he arose from the pallet cautiously and caught the pigging string that I tossed to him.

"Aye, and be careful now lad," I told him. "I would dearly hate to see that rifle setting next to him damaged by this buckshot. You'd best pick it up by the barrel and lay it over here next to me."

He moved slowly, picking up the rifle as I had told him and passing the butt end of it over to me. I grasped it with my left hand, and leaned it against the log that I was setting on, as he started tying Blake's hands. Moving one behind his back from the top of his head, and then the other.

When Blake was secured I felt better, although I had no reason to. I hadn't had an opportunity to see that he was tied properly, and he was a big man. Big enough that if he wanted to take the chance, he could have given me a rough time of it even with his hands tied. No man wants to face a situation of sure death, and that is just what I presented to these men. There was no option. They must comply or face two barrels of buckshot at close range.

When Bill stood up from tying Blake's hands, I tossed him another pigging string. "Now, tie up the one snoring there," I said a little louder. "Do it right and no tricks with you now."

He nodded his compliance to my directions, and went over to Melvin. Kneeling next to him, he had one hand tied before Melvin awoke.

"Say Bill," he said confused. "What you think you're doin'?"

Bill's eyes went from Melvin to me and he nodded toward me. His ponderous head rolled over to see me setting on the log, a shotgun in my hands with the hammers back, and his boss tied up and setting with his back against a tree.

"Aye and if you'll just behave now, nothing bad will be happening to you now," I told him in my normal voice.

The weather was getting closer to us now, the thunder rolled loudly and the lightening was seen coming toward the ground. I wanted to hurry this before the rains started, but didn't want to endanger my position, nor my advantage.

Bill rolled Melvin over on his belly, and then tied his other hand. This one I could see and knew that the knots were tight made and the pigging string securely wrapped around the wrist.

Completing his task, Bill stood and it made me wonder how I would handle securing him. If they only knew just how reluctant that I was to shoot or to kill, I would not have stood a chance with any of them. This Bill now presented a problem to me, for he was the smartest of the three I could see, and maybe I had underestimated the danger in the man.

I told him to set down and keep his hands in sight. When he complied, I lay the shotgun across my legs and taking a pigging string from my pocket, I fashioned a slipknot on one end of it. Blake was fully awake now, and the meanness in him was beginning to come out, for he cursed at every breath, his face flushed red with angry blood.

I stood and walked around back of Bill, commanding him to raise his right hand. When he did, I placed the shotgun barrel against his neck and placed the loop around his wrist, and then told him to move his hand behind his back and next to his left. I tied him as best I could with only one hand, and when I felt that he was sufficiently immobilized, I released the hammers on the shotgun and leaned it against the log, taking another pigging string, I tied him properly, and then checked Melvin's bonds.

Blake was cursing violently now, threatening me with every breath. I turned and smiled at him, a friendly and innocent smile that just seemed to anger him all the more.

"Aye, Mr. Thompson now," I told him. "And if it makes you feel better to curse and to threaten me then I don't mind. But there's nothing you could do to me that you haven't already tried now."

"You may think that Mick," he said bitterly, "but it's a long way back to Knoxville, and I'll make sure the job's done proper this time."

"And I doubt if you will have the chance now," I said picking up the shotgun. "For the first move that any of you make I don't like, I will not hesitate. You're worth as much dead as alive now."

He cursed me again, a hint of worry in his eyes for the first time. I did wish that I had another person with me to help out while we took our leave, but I had it alone, and alone I must take them back. They would be trouble, this I had no doubt, and would make every opportunity to try and best me or escape.

I searched through the camp and found all of their weapons, which I unloaded, all but one pistol that I tucked behind my belt. I found our money as well, and a good bit more with it.

The rain seemed to have passed off a little to the south of us, which I was grateful for. Leather, when it is wet will sometimes stretch and if they worked the pigging strings while wet, they may have been able to free themselves.

It was still hours before dawn when I broke camp, loading their gear on the wagon along with my own, and tying their horses to the back of the wagon, I thought it safer for myself to have them mounted, so I had them mount their horses, and then tied them securely to the saddles. While I was tying Blake, he kicked out at me at one point, hitting me in the side of the face and knocking me to the ground. He could not follow up on the blow, for he was already secured to the saddle, and even though the blow hurt me, I passed it off as nothing.

When we left the cul-de-sac, still at least an hour before first light and I picked up the bay as we left. He had made himself comfortable on the grass where I had staked him, and looked at me like I should leave him be when I retrieved him.

The sun arose as we passed the second campsite they had used on the way to their hideout, and by noon, we had reached the first.

Melvin had been complaining about letting him off the horse to relieve himself, but I knew better and told him to be quiet and use his pants. It surely could make him smell no worse than he did already.

We didn't stop for food, or for any reason other than to spell the horses. I felt that if we pushed hard, we could make Knoxville before sunset, and I didn't want to spend a night on the trail with these three cutthroats. They were relatively safe tied in their saddles like they were, and could do little to harm me or seek an escape.

■■

Chapter 15

We pulled into town just before sundown. The team was tired and pulling the wagon with their heads down and laboring at the task. As we started down the street towards the sheriff's office, the look on Blake Thompson's face had changed from haughtiness and arrogance to one of desperation, and his speech was filled with cursing as he talked with Bill and Melvin.

People saw the strange procession coming down the street and many of them walked out into the road for a closer look as we came to the sheriff's office. Noticing the gathering crowd, the sheriff, who had been in the General Store came out into the street with the others and, upon seeing the procession, broke into a broad smile.

I stopped the wagon in front of the office, tired and haggard from the long night and day, the tension and the constant threat.

"Seems how I underestimated you Philander," he said as he walked over to the front of the wagon. "Thought sure I'd seen the last of you, and you'd be dead and gone by now."

"Aye sheriff," I responded. "And it's dead I am for sure. Dead tired at least."

He held a hand out to me to help me from the wagon. I had sat on that bench for so long that my back cracked as I stood, and it felt as though I would never have feelings again in my buttocks.

Smiling broadly at me, he said, "well lad, you done it. You done it for sure," and then he slapped my back.

"Aye, and I got our property back from them now," I said. "And I can go home."

The sheriff turned and called for some of his deputies to take charge of Thompson and his men, and then to the hostler to take the wagon and the horses to the livery, telling him to rub them down good and charge the county with the bill.

We walked into his office and the sheriff got out a piece of paper to write out his report. I sat in a chair across the desk from him and passed the sack of money I had recovered from Blake Thompson over to him.

"They had this on them sir," I said. "Three hundred twenty seven dollars of that belongs to Bret Sullivan. It's what's left of the money after purchasing his supplies. One hundred and eighty four dollars is mine. I don't know who the rest belongs to, but it's in your charge now."

He dumped the sack onto his desk and counted out the money for Bret Sullivan and for myself, and counted an additional eight hundred and sixty three dollars.

"The folks this money rightfully belongs to are probably dead," he said as he wrote the figures on the report. "Blake Thompson didn't leave many witnesses behind."

"Aye, and it's a shame now for sure," I said. "I don't know how a man could take another's life."

He stopped writing and looked across the desk at me, a quizzical look on his face. "Philander, you mean to tell me you went out after this here pack of vermin without the intention of shooting any of 'em?"

"Aye sheriff, that I am," I responded. "If they had called my bluff I don't know what I would have done, for life is a sacred thing to me, and the only one who has the authority to say who lives and who dies is God."

He shook his head, a strange smile on his face as he turned back to the paperwork at hand. "Just wait until Thompson hears of this," he chuckled. "The meanest man these parts ever saw and he was took by a man who wouldn't have shot back."

It was full dark by the time the paperwork was completed and we walked across the street to the tavern for our supper. The tavern was full, and people turned their heads to see me as we walked in, most of them smiling and greeting me politely.

Mary met us at the door and led us to a table that was already spread with food and coffee. "It's a real service you've done for this community Philander," the sheriff said to me lowly, "folks'll rest easier tonight knowin' that Blake Thompson and his gang are locked up in the jail."

We sat at the table and I didn't realize how hungry I had become. It had been three days since I had a good meal, and I was feeling the effects of it. We didn't talk as we ate, paying strict attention to the food that was before us. Others came into the tavern while we ate, most of them greeting me as they came in.

"Aye and it's a bed that I need now," I said when I was through eating.

"We'll get you fixed up at the hotel in a bit lad," the sheriff said. "Still got a bit of business to talk to you about."

"All right sheriff," I said as I poured myself another cup of coffee.

"Do you know who those other two you brought in are?" he asked.

"One's named Bill and the other Melvin," I said.

"Bill and Melvin Long," he responded. "Melvin's got a one hundred fifty dollar bounty on him from killin' his Pa 'bout six years ago."

"He killed his own father?" I asked incredulous at the thought. "How could a man do such a thing sheriff?"

He shook his head, "don't know Philander. All I know is they're a bad lot, and deserving of the noose that they'll get after their trial."

This saddened me. To think that a man would kill his own father, his own blood was beyond my comprehension.

"You go and get you some rest," the sheriff said. "We'll talk tomorrow. I've got to get all the details for my report, and we have to arrange to pay you the bounty on these men."

"Aye," I said. "It's tired that I am and I could sleep through the morrow I'm afraid."

"Just look me up when you get ready to talk," he said. "The way that team looked you drove into town, they'll need a day or two before they can draw your wagon."

"Aye," I responded. "And I'm overdue at home. I hope they will not be to worried."

The sheriff chuckled, "If they know the same man that I do, they'll not be frettin' over you. Best get some rest now," he said as he stood from the table. "Mary, bill the county for this meal will you?" he said as he turned to leave.

When I went wearily to the hotel and found that the sheriff had one of his deputies put a room in my name, charged to the county again. I went into the room, totally beat, both mentally and physically. As was my custom, I washed thoroughly before lying down, my mind racing with the events of the past few days and in concern for Caroline. I knew she would be worried and as much as I hated to admit it, the sheriff was right; the team needs rest and feed. It will take two or three days before they will be ready to travel, and this will have me well over two weeks overdue at home.

There was no way that I could get a message to them, no means of communication other then a dispatch rider, a letter or by word of mouth. As I lay in the bed thinking of these things, sleep overtook me as a thief, and it was full daylight when my eyes again opened.

When I awoke I was confused, for to awaken after a full nights sleep to find the sun in the sky was unheard of for me. I had been a hard worker all of my life and one who understood the responsibilities of the debt that I owed to Bret Sullivan. I was aware that it had been a noise that had awakened me, and I sat up straight in the bed, listening and wondering what it could have been

There was s scrubbing sound from the hall, like one made by boots against a plank floor while one stands and shifts their weight, and then a light tap on the door. Rising from the bed quickly, I pulled on my pants. My feet were still tender from the long walk without the benefit of boots and I stubbed a toe against the chair leg. When I went to the door and opened it, I was surprised to see the sheriff, and standing behind him was Lem, a broad smile on his face and dust on his clothing.

Both entered the room when I opened the door, Lem looking like the cat that ate the canary.

"Philander," the sheriff said. "This here gent come to town a'lookin' for ya'."

"Aye Lem," I said. "And it's good to see you. Good indeed." I reached for his hand, which was taken in a firm shake.

"And Mr. Sullivan has been worried 'bout you Phil," he said. "You're overdue and he asked me to ride down and make sure you are all right."

"Aye," I responded. "And it's been worried I've been about things at home too."

"Tell you what fellers," the sheriff said. "Lem an' me'll go down to the tavern an' get some breakfast ordered. You get dressed an' meet us there an' we'll tell the whole story."

They left then, and I poured water in the bowl and washed the sleep from my eyes. I combed my hair and put on the clean shirt that the sheriff had given me three days before, and went to the tavern.

By the time I had got there, Lem and the sheriff were in deep conversation, Mary hanging over the sheriff's shoulder and hanging on every word. There was a pot of coffee and three cups and none had been poured from the pot, so I sat down and poured a cup to set and listen.

"…come ridin' into town in that there wagon, all of his gear recovered an' them three cutthroats hog-tied to their horses. Tied so tight it took three of my deputies 'most half an hour to cut them loose. Beats all I ever done seen in my whole life for sure. And then to beat it all, Philander tells me that he couldn't a shot 'em if'n he had too, feelin' like he does 'bout life an' the Bible an all."

Lem was grinning from ear to ear as he looked across the table at me. "Aye, and I'll be off again after breakfast then," he said. "There's a little girl at home who's worried sick and I need to relieve her mind some."

"And did Bret Sullivan send you now Lem?" I asked him.

"He was worried some, but knew you'd be along," he responded. "It was Caroline a frettin' around that made me decide to check on you. Finished with the hayin' and wasn't much else to do."

"It's going to take a few days to get that team back in the harness," the sheriff put in. "He'll also need a day or two to help me finish my reports and to collect the bounty."

"Bounty?" Lem said. "Aye lad, and these must have been some salty men then."

"They got the bark on," the sheriff replied. "Murderers, all five of them. If it hadn't been for Philander here, no tellin' how many more would'a been killed and robbed."

"Sheriff's making more of it than it was Lem. They were as polite as lambs while looking into the barrels of that shotgun. Gave me no trouble at all now." I stated dogmatically.

"That ain't exactly true," the sheriff said. "Took more sand then most men got to do what he done. Them's known killers, been robbin' and murderin' folks up and down the country for years. Took a lot in my book to take 'em, and to take 'em alone."

Finishing his meal, Lem bid us farewell and left the tavern. I looked across the table to the sheriff and there was that friendly smile greeting.

"Talked with the Judge last night," he said. "I can release your money to you, and Mr. Sullivan's as well. When you finish up, let's go over to the office and finish those reports."

"Aye sheriff," I agreed. "And it will be my pleasure to accompany you."

"You ever thought of becoming a lawman Philander?" he asked. "Pay ain't much, but it's a good livin'."

"No sheriff," I responded. "It's a good and honorable profession, and I respect the man behind the badge, but it's not my way. I've a beautiful lass that I'll be marrying soon, and my calling is to the Church now."

He considered my comment for a moment, and then shook his head knowingly. "You may be able to do more good in the Church than you can with a badge. It's better to stop crime before it starts by changin' the character of a man then to clean up the mess afterward I reckon."

I continued to eat in silence, and when I had finished, we left for his office across the street.

That evening when I got to the hotel, I was tired and ready for bed. I had checked on the stock and they were true to their breading. Strong and resilient creatures that recover quickly from a hard work, they would be ready for the trail again come morning.

Three hundred and fifty dollars was given to me by the sheriff as the bounty on the men I had brought in. With what I had left, it gave me a total of five hundred and thirty four dollars. It was a veritable fortune to a man who had never had two pennies to rub together in his pocket before, and I dreamed that night of a home of my own, and of Caroline and the life we would lead.

The sheriff had told me of land that was opening up down to the southwest. Fort Hampton south of the Tennessee River and on the Elk River in North Alabama had been dismantled and the lands to the west and south of the fort opened for people to settle. He talked of a region he had been through down there, a veritable paradise as he described it, of rich forest, of good grass and plenty of water, and of a multitude of game. The government had bought these lands from the Cherokee tribe in 1802, and the territory had been preserved as a refuge for the Cherokee, Chickasaw, and the Creek Indians until just a few years ago. The land he spoke of was called the Bankhead, and he mentioned different places that had been named there, one that held my mind was a place he talked about called the Double Springs.

▪▪

Chapter 16

It was an hour before first light when I pulled out of Knoxville for my home. I missed my Caroline terribly, and wanted to see her. Lem would answer their questions about what took me so long, and I hoped without exaggerating the truth too much, for he was a man who liked the sound of his own voice.

"Philander"

It was a pleasant morning, calm and cold, and I waited not for my breakfast before leaving. I chose rather to eat a little bread and cheese as I traveled, and to dream all the while of my forthcoming life with Caroline. Aye, a lovely girl she is indeed, and as pleasant to talk with as to look at. This was a rare thing for most women who know that they possess beauty have flawed personalities, but not my Caroline. She is gracious and kind, submissive and bold, beautiful and strong all in one.

It would be a year before we could wed, this I knew, but a year that held promise too. With the money in my pockets, I could by some stock from Bret Sullivan and start my own herd. Aye, and it would be small indeed, but would have a few years to grow, and with the proceeds from their get I could increase it, adding to the bloodline and improving it as we went along.

The first light of dawn's twilight exposed a frosty landscape that reflected the little light making it almost iridescent. Aye, and a lovely land we had come to indeed, in some ways similar to what I remembered of my homeland, yet so different, so wild and unoccupied. There were no lords here, none to have you thrown in prison for poaching game, none to hold you in bonds to farm a land you could never expect to hold as your own. Bret Sullivan had taught me that no man possesses the land, but rather they hold it in trust. Trust for future generations, for your children, and children's children. The land was to respect and to use sparingly and with care, for everything we do could affect the quality of life for our ancestors to come.

It was two hour past sunrise and the frost was just leaving the landscape when I passed the place where I had stopped and was beaten and robbed that fateful day. It was a peaceful setting on the banks of Clinch Creak, and one that should not have been disturbed by such violence. I resisted the desire to pull the team over and rest there. The team was fresh still and pulling well, yet it nagged at me, the desire to once again see the spot where I had been so despicably used by the bandits, and where they had tried to bury me.

It saddened me as well, to think that men could sink so low, to have such a disregard for life and property. It was not in me to understand the depravation of such men, nor to see how they could place themselves in the position of God by saying which person might live and who might die. It further saddened me to think that these men would soon face a jury and would likely be hanged their own selves. I held no animosity toward them and no desire for revenge. All that I wanted was to retrieve my property and that of Bret Sullivan, and to see these men taken out of circulation so that they could not destroy any more lives.

I thought on these things as I traveled, and tried within my own mind to place a value on life. It was impossible for me to do, for life is so precious, so rare that it was beyond any value that I could imagine. Bret Sullivan had taught me well indeed, and the ideas of civil liberty and Christian values were a part of my nature. If God had thought that life was so valuable that he would cloth himself with the flesh of a man, to suffer it's bonds and temptations, and to purchase mankind with his own pain and blood as he hung on a cross over Golgotha, then how could I place a value on life?

Deeply in these thoughts I traveled, and when I finally immerged from their depths, I saw that the team was pulling with their heads down and laboring heavily. It was in me to be angry with myself for being so thoughtless as to not pay attention to them, and I started to look for a place to make camp. It was mid afternoon now, and I could barely believe how far we had traveled, and with such a load.

A spring appeared to my right, a nice cove in the shelter of the hills filled with ancient Cedar and hardwood trees, a nice meadow to hitch the stock and allow them to graze and rest. I pulled the teem over and halted them not far from the stream, and then un-haltered them and allowed them to drink long and deep from the clear fresh water of the spring.

When I put them on the grass, they rolled and shook their gigantic heads as they settled in, glad to be through for the day, and then I started making my camp. It was foolish of me to not have paid them any mind, to allow them to tire to the point that they were, and I knew that tomorrow would be a day slow in travel and full of much needed rest for them.

Dusk had settled over the land before I had a fire going and a pot over it. I took some water from the spring, combining it with some jerky, a few potatoes and an onion and settled back to wait while a stew formed in the pot over the heat. I drank coffee and thought of Caroline. Soon we would be reunited; soon I would look into her lovely green eyes again and see my future, feel her hand tenderly touching my own.

The injuries that were inflicted on me by Thompson and his men were healing nicely, but there was a stiffness that settled in on me in the cool of the evening, and that stiffness was upon me now. I don't know when it was that I dozed off but I awoke with a start when the coffee in the cup in my hand overturned in my lap, sending cold chills through me. I jumped as one shot, and nearly fell when the soreness sent pains shooting through my body.

Looking around, I suddenly realized what had happened, and laughed at myself for allowing sleep to overtake me with the coffee in my hand.

It was late now, the stars were brightly shining in the crystal clear sky, and the moon was down. The stew had cooked to almost mush, but I ate it anyway, for I was hungry from the work of the day.

It was late the next morning when I put the team in harness again, and we traveled no more than eight miles this day. I had overworked them severely the day before, and it was a light day they needed, and rest to regain their strength.

Two more days we traveled, and should be home by tomorrow night. The camp I chose this night was next to the road and a creak, one that was often used by travelers and was well set up. It was a cold day and the night held the promise of even more cold as I huddled around the fire and drank coffee. My blankets were spread and it was getting late when I heard the patterned symmetry of horses coming up the road. There were two of them if my guess was right and they stopped near the creak adjacent to my camp.

"Hello the camp," I heard the voice of Bret Sullivan say.

"Aye now Bret Sullivan," I responded. "It is I, Philander Sherman indeed."

The horses started moving again and I watched as they entered the outer rim of the firelight. Bret moved on into the glow while the other rider sat just in the darkness of the night, the light from the fire lighting only the legs and chest of the chestnut horse they rode.

Bret dismounted and looked at me with a big smile on his lined and weathered face. "Aye and Phil now, it's worried I've been about you lad," he said.

"Sure and it's been a long trip now Bret," I responded. "But I'm no worse the wear for it."

"And is it that you're going to let me set on this beast all night in the cold now Phil," I heard in a sweat and gentle voice that sent waves of thrill through my soul. "Or are you going to help me down now?"

"Caroline," I responded in excited surprise as I stood from the fire and rushed to the chestnut. "Aye and it's good to see you darlin', but what are you doing here?"

I lifted her light frame from the chestnut and she melted into my arms before her feet touched the ground, her hand on the back of my neck and holding my face tightly against her shoulder before she let go.

When she did, her other arm was around my waste, and she backed off enough to look into my eyes. It was dark and the fire glow lighted her face softly at this distance, reflecting in her gentle eyes and I could see the makings of tears forming in them.

"Aye, and it's all right now Caroline," I told her gently. "I'm home now, and a better man for the trip."

Bret had moved over to grasp the lead line of the chestnut, and placed a hand on my shoulder.

"We've been worried lad," he said. "And when we heard of what you've been through, it was all that I could do to hold Caroline at home."

"Come," I said suddenly. "You'll catch your death out in this cold. Come near the fire the both of you and get some hot coffee."

Caroline's hand had slipped from my waist and was now holding tightly to that of my own as we walked to the fire.

I sat them both down near the fire and threw on a few more sticks of wood, and then found two cups and leaned across the fire to get the coffee pot when I heard a gasp escape from Caroline's lips.

"Oh Phil darling," she said in a tearful tone, "what is it that they have done to you."

Surprised I stood, the coffeepot in my hand as I heard her breath catch in a gentle sob. I realized that the light had been so poor that she could not see the bruising on my face until I bent over the fire, and was glad that the swelling was gone.

"Aye, and I'm all right Caroline," I responded. "It looks much worse than it feels now."

I handed the pot to Bret and set down next to Caroline on the log, placing an arm around her shoulders as she hid her face in the juncture between my shoulder and neck sobbing with less control. I could feel the warmth of her rasping breath as she sobbed and the warm wetness of her tears on my neck.

"There, there now Caroline," I said as I gently rubbed her back and let her cry it out. "I'm all right darlin', and I'm home to stay now."

She held her face tightly into my shoulder and sobbed until she could no more. And then I felt her relax, her breath still coming in catches. She fell asleep in my arms there, her head on my shoulder and it soaked with the tears she had shed over me. I felt love like I had never felt before, as her protector and her strength, and my own eyes began to tear at the thought.

All this time, Bret Sullivan had been setting across the fire quietly, drinking coffee and watching the drama of human emotion unfold before his eyes, touched himself by the display of love and concern for my welfare.

I looked across the fire at him, a question in my eyes and on my heart, and knowing me as deeply as he did, he caught the question without a word being spoken to him.

"Aye, and she's been worried to death over you Phil," he responded softly. "Hasn't eaten or slept since we heard the story two days ago, and wanted to come meat you. It was all that I could do to hold her back as long as I did, and when this noon I could take no more, we mounted to come and find you. You're a lucky man Philander Sherman, a lucky man indeed to have one who loves you so much."

"Aye," I responded as I adjusted her slightly to give her a little more comfort. "I don't know what I would do without her Bret. She's my life and my future indeed."

"It is my feeling that you two should be wed as soon as possible Phil," he said. "She's woman enough and will not be content until you two are together. I'll talk to her father. They've agreed to your marriage rightly enough, but wanted her to wait a bit until she's older and knows her heart more. I say, the lass knows her heart well and her feelings will not change with maturity now."

I nodded my head in response to his reply, and then gently slipped from the log, adjusting Caroline as I did, so that we were setting on the ground, my back against the log and her head still on my shoulder as she slept. Bret Sullivan arose and retrieved my blankets, spreading them over the two of us as she slept, and then unsaddled the horses and fixed his own bed across the fire from us. He placed some more wood on the fire, banking it so it would last long into the night and then rolled up in his blankets and was fast asleep in a few moments.

Caroline slept on my shoulder as I leaned against the log, not wanting to disturb her and wanting to see her rest. She had been through much more than I. Of this I was sure. The mind can be a cruel master, especially when worry causes stress and pain above one's own limits of tolerance. She had been in utter misery since I left on this trip and to find that I had been misused, robbed, beaten and left for dead by some ruthless thugs had burst the dam of emotion within her.

I thought of these things long into the cold of the night as she slept in my arms, and was overwhelmed by the emotions of love and concern for her. Such a frail and gentle creature she was, as fair as a newborn colt, as light as a wisp and as tender as Gods grace on man. How could I, a serf's son from the emerald isle, a bondservant with nothing and little future, be worthy of such as she?

■■

Chapter 17

"Philander"

I awoke with a start. Looking across the fire, I saw Bret adding water to the old coffee in the pot from the night before. I blinked the sleep from my eyes and looked off to the east. The sky was just turning a lemon yellow over the horizon of the mountains in the distance. Looking over at Caroline, I could see that she had curled up in a little ball next to me, her head still on my shoulder and slumbering peacefully.

Aye, and what a sight she was to my tired and lonely eyes. Her beauty was something to behold and to treasure I knew, for the hard times ahead would temper the gentle lines in the years to come. There was steel in her too, a metal that was uncommon, a gentle strength of will and of character.

Bret Sullivan had been more than a master to me as he was to all of us. He was family, and had treated us as such all the years that I had known him. When Mother died at the hands of the pirates so many years ago, he was there to fill the gap, being both a father and a mother to me, and even more. I could never repay his gentle guidance, the character he had instilled in me and the education and the use of my mind that was so rarely instilled in youth of the times. Father had started me on my road to education and Bret Sullivan had picked it up where father had left off. The moral values, religion, ability to analyze problems and to work out a solution in my mind were just a few of the things he had taught me.

I lay there enjoying the sweet smell of Caroline's hair, the feel of her warmth, and of her hair touching the bare skin of my neck as the sun slowly escaped it's confines and pushed the darkness from the landscape around us, changing it to a black and white world. Bret was busy rebuilding the fire and preparing breakfast. He noticed that I was awake a few moments before, placing a finger to his mouth in a sign to stay still and quiet, surely wanting Caroline to get as much rest as possible. A quick nod of reply acknowledged my own feelings and I relished the opportunity to enjoy her lying against my shoulder.

Bret came around the fire passing a cup of steaming coffee. I took it in my left hand and adjusted myself up slightly so that I could drink it, giving him a smile of gratitude, and being careful not to disturb Caroline. I sipped the hot brew and enjoyed the moment. Enough light had now trickled down to add colors to the scenery, and there was frost wherever I could see. The stream had a thin layer of ice at their banks, and the ground had pushed up cones of moisture at places that extended into white crystal cones maybe six inches high.

The sky to the east was clear yet streaming clouds left a sharp outline and contrast against the rich light blue and gold of the rising sun. The clouds thickened the farther west they extended into a billowing thick pillow of white, and it was still quite dark the further west I looked. Sipping the coffee while Bret sliced bacon into the frying pan, and then took a loaf of bread and cut thick slices from it, I watched the scene as the sun slowly peaked over the ridge of the mountain. The sky suddenly seemed to burst into brilliant colors of yellow, gold, pink and red that extended across the entire sky. A lovely sight indeed it was, but a concern to me as well, for I remembered what the saying was when we were aboard ship so many years ago. "Red sky in morning, sailor take warning" is how it went, and the saying always seemed to ring true.

I felt Caroline's head move slightly and then heard a quiet moan. Turning my head so that I could see her, she suddenly looked up at me and our eyes locked as sleep faded from her. A coy smile on her lovely lips, her eyes held the promise of my future and I loved her all the more for it. She sat and stretched then, placing her arms in a wide circle and arching her back as she worked out the kinks from the night. She suddenly stopped and looked at the beautiful colors overhead. So rich were the pinks and the reds that it caused a red pastel shadow across the landscape, filling it with the unnatural color. Shivering suddenly, she covered up in the blanket and leaned back against me. I could feel the spasms of chill from her body against my own as she tried to warm herself against me.

Bret poured another cup of coffee and brought it around the fire to her. She smiled as she took the cup from him, "thank you Mr. Sullivan," she whispered not wanting to disturb the moment, the serenity we all felt.

Bacon popped and sputtered in the skillet. The smell of the coffee, the frying bacon and the wood smoke in the still cold air caused my stomach to growl in anticipation, and I could not have been happier. I had nothing as the world counts as value, but I had it all at this moment. A fine friend and mentor across the fire from me, my life's love against my shoulder, the lovely smells in the clear frosty morning air, and the beauty of this remote wilderness sunrise was something that could never be valued, never be stolen from me all the days of my life. What an imagination God has, what beauty he can create with just the simple addition of the pastel red color across the frosty land.

It was cold this morning. Colder than we had experienced this year and it frightened me a bit seeing the heavy clouds above us. There was worry on Bret's face I could see, a worry brought about by the threat of snow and the cold temperature while still away from home.

"Sure and that is a heavy sky we have above us now Phil," Bret said as he turned the bacon in the skillet.

"Aye, and it's snow we're in for that I'm sure," I responded.

Caroline sat with the words and looked up. "Oh my," she said softly.

"We'd best eat and be moving on as soon as we can now," Bret said.

With these words spoken, I slipped from under the blanket, and then tucked it in around Caroline's shoulders. The stock must be tended to and hooked to the wagon, horses must be saddled and camp broken as soon as possible. Caroline looked into my eyes as I tucked the blanket around her, a soft smile on her sweat lips and a raging fire in her eye, yet a concern showing on her brow. The weather worried her I could see, and I tried to play it off nonchalant, although I was plenty worried myself. I had seen deep snow's come here, and it was the time of year for them. Snow and cold so severe that there could be no travel, and we were ill equipped to meet it out away from home as we were.

The horses were sensing something in the air as well, and were eager to be in harness. I'm sure they were thinking of their warm barn back home. They were nervous, snorting and stomping as I hooked them up, and ready to be underway. When I had them hooked to the wagon and the two saddle horses ready, Bret and Caroline were breaking camp. They had eaten as I worked, and when I walked back over to the fire, Caroline handed me a plate of the fare and a cup of coffee.

"And you set and eat now while Mr. Sullivan and I pack things away," she said.

I sat on the log that I had slept against the night before and ate the food I had been given. The bacon was already cold but good, and the air around me was bitter cold. Looking at the stream, I could see that the ice that had formed on it the night before was thicker now, and extended farther out into the current than it had just a half hour ago.

Caroline picked up my dish when I had emptied it and washed it, packing it away with the rest, and I continued to drink my coffee, warming my hands from the cup as I drank. When I was finished, so were they. I didn't hesitate a moment to climb on to the box of the wagon, grasping the lines firmly and being ready to go. Bret tied Caroline's horse to the tailgate of the wagon before he mounted, and I gave her a hand up to the box next to me. When she was seated, I wrapped her with me in the quilt I had been using in the box, and she cuddled close as I snapped the lines and the horses pulled against the weight of the wagon.

A few flakes of snow fell as we entered the road causing a chill to come up my spine, for I knew we were in trouble. If we were snowed in we would have little chance in the cold without a shelter and I feared for Caroline.

The snow started lightly, and continued so for most of the morning. We stopped to rest the horses at noon, but not for long. No fire was built, and we ate jerked meat and hardtack for lunch. We were nearing home now, and I could see a little glimmer of hope. The snow had held off for the most part, allowing an occasional flurry or two that frightened the three of us. The horses were eager to pull, wanting to be home in their safe and warm barn I was sure, and they were ready to go again with just a few minutes to blow.

My face was chapped from the cold and sharp winds. The bitter cold was almost intolerable at times and yet I never heard a word of complaint from Caroline. When the gusts would come she would cuddle a little closer to me, at times protection her face under the quilt that was wrapped around us. Her hands gently clutched my arm and she was constantly adjusting the quilt around me assuring herself that I was covered at all times.

It was around two thirty in the afternoon when the bottom dropped out of the sky. Huge flakes started falling thickly, so thickly that at times I could barely see the lead mule from the box of the wagon. Quickly it accumulated, and I pushed the team harder as the snow fell. We were close to home, so very close and yet still far enough away that we could still be in trouble should the snow continue at this pace.

Bret Sullivan had been riding lead and he dropped back beside the wagon now, a look of true concern on his face.

"Phil," he called to me. "Phil, pull up for a moment, the team won't stand much more of this."

Pulling back on the leaders I stopped the mules there on the side of the road.

"We're in trouble Phil, they're too tired to pull anymore today," he said.

"Aye, and this is my feeling too Bret," I responded. "There's the shelter of some trees off to the right there, let's pull over and make our plan now."

"Aye" he said and I started the team forward.

There had now accumulated between four and six inches of snow on the ground, and no break in sight. The horses could manage with a rider at this depth fine, but it was a drag on the team and making it hard work for them.

When I had pulled off, I motioned for Bret to come over. "Take Caroline and get her home now. The saddle horses should make it without any trouble. I'll stay here and wait out the snow."

"No Philander," Caroline spoke vehemently, "I'll not leave you here alone."

I patted her hand reassuringly, "I'll be fine now Darlin' and you'd best be off with Bret now before it gets any worse."

"Phil now, I don't want to leave you here alone. Let Mr. Sullivan go for help now, and I'll stay with you," she responded.

"I'll be all right now lass. Ride on with Bret to the safety of home now and you'll ease my mind Darlin'. There's not much you can do here, and you've a wedding to get prepared for," I told her with a smile and a gentle pat on her hand.

Her eyes came to mine, and I could see the concern in her. Words were spoken in that look, words that could not be expressed in mere language, for there was no word that could express the love held between us.

"Aye," she finally said, "I'll go Philander Sherman. I'll go because you've asked me and because I respect your judgment. But you take care now, for I love you."

"Sure and I love you too now Caroline," I said sincerely. "Be off with you now."

She smiled and I kissed her gently on her forehead, which drew a hug from her, which lingered in the cold of this day long after they had left. I knew that God had blessed me greatly with her, and I was so undeserving of such as she. The warmth of her love filled my heart as I worked in the bitter cold on a shelter for the team and myself.

There was a great old cedar tree there, and I took my hatchet and started chopping the low hanging branches from it, taking the branches and weaving them in the higher branches. The diameter of the great old tree was nearly twenty-five feet, and would serve the team and I well I knew. The branches I wove into the tapestry of the remaining branches fell toward the ground, making a frame of sorts and allowing me to weave more of the branches into them which would slow the wind and the airflow from the center of the shelter. When I had used up all of the branches I had chopped from the shelter tree, I went to another that was close by and chopped branches from it to further extend the shelter. When I was finished I had built a complete circle around the tree that was as fit and secure as most barns I had seen. I took the team under the tree, built a fire and using a large flat rock I had found I stood it on end to provide a reflector, and then went out and gathered wood to feed the ever-hungry fire.

It was a cozy structure when I was done, not as warm as a cabin or even a barn; it was still much warmer than the weather outside of it. Snow was still falling at a rapid pace and was building deeply over the landscape. The wind had picked up and was drifting the snow against any obstacle that littered the landscape. When I had completed gathering wood for the night, I could see that what I had done would become warmer as the snow fell, for the wind was impregnating the branches used as cover with snow, sealing out the harsh weather from entering.

I scooped fallen leaves and made myself a bed near the fire, placing a groundsheet over the pile of leaves and the thick quilt over the groundsheet. The smoke lifted lazily from the fire, dissipating in the branches above the fire, and finding it's way through the maze of branches and quills to the outside.

By the time I had finished my work, the twilight of evening had set on. There was little for the stock to eat in the shelter, so I fed them some dried corn and oats I had on the buckboard and hoped they would be comforted, and then I started a meal for myself.

The way it looked out there, I may be here for some time, for the snow was building and the weather colder as the minutes passed.

■■

Chapter 18

The snow continued to fall in the night, and it took an effort on my part to keep the fire fed. The fire’s insatiable appetite seemed to grow with the falling temperatures after the sunset, and if it had not been for the meager heat from the fire, and the warmth from the bodies of the team, I doubt if I would have survived the night.

I drank coffee and tried to sleep, lying close to the fire under the thick quilt. The snow was falling so hard that it made a sound in the stillness of the night. I would doze lightly and be awakened from the cold the minute that the flames went down on the fire.

I was worried about Caroline and Bret Sullivan. We weren't far from home, but what if they didn't make it? How could they survive such a night without proper shelter? It worried me and kept me on edge as the night slowly passed.

Along about midnight I was again awakened by the cold, and I reached my arm from under the quilt to throw a few sticks on the fire. There was something that was different than before. Something that was not the same as the dropping temperatures, and it worried me some, for I could not place what it was.

The fire suddenly blazed back to life, the flames reaching high into the air and there was an immediate rush of heat that helped to warm the side of me facing the fire. I looked at the woodpile I had gathered before sunset and saw that I had woefully underestimated the amount of wood I needed. There was no choice, as cold as it was out there, I had to get some more wood to keep the fire kindled. Grumbling to myself I threw the quilt back and sat up from the makeshift bed. I took another cup of coffee, sipping it gingerly and warming my hands from the metal cup. I had it to do, and I was never one to put off work no matter how difficult it was.

I reached into my saddlebag and retrieved a towel from within it. I then placed it on my head, wrapping it around the back of my neck and over my ears and folding the front into my jacket to secure it, and then placed my hat over the towel on my head. I took my hatchet and then removed one of the branch that was being used as a closure for my shelter and stepped outside.

It surprised me when I stepped out, for the snow had stopped, the sky had cleared and the stars and moon shown brightly. The full moon combined with the white of the snow that covered everything thickly; illuminated the landscape, and I could see easily. It was bitter cold, the wind sent a chill up my spine as I looked at the shocking beauty of the moment. God had painted such a picture on the tapestry landscape, the tree bows hung heavily with the accumulated snow, and there was a thick carpet of snow covering everything in sight.

It was a real effort to find wood in the thick covering of snow. Nearly a foot of the substance had fallen, and in places the wind had banked it to a good three to four feet in depth. Again I thought of Caroline and issued a prayer for her safety. If they did not make it home, they would be in trouble for sure, and it weighed heavily on my mind as I looked for wood to restock my stores.

I found a blown down tree not too far off and stripped some of the branches from it, my feet numb and hurting from the cold transmitted through my boots from the snow. By the time I returned to the shelter, the flames again had receded, coals glowing in the darkness of the night under the shelter of the tree. The wind was beginning to die down as I entered the shelter and lay the wood on the pile, then pitched a few sticks onto the coals, stirring them some as I added the wood. The flames returned gladly and I sat on the quilt rubbing my arms before the fire and trying to absorb some of the heat it transmitted into the crisp air.

Again I took a cup of the coffee and warmed my hands as I drank it slowly, my mind a swamp of worry over Caroline and Bret. There was steal in her I knew, but she was so fragile, so frail and gentle that I could not but help from the worry.

Covering myself again with the quilt, I lay on the bed, removing my boots and scooting my feet nearer the fire to try and warm them. It had been a long night already, and the night was not over by a long shot.

When I awoke again, it was nearly daylight. The wind had stopped blowing and the shelter held more of its warmth during the rest of the night, but it was still bitter cold. I pulled on my boots when I sat up and threw some more wood on the fire. My stock of wood was getting pitifully small again and I knew I would have to get some more before long.

Looking at the mules I could see that they were content. Huddled together to help each other warm as animals will do, they dozed three legged and seemed comfortable for the moment.

I cooked a small meal before I went out to gather more wood. I thought through what I would need, and decided to just get some more branches at first, and wait until it warmed up some before I tried to tackle cutting that fallen log with the hatchet. The log would make the coming night easier, for the thicker wood would burn slower and hotter than the meager branches I was able to gather the night before. I was here for a few days I knew, and there was no sense in fretting over it. I would have to make the best of it and trust that God had seen my loved ones safely home.

This was a harsh and a cruel land we had come to, and if one were to survive, they must not fight the elements, but learn to live with them. Aye, harsh and cruel as it was, it still was not as cruel as the Lords we had escaped back home, the serfdom that held a man by birth and disallowed him from advancing and bettering his stature, never allowing him to own land of his own.

The mules awoke while I was cooking and rolled their eyes at me, snorting and stomping their massive hooves. They were hungry I knew and letting me know about it. There was pitifully little that I could do for them, for the oats and corn would play out soon enough. I had not counted on encountering weather like this, and was ill prepared for it.

"Aye lads," I said to them. "This I know is hard on you too. I will feed you what I have in a bit, and you'll have to be happy with what there is now. I can't give it all to you in one meal now."

When I had eaten, I filled their feedbags and hung them from their ears. It would satisfy them for a bit, and we could possibly last two days with what we had, but not much more.

Caroline was beside herself with concern for Philander, and sat angrily staring at her father and Bret Sullivan.

"Father, and I just can't understand why we can't go and get him now," she said with a pouted lower lip. "Philander will freeze in this weather and he's all alone out there."

"Aye," he responded taking the pipe from his mouth. "That I know all too well now lass. But sure and if one of us was to go and try to help him, they'd be endangering the future of all of us now. We'll just have to wait out the cold spell."

"I never should have left him," she said more to herself than to the others. Tears started again to form in her eyes as she thought of him out there in the cold and the snow. Philander had always shown himself resourceful in everything he had ever done, but in this weather, and without the benefit of time or help, how could he have built an adequate shelter for himself? And his condition as well. It had been less than a week ago he had been left for dead by those marauding bandits.

"Aye now lass," Bret Sullivan said compassionately. "And we'll have none of that now. Philander can take care of himself, this I'm sure. And he'd be worried to know that you were upset about him now."

"And he's a fine and a smart lad," her father added. "He's found shelter all right, and is setting fine and warm inside of it now. He'll do in any fix, he'll surely do."

"But how do you know father?" she added. "How do you know he's not out there hurt or freezing to death while we set in our warm cabin and debate him his fate now. I don't want to become a widow before I'm a bride, and I can't stand the thought of him needing us while we don't even try." Tears were rolling from her eyes again now, and her breath was beginning to catch as she sniffed the tears back.

"And we surely don't know Dear, but we have to trust in the Lord at times like this. Surely God would not have delivered him from the hands of the Philistines just to have him perish by the weather!" Bret responded. "Have some faith girl. I've raised the boy, and Philander can take care of himself now."

Caroline arose in a flood of tears from the chair she was setting, and ran into her bedroom, slamming the door behind her. There was no use discussing it anymore with them, for their minds were made up. How could they do this to Philander? She thought. How could they just leave him out there exposed to the elements? Not knowing of his condition or his safety.

She ran to the window sobbing, and stood there looking out into the cold wonderland of snow and ice. Her mind was raising, in a whirl of concern and doubt. Surely Philander was a strong and a fine man as they had said, but he's injured too. The beating he had sustained less than a week before had sapped much of his strength, much of his endurance, she knew.

As she stood at the window and looked out, she could see long clear cycles of ice forming from the roof of the house, and it caused a chill to come down her back.

Her decision was immediate and without forethought. She never should have left him, never should have listened to the commands of others. Sure she was a bondservant as were her parents and as was Philander before his birthday, but in matters of the heart, and in matters of decency, she had the right to choose for herself.

Turning quickly, she looked through the things in her room and dressed, donning a quilted coat and a scarf tied around her head and under her chin, she eased the window open and was through it with little difficulty. Philander was her man, her chosen mate, and if she had to fight the fires of Hell for him, she would do it. He needed her now, she had convinced herself, and she would go and make sure he was comforted, safe and warm.

Surprised by the depth of the snow, Caroline walked quickly to the barn where she saddled her horse. She loaded some of the extra blankets on the horse, thinking they may be needed, and a pack of supplies that was always kept in the barn for emergencies, and then left through the back door of the barn that was facing away from the house. A skilled rider, Caroline knew where they had left Philander, and he was only about eight miles away. An hour, maybe two hours would have them together, she thought as she entered the woods off to the east of their home and unseen from the house, and then turned the horse back to the south, toward Philander.

The air was bitter cold, so cold that it even hurt her when she breathed in deeply. She took the scarf and pulled across her mouth, shielding her face from the bite of the air.

Her horse was making a hard go of it at times. The snow had blown in the wind and had settled deeply in the ravines and ditches. Even a small rock was enlarged greatly by the fluffy white pillow of snow that engulfed them. It worried her as she pushed the horse at times beyond its limits, intent on getting to Philander and being of some comfort to him. She did not imagine that it was as bad as Bret Sullivan and her father had expressed, but now a worry came over her, a worry for the horse she rode upon, and for her own welfare.

Caroline slowed the horse to a stop and allowed him to blow some. She realized suddenly that the air, if difficult for her to breathe, would have the same effect on the horse. She had pushed the horse for over a half-hour before she realized the situation, and that her life may depend on the horse's stamina. The snow was deepening, or so it seemed, and the cold relentless. The realization of her predicament caused a startling knowledge that her father and Bret Sullivan had been right. It really didn't look as bad as it actually was, and she angered at herself for allowing her emotions override good sense and logic.

Thinking that she was probably as close to Philander now as she was to home, she decided to continue, but would allow the horse to pick it's own trail, and at it's own pace.

Slowly she traveled, another half an hour passed, and she never felt so cold in her life. The wind had picked up again and ice crystals gathered by the passing wind burned the skin of her face that was exposed. Her feet were numb from the cold, her arms feeling almost like they had fallen asleep. There was no escape from the wind and the cold, it found every entrance that it could into her clothing, and she was constantly adjusting to try to keep it out.

Another hour found her close to Philanders camp. She was picking up the faint smell of smoke every now and again, but could not see it rising in the air. The tree that Philander had used to build his shelter dissipated the smoke through it's branches as it arose, not showing any definite telltale sign in the sky that could be used to direct one to the camp.

Things looked so different to her now than they had the day before. The thick blanket of snow covered the landmarks she had set in her mind when they left, and there was nothing definite to her location. A panic hit her as she looked desperately around, trying to locate the simplest clue as to where her and Bret Sullivan had left him.

Before her now was a stream. It was covered with snow, and she was sure that ice had formed thickly over its surface due to the cold. It was the first sign of recognition she had seen to understand, for it was just beyond the stream off the road that they had left him.

She stopped her mount and looked across to the other side and then into the depression that housed the stream. It looked all right, looked safe enough she thought, so she prodded the horse in its flanks to continue.

The snow had piled deeply into the banks of the stream. Much more deeply than Caroline could have imagined, and as the horse plunged into the depth, it labored hard, jumping to try and make some forward progress in the five-foot deep snow bank. The progress was slow, and when the horse finally made it to the water, he broke through the ice and went down, throwing Caroline from the saddle and into the bank of snow covering the stream.

Philander was about to go out to chop some more wood. He was just reaching to open the area he had been using as a door when he heard the horse scream in fright, and then the faint scream from a woman. Astounded at the sounds, he stood up straight and listened intently, and then heard a distant movement as the horse struggled to free itself from the confines of the snow bank and clamber up the side of the depression.

Quickly he went outside, and looked toward the direction of the sound. There, standing on the bank three legged, the saddle at an odd angle, was the horse. It was a horse Philander recognized immediately. One he had groomed and cared for a number of years. The horse belonged to Caroline, and a shiver went up his back.

The snow was pretty close to a foot deep in the flat, and was banking three to four times that against the trees, logs and rocks. Oblivious of the snow and the extreme cold, Philander ran as fast as he could to the horse. He saw the evidence he was looking for easily enough, for the blankets and food sack were tied to the now out of place saddle.

He looked from the horse, seeing the trail clearly where he had gone through the creak, a hole in the snow about four feet from the area that the horse had gone down.

Fear ran through him, fear not for himself, but for the welfare of Caroline. Plunging through the snow, Philander worked his way as quickly as he could to the hole. Caroline was there; covered in a layer of snow that had fallen in on her from the edges of the hole when she fell.

Philander worked feverishly to get her free. She too had fallen through the ice and was soaking wet and unconscious from the fall. Even though Caroline was petite, it took a great effort for him to extract her from her position. He finally got her across his shoulder, and then struggled in the deep snow trying to get her up the embankment. When he finally reached the top, he was completely exhausted. He grasped the lead from the horse and started in a quick walk to the shelter.

▪▪

Chapter 19

“Philander”

Philander Sherman worked feverishly on Caroline. Great spasms shook her body from the severe cold she had experienced, as she lay unconscious before him. She was soaked through and through from the dunking she had experienced in the stream, and he stripped the coat from her. Ice had already formed from the water in her coat and it was stiff as he removed it. He threw a couple of logs on the fire and removed the blankets from her horse, wrapping her tightly in one, and then placing two more over the top of her.

Quickly he made a fresh pot of coffee and then taking a cup, sat and placed her head in his lap. He poured a little of the warm brew into her mouth, and she coughed as the liquid choked her, opening her eyes with a flutter. She looked around, her pupils unnaturally large for a moment before she could focus.

Shudders of cold still rocked her body as she looked up into Philanders eyes and a quick smile lighted her face as she recognized him.

“And you’re all right then,” she said. “I don’t remember getting here.”

“Aye and you should not darlin’,” he responded. “Your horse broke through the ice and sent you spilling into the creak now. What were you doing out there? It’s not fit weather for man nor beast.”

“I was worried about you,” she said as she sat up slightly. She took the cup from his hand and drank from it, the hot liquid burning a path into her cold insides.

“Sure, and I you,” he answered. “But that was no reason for you to jeopardize your safety now. Never the less, I’m glad to see you Caroline.”

“And I you,” she responded as another shudder of cold rocked her body.

Philander stood suddenly and threw more wood on the fire. "I'm going to get some more wood," he said. "Get out of those wet cloths and wrap in a dry blanket now. When I get back, I'll fix you something to eat."

She smiled in response and he turned and went from the shelter. Caroline undressed quickly. The water had frozen in her clothing making them stiff, and her body was racked with chills. What a foolish thing she had done, and the realization of it struck her hard. If Philander had not been near, or if he had not heard the commotion as she was thrown from the horse, she surely would have frozen to death. God had been looking out for her she knew, for it was providence that had saved her life and no luck that she would award thanks to.

"Mr. Sullivan," Brody Shaw called out as he ran into ran into the cabin in a fever. "Mr. Sullivan, Caroline's gone now."

Mrs. Shaw came from the kitchen, her apron wound tightly in her hands and a worried look on her face.

"What," he responded as he took the pipe from his lips and folded the book he had been reading. "What do you mean gone Brody?"

"Aye, and she's no where to be found now. I thought she had gone to the barn to gather eggs, and when I went to look for her she was not there," he responded. "Her horse is gone also and there's a trail leading from the back of the barn into the woods now."

Lem had come in through the door. He had been working in the barn for nearly two hours and had not noticed that one of the horses was missing.

“And do you know anything of this now Lem?” Bret Sullivan asked.

“Nary a thing now Bret,” he responded. “I been workin’ in the barn for ‘most of two hours and she’s not been around.”

“Fool girl,” Brody said. “She’s liable to meet her death now, out in this cold like that. I knew she was worried about Philander, but I had no idea she’d pull a stunt like this.”

“Aye,” Bret said. “She’s a woman full Brody, a woman in love now. You’ll have to face up to that some time.”

“What will we do,” Mrs. Shaw asked. “She can’t take care of herself in this weather!”

“Aye, and this I know. We’ll just have to go fetch her and pray that the good Lord has seen fit to keep her safe now.”

“I’ll go,” Lem said. “I’ll get saddled and take out after her for you Brody.”

“And I thank you now Lem,” he responded. “But it’s my responsibility.”

“Aye, and you have a wife to comfort now Brody. She’ll be all right and we can’t be that far behind her now,” Lem responded. “Just tell me where it was that you left Philander now Bret, and I’ll be on my way.”

“It’s a good thing you’re doing now Lem,” Bret said approvingly. “Mrs. Shaw, fix Lem a sack of food while he saddles his horse now.”

Mrs. Shaw ran over to Lem and gave him a quick kiss on the cheek, causing him to flush and blush from embarrassment. “Thank you Lem,” she said. “Bring my girl home to me now, and see that she’s safe and unharmed.”

"Aye, and that I'll do. If she's made it to Philander now, she'll be safe enough ma'am. He's a good man and he'll take care of her now," Lem responded.

"Brody," Bret Sullivan said, "you'd best set down now. There's a thing I want to discuss with you."

"Aye Bret," he responded, "and I know what you are going to say now. If she's all right, they can be wed on her sixteenth birthday. It's about two months and I know now that she knows her mind, even if her judgment is not matured yet."

"She's a fine lass Brody," Bret responded, "and she could find no better lad now."

"Aye and that I know, I surely do now. I've watched the boy grow into a man, and the things you've taught him have seated deeply into his being. He'll make a fine husband and a good father to my grandchildren," Brody said.

Elm opened the door again and a strong gust of cold air followed him in the warm cabin. "And I'm ready now," he said as he shut the door behind him.

Ruby Shaw came from the kitchen with a flour sack filled with food. She was drawn from worry, but had overheard the conversation between Bret Sullivan and her own Brody, and she agreed wholeheartedly with their decision. Philander would make a fine son-in-law, after all, he was already a part of their lives and their family. She recalled how he clung to her as a lad when his own mother had been killed from the pirate's cannon. She had a special feeling for him ever since that time, when he clung so tightly to her, when he shared his emotions and his grief.

Philander had been mostly Ruby's charge until he was old enough to help in the fields, that is as a man. He was always a help to them all, and never shirked his work for a single moment.

"Aye and here's your supplies Lem," she responded back to him. "Be off with you know, and make sure my baby's safe and warm now."

"And I'll do my best ma'am," Lem responded as he turned for the door.

"And thank you Lem, take care of yourself too now," Ruby said as the door closed behind him.

I came through the doorway of the shelter I had built under the great old cedar tree, a load of wood in my arms, to find clothing hung from the branches over the fire. Caroline was there, and working over a pot of food she was preparing. I smiled as I placed the load of wood on the pile, and then returned through the door for another load.

The temperatures had changed little in the time I had been here. In fact, it was in my mind that they had possibly worsened. It was warmer in the shelter, much warmer, but still quite cold. Caroline had wrapped herself tightly in a blanket while her clothing dried out, and was working over the fire, but I was still worried as to the effect that the severe cold may have on her.

I had known people who had gotten as cold as she had been and had come down with the lung disease, which ultimately killed them, and I was worried. I must keep plenty of wood in the shelter, must keep the fire going even if I had to set up all night to assure it burned brightly. Caroline was my life now, and all that I had loved had been stolen from me by death. I knew I would see them again, and often thought about the reunion we would have in glory, but for now, I was tired of being alone and without a family of my own.

Bret Sullivan, Brody and Ruby Shaw and Mr. Tally had been my family, and tried their best to fulfill that roll with me, but there had always been something missing in my life. Ever since mother was killed there had been a deep and abiding whole in my life. Something that I tried to ignore and yet it clung to me as the scent would to a skunk. There was within me a loneliness that I just could not explain, and one that I didn't understand my own self, nor could I try to explain it to others. And yet it was there with me always, that is, until I fell in love with Caroline.

I had been there to help rear her, being a big brother and a protector for her since I was seven and she was just a sprout. A wee lass she had been, frail and beautiful all of her life, and as tender as a spring flower, and as strong as the mountains that surrounded our new land. It wasn't until she had turned fourteen that I noticed her as a man would, and it was a shame that came upon me at first, for I had always been her big brother. The shame though was short lived and we began a flirtation that lasts to this very day, and I hoped would never end.

Gathering the second load of wood, I walked briskly back to the shelter. There was only so much that one could stand of these extreme conditions, and I praised the Lord as I walked for his assuring that Caroline had made it safely to me.

"And the stew is ready now Phil," she said with a smile as I walked into the little shelter. Laying the wood on the pile, I reached over and took the plate from her she was offering, and then allowed her to fill it for me.

She had made corndodgers as well, and a fine fit supper it would be, with a fresh pot of coffee to top it off.

"It's grateful that I am now Caroline. My but this smells divine," I said as I sat down on the blankets. This pleased her and she smiled at me in a radiance I had not seen in some time.

"And are you warmer now?" I asked.

"Aye, but it will take my cloths some time to dry out. They were frozen stiff when I took them off," she responded. "I'm glad I came though."

"Aye, and does Brody Shaw and Bret Sullivan know that you are here now?" I asked.

Her head dropped a little as she answered. "No Phil, and they'll be beside themselves when they find out. It was a foolish thing to do I know, but I couldn't help myself. I was so worried about leaving you here all alone like we had done, and I feared for your safety."

"Sure and I can take care of myself now Darlin'. But I'm glad you came," I responded. "They'll be along after you in a bit, I'm figuring. They'll be worried for you."

"And I now that I have caused you all trouble," she said sadly.

"Aye lass," I responded with a smile. "But if this is trouble, I'll look forward to it every day now."

She looked back at me and smiled again. Sure she had run off into a dangerous situation, but it was something that I would have done myself. I understood her feelings, and in my mind she could do no wrong.

The sun was low and twilight was setting on when I heard noises off to the northwest. It came from the same direction that Caroline had rode in from, and I smiled to myself, knowing that someone from the ranch had come to make sure she was all right.

Donning my coat, I went outside, a cup of coffee in my hand and waited. I could hear his progress as he came through the deep snow, and heard as the horse entered the ravine that held the creak. The hot cup of coffee left a thick trail of steam in the frigid air, and then I saw Lem come from the ravine, looking over the tracks as he rode from it.

"Over here Lem," I said to him loudly. "And it's a welcome sight that you are now."

"Aye, and I can see she had some difficulty back there," he responded in a concerned tone. "Is she all right now?"

"Aye," I said. "Mad as a wet hen from her fall, but the only thing bruised is her pride."

Lem looked relieved at my response and rode on. When he came abreast of me he looked at the hot coffee. "Got any more of that?"

"Aye, but it's room we're lacking for," I responded. My shelter was small, big enough for the team and myself, but now we've added two more horses and people.

"And it's snug and warm then that we shall be," he said.

"Snug of that I'm sure Lem, warm remains to be seen now," I responded as I passed him the cup of hot coffee.

Lem dismounted and seemingly drank the whole cup in one gulp. He was cold I could see, his cheeks were bright red and chapped from the frigid temperatures.

I led the way to the opening and he entered, and then I led his horse inside. Feeding the growing number of stock in the tight shelter was going to be hard, and I knew there was not enough to go around.

Lem sat next to the fire, stretching his hands over it and rubbing them together, while Caroline refilled the cup for him.

When she started to hand the cup to him he said, "And it's a bit of trouble that you have caused for me this day young lady."

"I know Lem, and I'm sorry. I had no idea that it was as bad as it is out. It's treacherous out there," she responded.

"Aye, and no place for the likes of you, or any woman for that matter," he stated. "I'm awful glad to see you made it safely anyway."

"I had my moments Lem," she responded.

Lem chuckled as he recalled the whole in the snow and the ice at the creak. "Aye, and that you did lass, that you did."

We all laughed at that and I came next to the fire and sat. It was good to see Lem, and I was grateful that he had come after Caroline. If she had been in trouble on the trail, Lem would have found a way to help her out of it.

"And I'm a bit worried over the stock Lem," I told him. "I just gave them the last of the oats and corn, and pitifully little it was now."

"Aye" he responded, "They'll be all right. In the morning we'll stake them out in the field. They'll have to scrape the snow away with their hooves, but there's feed aplenty for them if they've the desire to eat now."

"Speaking of eating, is that stew in that pot by the fire?" he said.

Caroline jumped from her seat. She had forgotten that he may not have eaten, and I could see that she was embarrassed, Lem having to ask. Quickly she took a plate and filled it, passing it over to him.

"And I've forgotten my manners now Lem, please excuse me," she said.

"There's nothing to excuse Caroline, you've had a rough day of it now," he said gently. "I'm just glad to see that you're all right now. I don't know how I could face Brody again if you weren't."

Chapter 20

Morning broke seeing me setting over the fire. Lem and I had taken turns during the night sitting up and keeping the fire going, for the night had been terribly cold. It had taken most of the wood I had chopped the day before to keep some semblance of warmth in our shelter, even with the bodies of the horses and mules there to help out. It's amazing to me how much warmth can be derived from an animal like that, keeping them in the shelter with you.

I had heard of a man up north of us who had built a wing onto his cabin, a huge wing, and had built cages in that room whereby he raised hundreds of rabbits. What I had heard was that he hardly had to heat his home of a winter at all for those rabbits kept the place good and warm.

It was a clerk at the General Store in Johnson City that told me the story, and I didn't believe it at first when I was told about this fellow, but I asked Bret Sullivan his thoughts on it, and he did a little research. Seems as rabbits now, have body temperatures much higher than that of a man and that they cool themselves from their ears. Those ears now, act like radiators and transmit the heat from the rabbit's body to the outside air, cooling the rabbit and warming the air in the same process. Bret seemed to think that it was possible so I doubted the story no more. I figured that if I ever met this fellow I'd sure enough know him, if I was down wind from him, and I could ask him myself.

As dawn broke I set to fixing some biscuit doe. I always like biscuits on a cold morning served hot and with some coffee. I was wishful that we had some of Ruby Shaw's preserves to go with them, but we'd just have to make out with the biscuits on this morning. About the time I finished mixing it up and breaking pieces of that doe to put in the skillet, Lem awoke. He crawled out of his pallet and came to the fire, which was no great chore for the shelter was small. It had worried me all night, those stock being in there with us, that they might get upset by the smell of a cougar or some other animal prowling the night and start stirring around. With the little room available to us, someone could get trampled awful easily.

"Sure and it's mighty cold this morning," he said as he squatted next to the fire and put his hands out to warm them.

"Aye, but it's still a good forty degrees warmer in here than outside," I responded.

"That it is lad. I hope that it warms today, we need to get these supplies back home, and Caroline as well. This cold can come to no good to us," he responded.

"Aye, and I'm worried about her as well," I said. "She was soaked to the bone and the clothing frozen stiff before I got to her yesterday, and she needs the warmth and the care she can get at home now."

Lem took a cup and filled it with some coffee, warming his hands from the cup and sipping from the hot liquid. "Looks like we're low on fuel as well."

"That's something I will get started on as soon as we've had our breakfast," I responded. "There's plenty of wood out there, but it's slow cutting with just a hatchet. If I'd have thought that we'd have gotten caught out here like this, I'd have brought an axe along."

Caroline stretched and rolled over in her pallet. She was still wrapped in the blankets for her cloths had not dried completely the night before. I took my cup and filled it for her, and then walked to the other side of the fire near her pallet and squatted near her.

"And it's a fine morning to you," I said as I passed the cup to her.

She grasped the blanket around her so it would not open as she sat up, giving me a sweet smile and making me feel as only she could.

"Mmm, and is that biscuits I smell cooking?" she asked when she was fully seated and had the cup in her hands.

"At least I hope so," I responded. "My biscuits smell and look right, but they don't have the flavor that yours do now."

"And I'm sure they'll be very good," she responded with a smile.

When the biscuits were done, I cut some bacon and fried it up to go along with them, and we had a good breakfast. It was full light when we finished, and I donned my coat in preparation to cut more wood. Lem was preparing to set the stock out in the field so they could dig out a couple of mouthfuls, and Caroline was up checking her clothing, which had dried overnight from the heat of the fire.

When I stepped outside of our shelter, the shock of the cold air set me back for a moment. Snow crunched under my feet as I walked to the fallen tree that I had been cutting for our fuel. The morning was bright and clear, and held the promos of much sunshine for the day, and the landscape was lovely on this pristine morning.

I worked hard and as quickly as I could to chop up that log with the hatchet. Thank goodness that Bret Sullivan had taught me to keep my tools in shape, for the edge on the hatchet made the work some easier then it could have been.

When I stopped for a breather, Lem was walking toward me, and I could see that all of the stock was staked out in the field and were rummaging through the snow to find their own breakfast. There was plenty of grass here, long and brown from the natural dying back process of fall and winter, but it was buried under a foot of snow. They would have to work for it now, but it was there if they wanted it, and the way they were pawing back the snow, I figured that they did.

Lem gathered a double armful of wood and headed to the shelter to drop it off. He was a wiry old man, not so old as he appeared, slender from years of hard work and rough times, yet a good worker and a pleasure to know. I had learned much from him, about stock and the breading and care of mules, and I would be ever appreciative to him. He had taught me the way of a life, a career that could set my fortune and provide for Caroline and me our whole lives through.

When he returned to the small pile I had built there in the snow, he passed me a cup of hot coffee, and never had I tasted a cup that was better. The brisk cold air, the smell of the deep woods and the work caused the coffee to grow in flavor and comfort.

"And it's about time I had a try using the hatchet now Phil," he told me. "You can pack some wood or just stand and watch if you care to."

"Aye, and I'll tote the wood when I've finished this fine cup of coffee now Lem," I responded. "What do you think of the day now?"

He looked at the sky and tasted the air before he responded, and then told me; "Aye and it'll be warmer today and tonight I'm thinking. We should see some of this snow melt back from the sun this morning and by the temperature this afternoon."

"And you could not tell that from this morning now Lem," I responded. "I wish you'd tell me how it is that you read the weather as you do."

"Aye and it's only a feeling that I have lad. If there was a way I could explain it to you now I would, but it's only a feeling that I have and a gift for seeing the weather now. My mother had the same gift, and I think it's by birth not by what you know, but truly, it's just a feel of the weather to come now," he responded.

I finished the coffee and threw the dregs into the snow, and then picked up an armload of wood and went to the shelter. When I entered, I found Caroline there, fully dressed and looking as lovely as ever. The shelter I had made looked very large when I entered for the stock had been moved out in the field, and there was plenty of room now. Caroline was working over the fire, preparing a meal to simmer on the coals until noon, and by the looks of the pot, until supper as well.

It was colder in the shelter now, due to the stock being moved away, and I sat next to the fire across from Caroline and poured another cup of coffee. Caroline looked at me and smiled, and then went about her business. Aye, and a lovely lass she was now. Pretty and pert and feeling her oats as she worked in the preparation.

"Lem says he thinks it will warm today," I said as I sipped on the coffee.

"And I hope so," she responded, not looking from her work. "I don't think I've been this cold in my whole life through."

"The stock seems to be busy and finding enough to keep them satisfied. That's my main worry now, keeping them full and fit now," I continued. "They're a fine bunch of animals, and I'd not see them suffer."

Caroline looked from her work into my eyes, and we held the glance for a moment, both savoring the moment. I could see a look of worry in her eyes as we held the glance.

"Philander," she finally said. "What happened back there? In town I mean. Why did those men try to kill you?"

"They were after our supplies and our money now," I responded. "Those men would have cut the throat of a Preacher if they thought he had a penny on him."

"Aye," she said thoughtfully. "And how was it that you came by regaining possession of the supplies and the money again?"

"Why, when I was able, I went after them now," I responded.

"And you risked your life against them, is that right?" she asked.

Puzzled, I looked deeply into her eyes. Where was this conversation going?

"It wasn't much of a risk now, Caroline," I responded to her. "Aye, and I was sure that when I approached them that they could do nothing, for if they had tried, the barrel of my gun was upon them now."

She stood from the fire and came over to where I was sitting and sat beside me. Taking my hand in her own, she looked deeply into my eyes before she responded.

"Phil," she started. "I've known you most of my life. You're not a man of violence now, nor will you ever be. What would you have done if they had challenged you?"

I was taken aback a bit by her question, for it was not in me to shoot another being, and she knew it.

"I truly don't know Caroline," I responded. "I suppose that I would have tried to bluff them into submission again, maybe putting a load of the buckshot into the ground at their feet or the like."

She shook her head, the smile had faded and been replaced with a serious look that I had never seen in those dark green eyes before.

"You risked your life, and both our futures on a bluff now," she said. "And for goods that could have been eventually replaced. Is there anything here of such value that it could never be earned again?" she asked.

I now saw where she was going, and believe me, I had been asking myself the same question ever since I went after Thompson and his men. It was a fool thing to do, this I knew, and it was something that I should have thought through more thoroughly before I took out.

"Aye, and the trust and respect of Bret Sullivan," I answered stubbornly, not wanting to admit my folly to her.

"And you think that Bret Sullivan would have thought the less of you now?" she asked. "And I know he would never have asked you to do anything he would not have done his own self, Philander."

Her response shamed me some, for I knew that Bret would not have wanted me to go after them. He would have counted it as loss and given the Lord praise through it all. I hung my head then, feeling empty inside and a bit guilty from both my actions and my response.

"Phil," she said to me. "Phil I love you. And I cannot bare the thought of living my life without you. Promise me Phil, promise me that if faced with such a thing again that you will think of me and just let it go."

It was shamed that I was now for sure. I hung my head like a small child would do when being chastised by his mother, and from this position responded, "Aye, and I will think of you now and always Caroline. I'll not do this again."

She reached over and took my face in her gentle hands lifting my head so that I would be looking her in the eyes, and then leaned over and gave me a quick yet tender kiss on the lips. When she backed away a bit so we could again look into each other's eyes, I said; "this I promise Caroline."

She smiled then, a smile that lit up my life and drove the feelings of guilt from me. Aye and her smile could rival the Angels in glory, for she could light a room from the glow of it, and fill my heart with warmth.

"I do love you Caroline," I said to her. "I really do now."

"Aye, and I love you Phil," she responded. "You'll always be a little boy inside now. One that I'll have to raise as my own and chastise occasionally to keep you out of trouble, but the Lord help me, I do love you."

Lem came in with a load of wood in his arms then, and I was somewhat grateful, and somewhat remorseful at the same time. No man likes to have his decisions challenged. Not by those he loves, or strangers for that matter, and this was why I was grateful. It was a rare thing to be alone with Caroline, to feel her presence and to talk deeply from the heart, and this is why I was remorseful that he came in.

It was a lazy for the rest of the day, for there was little else to do. We sat around the fire and talked, and dozed as the day passed. Between Lem and myself we had accumulated enough wood in the shelter to last a few days if needed, yet the temperature had risen considerably as the day went by, and between the temperature and the bright sun, better than half the snow had melted during this day.

At dusk we brought in the stock, and content and happy they were. There was plenty of feed left for them out there, and their work to get to it had not been too difficult for them.

■ ■

Chapter 21

And the morning was bright and fair as we hitched the team to the wagon. They snorted and pawed at the ground, anxious to be on their way and to the security of their barn and the other livestock.

Caroline had been up for hours and had prepared us a good breakfast in the way that only she could do. A fine and pretty cook she was with a bright smile in her eyes and on her lips as she worked and hummed over the fire. Aye and I knew I was a lucky man. Lucky, for I would see her this way every morning soon, as lovely and as fresh as an Angle, shaming even them with her beauty. I enjoyed watching her, listening to the melody that she hummed as she worked on the food, enjoyed the redness to her cheeks, which was caused by the fire and enhanced the features of her small face.

It had stayed much warmer last night, just a little below freezing, and it was in my mind to hitch-up the team and be on our way early before the ground had an opportunity to thaw. We would have a rough day of it with all of the moisture from the snow if it melted before we made it home, for the road would turn to mud, and the team would labor hard before making it. Aye and I knew that we would have a rough time of it as well, for if the road were mud, it would cause us much delay, and we'd have to walk a goodly way and perhaps have to free the wagon from sinks as we traveled.

With breakfast completed, I took the team outside and hitched them to the wagon. The sun was just peaking over the distant mountains to the east as we mounted to leave. Aye and God had painted us a beautiful picture this morning on the canvas of his sky indeed. Deep blue, red, yellow and pink shown through the rich green of the pines and cedars from the mountains and in the valley below.

The team was anxious to go, being well rested, and wanting to get back to their safe haven, the barn and their companions. They pawed the frozen ground and snorted as they waited impatiently for us to move out.

With the last of the supplies loaded, I helped Caroline to the seat beside me, and the team pulled at their bits nervously until I gave them their heads and we were off. Already it was hovering just about freezing and I knew that as soon as the sun began hitting the ground the mud would start to appear as the snow melted. Without obstacles we were probably only a couple of hours from the farm and our safety, but mud can be a big obstacle, and I was fearful that we would have difficulty. The snow had melted down by maybe half of its depth from the day before, so should not slow our progress much, unless we hit a deep bank of it that was shaded and had been piled from the winds of these past few days.

Crossing the creek was a chore. The snow was still deep in the valley of the creek, and the stock labored heavily, not so eager anymore to be on the road. When we had passed the creek, we hit a long space of even ground that was good traveling. An hour out from our makeshift shelter, I motioned for Lem to come abreast of me. He kicked his horse in the flanks to get it moving and pulled up next to the wagon.

"Lem, the ground's beginning to get soft and I'm worried for the teams sake. Why don't you ride on up ahead now and come back with a good wagon and team," I told him. "We'll split the goods between the two wagons and have less trouble now."

"Aye, and I'm a bit worried about the ground too," he responded. "That's a heavy load now and it's much warmer than we expected it to be. You stay on this route and I'll be back before noon to meet you."

"And be off with you now," I said concurring with his thoughts. "We'll be right along behind you."

With that said, Lem put heals to the mount and galloped ahead. At the rise ahead of us, he looked back; taking his hat and giving us a wave before he put heals to the mount again and disappeared into the horizon.

We continued making slow progress; the team struggling at times and making a hard go of it in the deepening mud. By mid morning, the sun had worked it's magic on the snow, causing it to retreat, and leaving the ground soft and wet, which soon turned into mud.

Twice I had to dismount off of the wagon and lever a wheel while Caroline worked the team, and it was brutal work, but if we were to continue, it was the only way.

By 10:00 we were both walking next to the wagon and I was driving them from the side. The mud was so deep in the lower places that we sank deeply into it and had to struggle to free ourselves from its grasp. Finally, Caroline stopped and I turned to her halting the team.

"Philander, I just can't go on now," she told me. "I've got to rest a while."

"Aye Darlin', we'll pull up for a bit and let the team blow now. They've had a rougher day than that of our own now. If you will, start a fire and make us some coffee now while I unhitch the team and stake them on the grass for a while."

"Sure, and a bit to eat now as well," she responded.

I started to work, loosening the team and ground hitching them in a field that showed grass through the snow now. It was strange to me, the snow melting away as fast as it did. Everything had been covered with a thick blanket up until yesterday afternoon. The sun worked magic on the snow, and the warmer temperatures caused it to melt quickly in most places, and yet, in the gullies, the streambeds, and where it had been so thickly accumulated because of the wind that piled it high, it seemed almost untouched. Especially in the shadowed areas where the temperature was the same, it seemed that if the sun did not show on it directly, the snow remained as it had been.

When I finished with the team I walked to the campsite that Caroline had chosen. She was there, a pot of coffee boiling on the fire, and slicing bacon into a frying pan. There was a log that she had brushed the snow from and had placed a quilt for our setting, and it was there that I sat.

"And the coffee is ready Phil if you'll have a cup of it now," she said with a smile as I looked into the fire.

"Aye and I thank you now Darlin'," I responded as I reached for the pot from my seat. "Sure and it smells lovely now."

She smiled at me as she continued to work over the skillet. Aye, and this is the way it should be, the two of us together, working for the same goal and sharing the load now. I tasted the coffee, and then tasted it again as I enjoyed the sight. The mules contentedly cropping in the field near us, the white under the rich green of the pine and cedar trees, the rich blue of the sky, the crackle of the fire and the smell of the coffee and bacon sizzling in the pan mingled with the smell of smoke and of the pines growing around us. This was a memory that I would have always with me.

The smells of this moment would be forever etched in my mind with the feeling that it brought. There was always certain smells that brought back pleasant memories, feelings that one could not explain. Aye, and this one would be one of my better memories, even with the hardness of these past weeks.

To think that only a week before I had been fighting for my very life. Unknown to me was the thought that I could ever have such a feeling again, or see and enjoy the beauty of God's creation, the simple pleasures such as I was experiencing now. Life is such a fragile and precious thing and I realized that we were not promised even the next moment. Death comes to everyone in their due time, as it had come to my father first, and then to my mother. "And as it is appointed to every man once to die, and after this the judgment," was a scripture from the book of Hebrews that went through my mind. Aye, and we'd best enjoy our lives while we are here below, for no man knows the moment of their death nor the course of their lives to come. I had been lucky I knew, or maybe it was not luck but the act of providence that saved me. Surely the beating I had sustained would have been enough to snuff out the fire of my life, but it did not. Surely the facedown with Thompson and his men could have gone the other direction if they had called my bluff, for it was not in me to take another mans life now. I had faced my own mortality this past week and had to come to grips with it.

"Aye, and it's a better man that I'll be now Lord," I said softly to myself. "A better man that will serve you than has served you from this body in the past."

"It is sorry that I am Phil," Caroline said to me. "What was that you said now?"

I looked at her puzzled for a moment as I was snapped out of my thoughts, and then I realized that I had spoken rather than thinking. She stood over me, a plate of the food in her hand and a slight smile on her face reddened from the fire. How lovely she was, how fresh and innocent in this hard and cruel world.

I returned the smile and accepted the plate. "It was nothing Darlin'," I responded to her. "I was just reflecting on life and on this past week now, and I guess that I spoke my thoughts."

She sat next to me, her side touching my own.

"Tell me your thoughts Phil. I want to know everything about you please," she said to me.

"Aye, and it was nothing now, just the peace of this moment, the mules cropping their grass in this lovely valley, the richness of the sky, and the beauty of my life's only love working around the fire to prepare me some comfort now. These are moments that shape a mans life now, and I feel truly blessed by them," I responded.

Her hand touched my own and I looked into her eyes. There was a tear forming in them as I looked deeply into them, and realized the seriousness that was behind them.

"Thank you Phil," she said to me. "I want you always to be yourself with me, no pretenses now, just your honesty is all that I ask of you. I do love you now, and I always will."

With the plate in one hand and the coffee in the other I bent over gently and touched her lips to that of my own. A kiss that was gentle and yet so filled with promise for our future is what we shared. Drawing back, I again looked into her eyes that were filled with love and a passion that I would treasure always.

"And that's what you'll have from me then Caroline," I said to her. "I will share my thoughts with you as we share our lives together now. Love is to mild a word for what I feel about you now, I cherish the very ground that is under you."

She smiled again, and placed her head over on my shoulder. "Aye and you'd best eat while it is still hot now Phil, and thank you, for it's a rare man who will open his heart to a woman now."

I started to turn again, for it was in my mind to taste her lips again, when she stopped me.

"Eat." She said firmly. "There's a plenty of time for the rest of that now after we are married."

▪▪

“Philander”

“Philander”

Chapter 22

We ate, drank a pot of coffee and rested there for almost an hour, talking and enjoying each other's company before we heard the jangle of trace chains and the rumble of wheels in the distance. I stood from the log where I sat and looked to the north, and saw Lem with a wagon coming on. Bret Sullivan rode a horse beside the wagon, and on the other side rode Mr. Shaw. They were still some distance off when I saw them, and it was clear to me that they saw the smoke from our fire.

"And you'd best put on another pot of coffee," I said to Caroline, "for they'll be here by the time it is done now. Lem, Bret and your father it appears. I'll go and hitch the team, for they've had enough rest now."

Looking overt at Caroline, I could see paleness had set upon her face, and a worried look in her eye.

"And I'm sure it will be all right now Darlin'," I told her. "You're father is a reasonable man, a good man, and he'll think no bad of you for coming to me."

"Aye," she said softly, "it's not that I fear him Phil, it's that I disobeyed him."

I walked away then for there was nothing I could say to comfort her. She would just have to face him, and then things will be all right between them again. The stock was not so eager to be hooked to the wagon this time, for the morning was a rough go of it, and they knew that the conditions had not changed.

By the time I had the team hooked up, Bret Sullivan and Brody Shaw had ridden into the camp. When I looked to the camp, Caroline was in Brody's arms crying, and Brody was trying to console her as much as he could. Aye, a good man and a loving man to all his family and friends, I knew he would harbor no ill will toward Caroline.

Lem brought the wagon on and backed it to that of my own, and then we started splitting the load of goods between the two wagons. Brody Shaw came over when he saw our work and jumped right in to help. It didn't take long to split the load, and when we were finished, Brody took me by the hand, a great smile on his face, and shook it vigorously.

"And it's good to see you lad," he said genuinely. "Aye and it's worried I've been about you now."

"It's good to see you again too Mr. Shaw," I responded with a smile.

"Come lad, come to the fire, for it's hot coffee we need now before we start our journey home. Ruby's busy baking for your return and an appetite you'd best have or she'll have her feelings on her shoulder now," he said as he turned to walk. "As well, there's a piece of business we must discuss, and discuss it we will now."

I followed him to the fire. Bret Sullivan was already setting there with a cup in his hand as Caroline busied herself in packing things away to leave. Lem followed us to the fire and immediately took a seat next to Brody and Bret.

When Brody had seated himself and had a cup in his hand he called to her; "And Daughter, I've a thing or two to say to you now, so come to the fire."

Caroline came over, her head down somewhat as that of a whipped puppy, and she stood next to me.

"And it's a matter that must be discussed and brought straight immediately, for I'll have no daughter of mine traipsing off in the snow to follow after a man that she's not wed too," he started sternly. "Aye, and if your grandmother could have seen this day, she'd have rolled over in her grave now."

Surprised by the coarseness of his tone, I looked over to Bret Sullivan, who was trying to look stern, but had a bit of a smile on his lips. Caroline had moved closer to my side and I could tell that her feelings were hurt by the talk.

"And what should we do with you two now?" Brody continued.

I felt her hand slip into mine, her fingers interlacing with my own, and I felt like a 10 year old child who had misbehaved and was now being chastised.

"And it's a problem for sure now Brody," Lem said. "I was there with them and they never left my sight now, but how will the community view this matter?"

"Aye," Bret Sullivan said. "And Philander speaking in the Church of a Sunday and all now. We've our reputation to protect Brody, and the community's acceptance to consider as well now."

"Now look here Brody…" I started to say in defense of Caroline. Brody held up a hand cutting off my words before I could continue.

"It's a grievous thing now Philander, and you two will have to pay the consequences now. I've thought this over thoroughly and discussed it with your mother Caroline. She is in full agreement now, and she's busy baking and preparing a wedding feast. You two will marry this evening, and I will not consider another option. Pastor Barrow will meet us at the house when we return." With this said, he broke into a smile, and Bret and Lem chuckled under their breaths.

Caroline's hand tightened around that of my own as a wave of relief swept over me, and I felt her knees weaken at her father's words.

"Aye, and it's a cruel trick that you've done to us this day to us Brody Shaw," I said.

He chuckled for a moment, "Yes lad, but deserving my daughter is of it now. She ran off, followed you and endangered herself, and more over, caused Lem to endanger himself. Aye, and if a daughter of mine thinks so little of her own safety for the love of a man, I'd rather it be you Phil, and I'll not stand in her way of having what she wants now."

"Oh father," Caroline said as she released my hand and ran to him.

Brody opened his arms to her and cradled her in them as she wept in joy, rocking her as he did when she was a toddler.

She gave him a kiss, and then stood and passed a cup of coffee over to me, her eyes filled with tears and a glow on her face such as I had not seen on her before.

Bret Sullivan stood from his seat and in one gulp emptied the cup in his hand. "And it's enough talk we've had now. We've a chore to do and we'd best be at it now."

"Aye" I responded and drank the hot liquid from my cup, throwing the dregs into the fire to empty the cup, and then passed it to Caroline.

Two hours later found us entering the yard of the farm, and a lovelier sight I had rarely seen before. It had been a long trip and a hard journey. Eventful, yes, and filled with danger and intrigue, yet home never looked so good to me. Caroline had ridden on the box beside me, clinging closely to my side throughout the last few miles, and the glow of happiness had not left her eye for a moment. Hardly a word had been spoken these last two hours as we made it a bit easier with the load lightened and with the extra help to pry the wagon loose from the mud when it was bogged down.

It was early afternoon, and as Brody Shaw had said, Pastor Barrow was there when we arrived, along with his wife and two of the elders from the Church. I stopped in front of the house, and let her off before I proceeded to the barn to park the wagon and to unhitch the team. They worked hard this day, and deserved a good rubbing and bait of corn and oats, and I would make sure they had it now.

My mind was still spinning from the events of this last two weeks. All that had happened, and all that had been experienced. My side was still sore from the beating I had received, and my face was still bruised and swollen, although much of the swelling had gone down.

It was in my mind to talk to Bret Sullivan, to make an arrangement for the purchase of some of the stock. Breading stock was what I wanted, and the little money I had would start my heard. Busy in thought I was as I worked over the mules that had been my team these past weeks. I curried them well, for they had served me faultlessly, and were deserving of the attention.

"And are you going to waist the whole day at that now lad," I heard Bret Sullivan say from behind me.

"Sure and they've been through it these past few weeks now, Bret," I responded. "And a little pampering would do them no harm."

"Aye, their good stock now," he said. "But I'm sure you have more important things to do now Phil. You've a marriage to attend to, and just a little time to get prepared for it."

"And that I will Bret. But there's a word or two I'd have with you if you don't mind now," I responded.

"Aye, and let us set over on those bails now," he told me. "You can talk until your heart's content now. Is it the wiles of a woman that you want to know about, or the depth of love that will be shared by you two? I've been a father to you now lad, for most of your life now, and you can say anything to me that you could to your real father now."

I was flattered by his offer, although I had been around breading stock all of my life, and the wiles of a woman were not on my mind this day, and I smiled as I moved to the bail and set.

"The thing I wanted to talk to you about was the stock Bret, I'd like to purchase a couple of mares from you to start my own heard now. I've the cash that I got as a reward for capturing Thompson and his outfit, but I don't want to spend all of it right now," I told him.

He shook his head knowingly. "Aye, and it's a wise lad that I've raised for my own now. To look to the future lad, that's what you are doing when most young men's heads would have been spinning in preparation for their wedding now.

"If it's stock that you want lad, it's stock that you shall have now. Three mares at first, and you can bread with my stud, any one of them that you desire, and I'll leave you with one hundred and fifty dollars in your pocket now."

"Aye, and that's more than fair now Bret." I responded shaking his hand. "Two I will bread to the Donkey stud for Mules, and one will be bread to make more breeders."

"And that's a good plan lad, to start your future and to continue to grow your heard. My offer of a few weeks back still stands. After you have worked off Caroline's debt, you may continue on here and earn a larger heard if you've a mind to. I'd be honored if you'd stay with us forever in fact, after all, I could not have built this place without your help now, you and the Shaw's and poor Sean, " he told me.

"And it's been on my mind Bret," I responded. "I don't know just what I will do in the future as yet, but I have a dream; of a home of my own settling, and of land that I worked from the wilderness with my own hands. In my mind's eye, I can see it at times, Caroline and I working together to build something for our children and our children's children."

"Aye," he said a bit subdued. "It's a dream that most good men have now. I myself had that dream now, and then I lost my wife in childbirth. But I fulfilled it anyway, and the evidence is where we are living now. But I had to leave the land of my birth, and yours as well for this great land. For there was no hope under the Lords of the land at home, no hope but to live in the position in which we were born to.

"A good dream lad, and I hope that you and Caroline can live now to."

"And the sheriff in Knoxville had told me of a land just opening up. It's called the Bankhead on the other side of the Tennessee, and he said it was a veritable paradise. The land had been held for the Cherokee, and Fort Hampton built there to keep settlers off and to protect their lands now, but the government has changed it's mind, and is opening up that land," I told him. "Aye, and it's the Bankhead to which we'll go when we've completed our service here Bret. What a lovely name for a land indeed."

Lem had walked up behind us as we talked, unnoticed to us. He was standing just behind us and overheard the conversation.

"What the sheriff told you was true," Lem interjected. "A better land I've not seen than that of the Bankhead region. There's great forests, old and tall, water a' plenty, and the game, why there's dear and turkey and mountain Buffalo so thick their like fleas on a hounds back. There's a great spring there, and some day there will be a town around it. Two springs together now, with water clear and cold running in a constant stream. Aye, a beautiful land that will need good decent men to settle."

"Tomorrow Lad, tomorrow we'll pick out your mares now. You can brand them with a brand of your own making, and start your future in trade. But this evening, it belongs to you and Caroline. There's the cabin that Sean lived in over yonder, and that will be your own as long as you want to stay now lad, you and Caroline's. Ruby and Brody have fixed it up for you now, while you were stranded in the snow. It's not much, but it will be your home now," Bret told me.

I was a bit overwhelmed by the things that had happened these last weeks, and especially the change of heart that Brody Shaw had toward Caroline and our marriage. There had never been any animosity on his part, just a concern for her welfare, and not wanting her to make a mistake due to her age. I thought about this for a moment in the silence of the barn.

"Bret," I finally said. "What changed Brody's mind about the wedding? I knew he was for it, but was determined that we should wait at least a year."

"And it was her running off after you Philander," he responded. "Ruby and Brody were beside themselves with worry over her, afraid that she would not survive to get to you. We talked, and they decided that it would be best for you two to get married. Aye, and she loves you lad, and that kind of love only gets stronger as the years pass, not weaker."

The answer satisfied me, and the doubts left me immediately. Oh, I wanted to marry her, but the doubts in my mind had to do with the Shaw's accepting our marriage. I didn't want anything between Caroline and myself, including resentment from her parents.

Slapping my hands on my thighs, I stood from the bail suddenly. "Sure and there's a wedding I must prepare for now, by your leave Bret."

"Aye, and you'll find your gear in the cabin lad, for that's where we moved things," he responded with a smile.

■■

Chapter 23

And it was a simple wedding we had that evening. Nothing fancy, no frills or ordinances, just plain and simple, as were most weddings of the day.

Caroline was dressed in a flowered gingham dress that her mother had made for her months before, a lace shawl gently placed which was used to adorn her head in a vale and provide her train. And a lovely sight she was now for sure. I was dressed I the best that I had, a pair of broadcloth pants and the white shirt that I would ware to Church of a Sunday.

Aye, and simple it surely was, but she was a lovely sight to behold, and the wedding was as pleasant as ever I had seen now. Elders James and Hawkins had brought their wives with them, and they made quite a fuss over the wedding and the execution of it, which added to the excitement and enhanced the glamour of it for Caroline. It was a special time, a special day that a woman looks forward to all of their lives, and the moment should be one that she can savor during the long hard days before her, remember as the hardness of life engulfs her. Aye and that's what they provided, that element of excitement which would make this day special and warm the cold nights in years to come with fond memories.

The following month passed quickly filled with work in the day and quiet evenings at night. The cabin was warm and snug, but it took much work for me, for there was a supply of fuel to build for the added cabin, and it was a cold winter. It was also the happiest time of my life, for the first time since my mother died I felt complete and contented.

And the winter was cold, much colder than those we had experienced before. The water was continually frozen and I had to bust holes in the ice with an ax each morning and afternoon to make sure the stock was watered properly. There was also an abundance of snow this year, and we were going through the hey we had cut much faster than we had imagined.

One night in early December, Bret Sullivan summoned us to the big house for supper and a meeting. Ruby Shaw was quite the cook, and had always set a good table. Caroline had learned much from her as her daughter, and was as good a cook as her mother, yet this night was special, for it was a meal she would not have to prepare herself and she looked forward to it especially.

When supper was complete and we had our desert and coffee, the ladies excused themselves to the cleaning of the kitchen and the pots, and Bret Sullivan sat sternly at the end of the table until they had departed.

"And there's a matter we must attend to men, for our meat supply is dwindling fast now. Winter has taken it's toll o our supplies already, and I'm fearful that we will run out of meat and then we'll be left on short rations now. The stores of flower and dried vegetables will dwindle quicker without meat, and we've a long way to go before spring arrives."

"Aye," Brody said with concern. "I've been watching our supplies closely myself, and I'm worried for the sake of the stock now as well. With the deep snow we've had to depend too much on the hay we've set by now."

"It would be impossible to purchase hay from Johnson City now," Lem added. "For all of the farmers are in the same dilemma that we are facing. Their building a railroad from Charleston to somewhere in Tennessee, butt it will be years before it is complete now, and 'twill be too late to help us now."

"And of Knoxville Bret?" I asked.

"Aye, I've considered that, but we'd never get wagons filled with hay through in this snow. We'll just have to trust the good Lord for the stock and allow them to forage in the snows now. We'll move them to the South section of the mornings now. We've done no cutting there this summer, and they'll be plenty of graze for them when they dig it out. My real concern with this is that we'll have to drive them there every morning, and back to the warmth of their barns before night now." Bret shook his head worriedly. "It will be quit a job for just two of us now."

"And that it would now Bret," I said. "But there's four of us to share the work now."

"And that there be laddy," he said, "that there be indeed. But what of the meat now? Two of us must go hunting lad, two and not one only, for there is danger in this cold. And if one were injured, he'd never return to us safely."

This I had not considered, probably from my youth and lack of experience, but consider I did now, and it made the only sense. "Aye," I said shaking my head in agreement with his logic. "And that I had not thought of now."

Caroline and Ruby had come from the kitchen and were listening to the conversation. When I looked at them, I could see the concern in their eyes, yet they said nothing, for they knew that all of our survival may depend on the decisions that were made here tonight. Ruby Shaw had a way of expressing her concern over things, she would hold the lower end of her apron and ring it her hands, which she was doing at this moment.

"We'll have to split up," Bret continued. "Two to hunt and two for the stock now. Those of us for the hunt will have to travel to the lower lands to the South to find any game now, for they've all left the hills for the winter. Best take a number of the horses to haul it back on."

I looked up into Caroline's eyes and met her own gaze. There was almost a pleading look to her as we talked, and I tried to console her in my stare.

"I've thought it over for the past few days now, and the plan that I have is that Brody and Phil will go on the hunt. Brody's the best shot among us, and Phil's almost as good. Lem and I will work the stock and keep the fires burning at home now. Caroline had better move back up here while you two are gone now," Bret said.

We shook our heads in agreement, although I would rather of had Lem with me on the hunt. Brody was much like Bret Sullivan. Rheumatism was catching up to him and he had trouble moving about at times, yet I could read Bret's judgment in the plan. Lem was still strong, as was I, and he would split us up so he could make sure that jobs would be done. Brody was a wise man and experienced in the field. He would apply judgment to his decisions tried over many years of experience. The same was true by leaving Lem to work with Bret.

"And what of mother and I now," Caroline interjected. "We can work as hard as you men can, and can stand as much now. We could help to move the stock when the time comes for it, and one of us should go on the hunt to help in the preparation of the meat now."

"Aye," Ruby said. "Caroline is right. Sure and we're all in this together and the work should be equally shared now."

"Maybe you're right," Bret Sullivan said. "We'll only use you now when we need you, but here at the farm. It's far too dangerous for you in the field now, and I'll not allow it."

"And daughter," Brody said. "You're a married woman now, and I'll not have you traipsing out as you did before. You will stay here at the farm and do what's needed here."

"Aye father. I'll do as you have asked this time," Caroline responded.

"Good then, and we'll be off then in the morning," I said. "I'll get Caroline's belongings and bring them up before we depart then, and you'll stay here with your mother until we return."

"Aye, and there's much to be done and little enough time to get it done then," Bret said. "We had best be at it."

We all agreed, and I took Caroline by the hand and headed home. She was quiet this evening; the trip baring on her mind I was sure. It was not fair, this I knew, but even so, how fair is life? We had been married just these few weeks, and now to be separated for a while.

"Philander," Caroline finally said to me after we had been busy packing the supplies Brody and myself. "I will miss you."

"Sure and I will miss you too Darlin'," I responded taking her in my arms. "But it can't be helped. If we don't do this thing, we've a chance of not surviving the winter now."

"And I understand," she responded. "Just…, just be careful and come back to me as safely."

"Aye lass, and that I will do now."

"And Phil," she continued. "Watch out for father, I'm worried for him."

"Don't fret now Darlin'. He's a good man and one that's not likely to give up on things. Sure and he can take care of himself now, but I will watch for him," I responded.

"And he is all of that Phil, he's just getting up in years now, and I can't help but worry for him," she continued. Before dawn had broken, I had moved Caroline's belongings that she would need into the main house, and had saddled the horses. I picked four of the big mules to take along and hopefully carry our meat back with us.

"Philander"

It was a cold morning, and the warmth of the main house felt good to me as I sat at the table to eat my breakfast. Sipping a cup of coffee, it was a pleasant thing to hear Ruby and Caroline working in the kitchen.

It wasn't long before Brody and Bret came down to join me, and Lem came in the door a moment later, taking a cup of the hot liquid and nursing it as he stood by the table.

"And I hope you have packed warmly Mr. Shaw, for there's quite a chill in the air this morning now," I said to him.

"Aye lad, and it's a chillier time that we'll have of it before we make it back now I'm thinking," he responded. "We'll eat and then saddle our stock for the trip."

"And their saddled already, the supplies are packed with the exception of your own gear now," I responded.

He looked a bit surprised and then a knowing look came over his face and he nodded his approval. Nothing that I would ever do could surprise him too much, that is when it came to work now, for I had always been the first in the field and ready to pull my own load.

The sun was fully in the sky before we started out, and we traveled hard most of the day. We wanted to complete our task as quickly as possible and return home again. There was much meat we would need before winter's end, and a good hunt we would have to accomplish.

We moved swiftly to the flat lands of the southwest, assured that the game would be there, for no animal would stay in the mountains during this winter, unless hibernating. There were still Buffalo in this land back then, not as thick as they had been before the white man came to these shores, but still present, and it was in my mind that this was the meat we needed to find. Three good size ones is all that we could carry back, and would be a successful hunt for us now.

It was evening before we stopped, to make our camp and we decided to make this place our base for hunting. We were on the flats and were starting to see signs of game. Before nightfall, I killed a buck and it would provide us with our meat while we were down here.

It was a cold night, even for the flats and we got little sleep from it. Both of us dozed some while the fire was up, and would awaken when the fire went down and the chill of the night set on us.

It was a good campsite we had found, in the turn of a creek and where much wood had been washed up during the rainy periods. The bank had been eaten away through the centuries and by floods past, and a deep hole had been cut into the side of the hill that was possibly fifteen feet deep, and twenty to twenty-five feet wide in the limestone rock face. We used the back wall of the cave as a reflector for our fire, and as long as there was flame, it warmed us well. Yet when the flame died away, the chill from the wide opening at its mouth would flood through the opening and cause us to awaken chilled to the bone.

I thought of Caroline as I set in the cave that night, thought of the warmth of her love and of our cabin. It wasn't much, but it was our start and a fine start we had. The stock Bret Sullivan had sold me were already carrying, and this spring, my small herd would double at least, if all went right. By the time I would be able to purchase Caroline's freedom we would have a considerable herd, and with the get of mules, would not be short on money as well.

Did you ever notice that the coldest part of the night is the hour before dawn? I had over my short years, and this morning proved to be true to my observations. The last hour before sunrise it seemed that even the fire could not help our misery this day, and I cooked some coffee and breakfast for us to help to warm us up. While we ate, Brody and I talked some and made plans for the day. We would go in separate directions and attempt to find some game. If one of us heard a shot, we would follow the sound of it so that we could help the shooter dress their kill.

Three Buffalo was what I wanted and I told him so. Yet we both knew the odds of that were slim, and it would take six times the number of dear if we could find none, for the amount of meat on a dear is so much smaller than that of the Buffalo.

While the sky was turning the first color of the morning we headed out on foot. It was a light step that I needed this day, and we both donned our Cherokee moccasins to walk in. Through the woods to the southwest I went as Brody Shaw went on west. There was a great field to the west of us, about four or five miles off, and we knew that if any Buffalo were in the vicinity, it was there that we would find them.

Like a ghost I moved through the woods, careful not to step on any branches or make any sudden movement or noise. Although the Buffalo were not a skittish animal, dear were, and it may be that this would be the only meat that we would find. It doesn't take long for game to avoid you if you announce your arrival, and it was game that we needed now.

It took me nearly two hours to get to the field, and in all of this time the only noise that I heard was that of my own breathing, and the occasional sound of a bird singing. It was still cold, even though the sun was well into the sky, yet not as cold as home, and the snow was very thin here.

As I edged myself to the break in the woods and the long, wide field that we planned to hunt, I slowed my pace considerably, stopping behind trees and logs or rocks and looking thoroughly before stepping out.

Aye and it was a grand sight that I saw as I came to the field. Before me was a small herd of dear, and beyond, toward the north and still a good way off, I could see the bulking dark form of a buffalo. He was a huge beast from the look of him and with his head down and grazing easily on the dried grass of the field.

Knowing that the Buffalo was not likely to bolt or run upon hearing the sound of a shot, I lifted my rifle slowly to my shoulder, and with extreme care, using both hands to muffle the sound, I pulled back the hammer ever so slowly. The head of the big buck came up at the clink of the hammer cocking the rifle, and I sighted down the barrel, being sure not to move so as not to frighten him. Easily I pulled the slack from the trigger and took a deep breath and squeezed the shot off.

The Buck leaped forward at the shot, bounding once and then twice, and then crumbling to the ground as his heart stopped beating. The rest of the heard was gone instantly, running across the field in the opposite direction.

"Philander"

I looked anxiously toward where the Buffalo had been and spotted him instantly. His head was up and he was looking off in the direction of the disturbance curiously. He looked for only a moment and then must have decided that the disturbance had nothing to do with him, and lowered his head again to the grass.

I circled around a big Oak that was near by' placing my back against the tree and out of line from the bull Buffalo should he look up. Quickly and efficiently, I placed powder, ball and wadding into the rifle barrel and rammed them home and then primed the hammer. Knowing the nature of the Buffalo, I decided to walk into the field toward him, rather than try to sneak up on him. He was out too far for a clear shot in the field anyway, and I knew that the only thing that might frighten him would be a pack of wolves, or a scent of an unseen animal that was strange to him. The Buffalo had few natural predators save the wolf pack, and was mostly fearless toward things they could see.

Stepping out from behind the tree, I walked slowly into the field toward him. He ignored me for a moment as I walked on, and then when he thought I had come close enough, his head raised from the grass and he watched me intently, snorting occasionally and pawing the ground in a sign of aggression and warning.

When I was about thirty yards off from him, I stopped and lifted the rifle. If he charged at this range my shot had better be true, for he was a huge beast and could proof dangerous if he charged.

Carefully I sighted onto him, picking my spot for the bullet to take him, and slowly squeezed the trigger. The hammer came down, and a second later the rifle leaped against my shoulder as the big bull went to his knees and then slowly fell over on his side.

I reloaded my rifle quickly before I approached him, for I had seen beast arise after a bullet had taken them and become fierce with fight, yet as I approached him, I began to relax for there was no motion in him at all.

Pulling my knife from my belt I cut his huge throat to let him bleed, and then turned toward the dear I had dropped. He would need hanging before the blood settled in the meat, and I worked on him first. I had just about finished dressing out the dear when Brody Shaw arrived.

Looking at the dear hung in the tree and then to the bulking form of the Buffalo lying in the field, he smiled broadly.

"Aye and its good fortune that has smiled on you today now," he said to me. "A good dear and a large mountain Buffalo for a starter. A fine piece of work now lad, a fine piece of work indeed."

"Sure and I was lucky now Mr. Shaw, but we'll need some of the horses to skin the beast and carry the meat back into camp now," I said.

He pulled his knife from his scabbard and started toward the Buffalo, "and I will start to work on this beast if you will retrieve a horse for us now lad. You've done enough of the work for one day and the rest you'll leave to me now."

"And that sounds the plan to me now Mr. Shaw," I told him as I took my knife and thrust it into the soil at my feet a time or two to clean it before I replaced it in the sheath. "It will take me most of an hour to get back now."

"Aye and I'll be ready for you when you return," he said.

Chapter 24

It took us most of the day to prepare the meat we had gotten, cutting it into strips when we got back to camp, and making racks to dry it over several fires that we had burning. We set to the task, making racks from branches we cut from trees and small willows from the streambed, tying them together in a teepee fashion, and then setting over the fires to smoke and dry it for keeping.

It was well after dark before we settled in for the evening, and it would take us all night and a good bit of tomorrow before we would be through curing what we had. We decided to work in shifts this night, me taking the first shift, keeping the fires burning and changing out the meat when it had dried, and then Brody would relieve me around midnight.

It was a job we had, keeping the ever-hungry fires burning and a watch on the meat to make sure it was cured properly. There would be little rest for either of us this night, of that I was sure, and there was still much more meat that we had to get before we could return home.

There were always the predators that had to be watched out for as well, for the smell of the fresh meat would draw them in, thinking they had an easy meal of it. Wolf packs were not uncommon to the region back then, cougars, bobcats and bears were in profusion, and I was glad for the cold this night, for the bears would surely be asleep for their long winters rest.

And there were predators around that night. It was still early in the night when my first encounter came. Brody had been asleep for only about an hour when the horses got nervous, stomping and blowing, as was there fashion when they were afraid. I was up quickly, rifle in hand when I saw their heads come up, nostrils flared and ears back and I knew that we were being stocked. And then came the growl, a shrill cry that echoed back from the walls of the rock face cliff and sent a chill through me. A cougar it was, and hungry for what we had. The smell of blood attracted him, but the smell of man had made him wary as well. He kept his distance and prowled the outside perimeter of the camp for better than an hour before his courage and good sense caused him to seek easier prey this night.

It was full light when I awoke the next morning, and Brody was diligently about his business of keeping the fires stoked and a check on the meat. The coffee tasted good this cold morning, the sky was brightly blue and clear against the white of the landscape. I pulled on my boots and got a cup of coffee, and then walked outside of the cave to see if I could find the tracks of the beast that had prowled our camp the night before. I was glad that it was a cat and not wolves, for I was sure that we would have had a fight on our hands should a wolf pack had come. They are almost fearless in numbers, skilled at the art of teaming their prey, and it would have taken an effort on our part to contain them.

The tracks were plain enough in the snow, a huge beast by the size of the tracks, and a male I was sure, for he had marked this area as his own territory to caution other cats away. A patient beast he had been, old and experienced by the marks he had left. There was little pacing he had done. He came in, marked the territory and then sat patiently back in the snow and waited for an opportunity that didn't come to him.

"And what is it that you see now Phil," Brody said as he approached me with his own coffee cup in his hand.

"Aye, and a wise old cougar that has been watching us this night," I responded. "Look at the tracks yonder. An old and a wise cat he was now. No anxiousness or pacing about him. He just sat and watched looking for his opportunity now, and when it didn't come, he went on."

Brody looked over the tracks through the steam of his coffee. "Aye lad, the tracks do tell the story now. A big brute he was, and he marked us for later now to keep the others away. Look where he marked that tree yonder, showing his size by the claw marks on the trunk of the tree. He's big, that's for sure now, and there won't be another to reach those marks and feel they can offer a challenge to him."

"We'd best hang the meat we've cured in a tree Mr. Shaw. I'd bet that he's got an eye on us now, and as soon as we leave he'll be in our camp and about our goods now," I responded.

Brody shook his head in approval to what I said. It worried me for the stock, but not all that much. It would take a desperate animal to attack those big draft horses, for their size alone was intimidating. A pack of wolves would try it and would succeed, but a lone cat would not, unless injured or starving, and there was easier game at hand.

We walked back to our camp and fixed our morning meal. There was much to do, and we needed to be about it, for there was more meat to gather and cure before we could head home, and it was our home that was on my mind now. I missed Caroline and was concerned about the women helping with the movement of the animals. They were capable enough, but it was the work of a man they were about.

When we had eaten, we restocked the fires and changed out the meat that we could, and then bundled the cured meat into burlap bags and hung them from the trees to keep them out of reach of the animals. When we had finished this task, I took my axe and went out to cut more wood.

It was mid-morning before I had gathered enough wood, and Brody suggested that I take a horse and see if I could not find some game, and so I loaded up two of the horses and went off. I stopped the horses outside the field we had hunted the day before and tied him off, and then slowly approached the underbrush at the field’s edge, keeping low and quiet as to not alert any animals that may be present.

Aye and a lovely sight it was when I got there, for not more than a hundred yards ahead of me was a small herd of Buffalo. Six beasts in all, three cows a bull and two calves about half way grown. The Bull was as large as the one I had killed the day before. They were within range and I set myself against a tree to steady the rifle for the shot. It was the bull that I wanted and he who I sighted down on.

Cocking the rifle, I slowly pulled the trigger and then the primer went, followed by the concussion of the blast from the rifle, and the bull set down and then rolled over. A clean shot it was, and there was plenty of time to get another, for they stood about and looked at the bull for a moment, and then went back about their grazing.

I could not handle another beast this day, not alone and with only two of the horses. If I had taken another, I was sure that a predator would be about it before I could return, so I stood and started to walk into the field. The heads of the other beasts arose from the ground where they cropped the dried grass, and as I approached they started slowly moving off. Buffalo seemed to have no fear, no natural aversion to man, and I'm afraid that this would be their undoing, for as man increased their need for meat would have it's affect on the population of the creatures. I slit the bull's throat with my knife and then went back and retrieved my horse before I got to work dressing out the meat.

It took some time to dress out the beast, and was well into the afternoon before I started back to camp, walking the horses that were loaded with the meat and hide from the beast I had killed.

An hour later found me outside of the camp and I could see that we had some visitors by the tracks in the snow. It appeared to be three who had come, and I feared immediately that something had gone wrong at home. My fear overrode my good sense and I came into camp at a run calling out for Brody.

I stopped suddenly as I entered the cave, for there before me were Bill and Melvin Long, two of the men I had captured with Blake Thompson and turned in to the sheriff in Knoxville. Brody sat on a log and Melvin had him covered with a rifle.

Bill Long showed his green teeth in a smile at the sight of me and immediately lifted a handgun toward my chest. The shock of the sight of them set me back, for I surely had thought that these two would have been hung by now, and I never expected to see them again, not in this life anyway.

“Philander”

“Well now,” Bill said through the green teeth. “Looky here Melvin. Did’ya ever guess we’d a’ come along over this her feller’ again.”

Melvin’s eyes lifted from Brody and to my own. A sadistic smile filled his face of a sudden, and I felt my heart flip and my stomach turn. I knew too well the cruelty of these men, the total disregard for the lives and sanctity toward other men. I heard the crunch behind me from a foot stepping on a twig, and then felt a blow to the back of my head that caused the lights to fade as I was tumbled toward the rock surface of the cave floor. I struggled for a moment to keep consciousness, but lost the battle as I drifted off into the oblivion of darkness. My head hurt something terrible, and it was the last thing I realized or remembered for some time.

When I awoke it was full dark. I awoke slowly from the oblivion, blinking my eyes and trying to get them in focus. There was a sticky feeling to the back of my head and neck, and my stomach turned slowly in sickness from the blow I had experienced. Fighting to bring things into focus and finally succeeding, I almost wished that I hadn’t tried so hard, for there setting on a log above me set Blake Thompson himself, a wicked and mean look about him.

Glancing around the campfire, I could see Bill and Melvin as well, and off in the corner was Brody, feet and hands tied securely, lying in a pile at the base of the cave wall.

I looked up again and into the cold eyes of Blake Thompson. “So, you awake now are you?” he said with a cruel turn to his lips. “Been keepin’ us waitin’ boy. Waitin’ too long for us to have our fun with you.”

I could hear a sadistic laugh from the fire and knew it was Melvin Longs laugh. "We goin' to start on him now boss?" he asked.

"Naw, we'll tell him what we're goin' to do to him and let him think on it over some. Let him worry 'bout it 'afore we get our pound of flesh off'n his hide," he responded. "Boy, you done us wrong, an' we're goin' to skin you alive 'afore we're through with ya. You're goin' to wish your Momma ain't never met your Papa 'afore we finish," he said to me in a mean low tone, and then he lifted a foot and kicked me hard in my chin. That kick was like something from a mule and it caught me unaware. I saw bright lights flash in my eyes from that kick as my mind again drifted into the oblivion from which I had awoken from just a minute or two before.

It must have been the cold that awoke me from this unnatural sleep, for when I awoke again the fire was down to embers. Slowly and not to let them know I was awake, I looked around the encampment. Three dark forms lay stretched out around the fire, and I could see Brody was still in the same place. My mind was foggy from the blows I had received, and it was hard to focus again, yet I could make everything out. It worried me why they were here, how that they could possibly have escaped the situation I left them in down in Knoxville, and what in the world they were doing here.

My body shook uncontrollably from the cold. My hands were bound behind me and my coat was gone, as well as my boots. My head felt odd, like some heavy useless thing that was attached to my shoulders, and I could not move it without pain.

Fear gripped me, and I knew that I was in real trouble. I knew too well of the cruelty of these men and had experienced one attempt on my life already. Aye, and I didn't hesitate at all to acknowledge the fear that gripped me. Fear for myself and fear for Brody Shaw as well.

Lying perfectly still, with the exception of the shaking from the cold, I started to work on the knot that bound my hands. The others were a good fifteen feet off, and were all sound asleep I could tell, for they were motionless under their covers, and the sounds of snores and deep breathing came heavily in the silence of the night.

My fingers were already numb from the cold, and hurt when I moved them, but I had no choice. I knew the coldness of these men, and knew what they would do to me and to Brody in the morning, and I had to take my chance while I had the opportunity.

Looking at the stars, I could see that it was around midnight. The stars shown brightly in the cold of the night, twinkling in the vast blackness that surrounded them.

It didn't take long before my hands hurt terribly from the work behind my back, yet I was encouraged for I could feel the knot start to loosen some. I continued the effort, working feverishly over the knot and spreading my hands somewhat to try to work free from the bonds.

Off somewhere in the blackness of the night I could hear that big cat that had visited the night before prowling, looking for his opportunity to get at the meat that it smelled. Thompson's bunch hadn't helped matters with that cougar either, for they had lain the meat on a groundsheet instead of hanging it, and the cat was tempted. I figured that the only thing holding him back from the easy meal was the man smell, and there was more of it tonight than the night before. I heard him growl in frustration, and then saw Bill Longs head came up from the pallet. He looked around the camp and I lay totally still, stopping the work while he looked over the camp.

Reaching an arm out from underneath the blankets, Bill picked up a few sticks of wood and tossed them into the fire which caused it immediately to flare up and lighted the small cave in which they lay. He at least was a man of the wilderness, one who slept light and listened for the sounds that did not belong, even while he slept. Blake Thompson and Melvin were unmoved, their snores continued through the slight noise of the cat and then the sounds of the wood being thrown on the fire. A moment later, Bill's breath was coming in long even breaths and I knew it was safe again to continue my work.

If I could be so fortunate as to get the ropes loose to escape, it may be a chore getting Brody free with Bill's alertness, and I prayed as I worked. I prayed for my success with the ropes, and that somehow I might be allowed to free Brody Shaw, for I surely would not leave him alone with these men and knowing what he would face when they awoke.

It was coming up on about three in the morning when the knot finally yielded and the rope came free. I looked cautiously at the three forms that lay around the campfire. The fire had gone back to coals, providing no light in the camp, just a red glow where the fire was built. Their breathing was steady and slow, and I knew they were in deep sleep.

Rising carefully from the ground, I stayed perfectly still for a moment before I moved. I hesitated even to breath at this point, for I was desperate to make our escape good. My feet were numb from the cold, and it was hard for me to feel anything underneath them, yet I must somehow succeed. Stepping on a twig, or some gravel that would grind and make noise was out of the question, and I started a slow, painstakingly movement around the camp to where Brody lay.

It took me a considerably long time to get to him, and I knelt over him for a moment before I placed a hand over his mouth as to quiet him from making noise when he awoke. Brody's eyes popped open, and he immediately recognized what I was doing, and gave me a slight nod with his head to assure me, and then I went to work on the knots that held him.

It took but a moment to free him, and I helped him to stand, placing a finger to my mouth as he stood to alert him that we must walk quietly. Brody acknowledged with a quick nod of his head, and we were off. We moved slowly, cautiously as we made our way through the small depth of the cave. I knew that we had but one chance and that was to escape them quickly and silently. We must put distance between us immediately and find a safe haven in which to hide before they awoke. We must also be careful to leave no tracks, no trail for them to follow.

The big cougar that had been staking out our camp the last few nights worried me now, but not that he may attack, for they tried to avoid man, being fearful of them and a cautious beast. What scared me about him was that he would growl or make some noise before we could make good our escape, and good reason it was too, for he had awakened Bill Long earlier that same night.

I took no time for supplies or for a coat or weapons. These men were too dangerous to take chances with, and I only wanted to make good our escape. I dared not even to breath to deeply, afraid that the sound might awaken one of these men. Each step was carefully placed, easing my foot down to make sure there was nothing underneath that could cause a sound.

Man was the only animal beside a horse that naturally walked without regard for silence. Each of God's creation was careful of where they placed their foot, what twig may give away their position, both predator and prey. Those who survived were those who were careful, and those who could silently come and go, leaving little except scent behind to be followed. This I had learned early at the feet of Patrick Talley, probably the best woodsman I had ever been around. The Cherokee had taught me as well, and I was an eager student, learning how to walk leaving little or no trail to follow, and being silent enough that I could almost pet a dear coming from the up wind side of them.

And now my skills would be tested. How much Brody Shaw had learned I had no idea, but would surely soon find out.

▪▪

Chapter 25

We picked our way carefully, silently, until we were well out of the encampment. Aye, and it was evident that Brody Shaw had learned a few things from Patrick Tally as well. He moved as silently as myself, almost as a ghost as we made our way from the camp and into the woods that lay beside it. As soon as we were out of normal earshot from the camp, I broke into a jog, a space-eating run that the Cherokee had taught me, and Brody Shaw did the same. I was wishful of my boots or moccasins, and a coat, but there was no way of getting these without giving away our plan of escape, so I put the cold out of my mind.

We ran for nearly an hour before I saw that Brody could take no more and stopped. Brody was a tough man, but the years had taken their measure of him, and it was evident to me that he was all in.

"We'll stop and rest here for a minute or two now," I told him.

"Don't stop for my sake now Philander," he responded. "I'll get my second wind in a moment if we keep moving."

"Aye, and I'm sure you would now Brody. But we've moved fast this last hour, putting some distance between us," I stated. "And now it's time that we disappeared, left no trail for them to follow. We'll rest here for a while, catch our breath, and then move on slower and more cautious now. We must be careful to leave no trail for them to follow, not a bent twig, not a scuffed rock, no print that can be distinguished at all. I'm grateful for cold now, the frozen earth will help us if we are careful of where we step."

"Aye and that makes some sense to me now Phil," he said collapsing against the base of a tree.

I leaned against a tree myself to take some of the weight from my bare feet. The stockings that were on them were almost worked through, and I would have to do something before long, or my feet would be in a terrible mess.

"And the thing that I can't understand is how they tracked me down now Brody?" I stated more than asked.

"Aye, and they didn't know it was your camp when they came upon us," Brody responded. "I heard them talking after Blake Thompson laid the butt end of his rifle against your ear."

"And what did they say now Brody? I can't help but wonder how they got away from their predicament down in Knoxville now. They were to be tried for their crimes and most probably hung from what the sheriff told me."

"Sure now, and that they were. Tried and convicted, sentenced to hang within the week, but they overpowered a guard one night at the jail and escaped is what I overheard them saying. That Blake is a mean one, mean for sure I say. When he saw it was you they had all that he could talk about was getting his pound of flesh back, and out of your hide is where he wanted it." Brody said.

"Aye, I've faced the man before," I said. "He's the one who beat me and left me for dead. If I know the evil inside of him, he won't rest until he gets even in his own twisted way."

A wave of tremors came over me from the cold, or from the dread of facing Blake Thompson again, which one I did not know, but the cold was intense and I was ill prepared to meet it. Brody saw the tremor, and he dropped his head.

"And we need some warmth for you now Philander. They've taken your coat and your boots and it's the lung fever you'll have if we don't get you taken care of," he said.

"Aye, and I'll be all right now," I responded. "It's a place to hide out that they cannot find we need worse. It's only an hour or so until sunrise, and it will be warmer then. And Blake Thompson will be looking then as well. We need some more distance, and with no tracks to give us away now, and a shelter that is hidden well."

Brody stood and took off his coat. "At least you can wear this for a while and get yourself warm now," he said.

"No Brody," I responded. "I'm a bit younger and stronger than you are, I'll be all right now."

It seemed as an inspiration hit him of a sudden, and he removed his shirt, placing his coat back on. "Here," he said. "You will take my shirt. It's buckskin and will stop the cold from penetrating. The tail is long enough to fashion a pair of moccasins from to protect your feet."

Reaching into his pocket, he brought out a small knife and handed the shirt and the knife to me.

These I took and gladly, for my feet were both sore and numb at the same time. There was no time for fancy work, I just cut off the tails of the shirt and wrapped the leather around my feet, cutting a pigging string from the shirt to tie them in place, and then donned the shirt over my head. It was a bold and noble thing that Brody had done for me this hour, and it would save some of my energy for the task before us.

When I completed the task and donned the shirt, Brody looked over at me and smiled. "Caroline would never forgive me If I let anything happen to you now Philander, and I could scarcely forgive myself as well. You're more a son to me then an in-law now."

"Aye, and you are more a father to me," I responded and stood. "We'd best be off, slower this time and careful to leave no track now."

Although there was a light layer of snow on the ground, it was possible to move quickly and almost without leaving a track to follow, for this was a heavily wooded area that we were in. The flat land between the mountains surrounding our home and Knoxville was a long rolling valley. The Tennessee River flowed here, along with countless streams, and the landscape was filled with trees. Old and thick was the forest, and filled with Oak, pine, Hickory, Chestnut and Cherry. The underbrush was thick in the spring and summer was sparse at this time of the year. It was fragile and dry and easily broken by animals and humans as they passed if not careful.

We moved swiftly and careful not to step in any spots of snow, choosing rather the loose leaf's that thickly carpeted the ground in the forest.

As the sun came from it's hiding place of night, bringing with it the first twilight of morning; we had put a great distance behind us from the camp we had established. I wished for a rifle or my shotgun, and I wished for my stock, for it was my own stock we had brought with us on this trip, and not that of Bret Sullivan. If it had been Bret's stock that we had brought, I might have tried to escape with them, even knowing that it would have awakened the men who held us captive.

An hour after dawn we stopped again. This time however, was to assay our situation and our position, and to attempt to figure out what to do.

"And I was wondering what your plan is now lad," Brody Shaw said. "We're too far from home to expect any help from there, and it would be a long hard journey for us to try and walk it now, especially without supplies and in the cold. We can expect a snowfall at any moment."

"Aye, and it's been on my mind as well now Brody," I responded. "I think that the best thing we can do now is to find a shelter, a place we can have a fire that is unseen and where we can snare some game for our food. And then I'll go back and get out supplies."

He looked at me almost incredulous for a moment, the shock of my statement sinking in. Shaking his head no, he said; "Now lad, I don't think that is the thing to do now. You'll surely make my daughter a widow if you try to play games with that bunch now. There was murder and Larson in their eyes and you'll surely meet your doom lad."

"Aye, and I've been up against them before now Brody. They are mean for sure, but they are not smart. They do not post guards, and would never expect us to come back for our property, of this I am sure. We'll find a shelter, and then I will leave you for a while and retrieve my stock and our supplies," I said confidently. "Beside all of that, if I know Blake Thompson he will be out looking for us. His bitterness will drive him to take chances and they'll be out every day until they work out the trail."

"Laddy, you'll surely meet you're end, but if you are bound to do this thing, then I will join you," Brody said. "We'd best go now, work out our way back slowly and we'll be back early afternoon. If they're out of camp hunting for us it will be our best opportunity."

"Sure and that makes sense now Brody," I responded. "They're in a blind rage now and will not expect us to double back on them. We've covered our trail well and it will take time for them to work it out now. My future is at that campsite now Brody, mine and Caroline's future is tied up in that stock now, and I must get them back."

We rested for about fifteen minutes before we started out. We knew this area well from previous hunting trips, especially in the early spring and fall, and knew of many trails that would lead us back to our camp.

As a child, Patrick would bring me here hunting with him, and this was my main training ground. He'd leave me, giving him a head start and then I would have to work out his trail. He taught me much in the few years before he was mauled by that bear that took his life, and I missed him always.

We didn't worry so much about our trail this time when we started off. By they time they had worked out our trail to this point, it would be late afternoon, and we should be well away with our stock and supplies.

“Philander”

I could tell that Brody was tiring and just about given out before we got to the campsite, but there was no complaint from him. This was a hard journey for a young man, and a fast pace as well, and Brody was getting up in years. It may have been two o’clock before we reached the camp, and we both hunkered down in the brush to watch for a while before we dared to enter.

All was still and quiet, the fire still smoked, although it was plain to see it was well spent. Some of our gear had been gone through, and they were scattered around the campsite. The meat we had dried was still hanging from the trees, but that cat had made into the Buffalo I had killed yesterday and had drug off a big chunk of the meat. He would not have come if there were anyone near camp, so I stood with confidence and started in and Brody following now.

My boots were still there, as were my coat and I donned them hastily and then retrieved my shotgun and my rifle immediately and placed them close at hand just in case they returned before we were through.

We made a hasty job of gathering our supplies and packing them up on the stock. Thank the good Lord that our mounts were still there. They had taken off in a rage, it was plain to see, and never in their wildest imagination did they figure that we would return.

When we pulled out we looked as a rawhide outfit, for our gear was hastily packed and not too well indeed. We moved quickly in the opposite direction from the way they had gone chasing us. With all of the horses and gear, there was no way of not leaving tracks and it was in our mind not to stop for a long time. Our mounts were fresh, and theirs would be tired by the time they made it back to camp. Ours were excellently bread and fine stock with bottom and heart and could take the punishment we intended to place upon them. It was not our home for which we headed for we had no intention of leading this evil upon our loved ones. We were headed toward the direction of Knoxville, and it might be just the best for us to go there and report the whereabouts of Thompson and his men to the authorities.

We traveled hard, and both Brody and I was bone tired from the lack of sleep the night before and the journey we had made to evade Thompson's men. It was hungry that we were, and tired to boot and around ten that night I pulled over to the side of the trail in a place that was a good camp sight.

"Aye, and it's a good meal we need and a little rest now Brody," I told him. "We've put more than just a few miles between us these past hours, and our stock needs to feed and rest before we go on."

He looked back at me in a tired and painful expression, yet a smile was in his eye. "Sure and you're right now laddy. I've gone about as far as I can without a little rest now."

"And will you lay down for a while 'till I get us some hot food and a little coffee prepared?" I asked him.

"Aye lad, that I will do, but I'd prefer tea if there is any. It seems to warm my soul on a cold night and a little warmth could not hurt us," he responded smiling.

"We'll leave the stock loaded just in case," I told him. "They can graze and blow with their packsaddles in place now, and it won't hurt them a bit now."

"Aye lad, Aye," he responded as he more fell from his horse than dismounted. He leaned against the horse for a moment before he untied his roll, and I was worried for him. Brody was no young man and I knew how it was that I felt.

I unpacked just what we needed for a meal and built a fire while Brody rested. He was asleep immediately and it was sleep that I was fighting myself, but it was food that I needed more. It had been noon the day before that I had eaten, and I was sure that was the case with Brody as well. It was in my mind to stay here longer than a hastily fixed meal. I was sure that their horses would give out on them and there would be little pursuit this day, once they returned to the camp sight and seen what we had done.

It was fresh Buffalo steaks that I cut from the meat we had loaded, and I sharpened some sticks on both ends and pierced the meat. The ground around the fire had thawed from the flame, and I set the sticks at an angle over the fire to broil the steaks, and then went to the spring and filled the coffeepot with water. It was coffee that I preferred, but I yielded to Brody's request and put tea in the pot when it boiled, and then removed it from the fire to simmer.

It was coming of midnight when I awoke Brody for his meal, and he got up slowly even though I knew he was hungry. The day and night had been hard on him, and with just a little sleep. The tea seemed to brighten his spirit and he drank a cup almost non-stop before pouring another and taking a bite of the meat I had broiled. All was quiet as we ate, and of a sudden I noticed, too quiet.

"Philander"

Slowly rising from my seat, I backed away from the fire and toward a tree that my shotgun had been rested against. Trying to seem as though I was walking out of camp to relieve myself, and when I came near to the tree and the shotgun, the night seemed to explode with the sound of running feet and loud voices.

"Don't take another step Mister, unless you want to ventilate your inert's some," a voice said loudly.

Raising my hands to my head and slowly turning I said, "Sure and you wouldn't want to do that, I'd most likely leak all over the place and a fine fix you'd be in now."

"Is that you Mr. Sherman," the voice responded from the night. "It's all right men, drop your weapons. I know this man, and he's the one who brought in Thompson 'afore."

"Sure and I'd be pleased if you and your men would come in for a cup of tea now sheriff," I said as I dropped my hands to my side.

"Come on in men," he said loudly. "Jim and Hiram, you stay out on watch. I'll have someone bring you some tea."

"And you boys are welcome to cut you a hunk of that meat yonder and broil it over the fire if you care to," I said.

He walked into the light of the fire, a tall and lovely sight to me, for I knew our run was over. A smile on his face, he removed a leather glove to extend his hand to me.

"Philander, good to see you boy," he said as he extended his hand.

"Aye, and you're a sight to behold now yourself sheriff," I responded taking his hand in a strong grasp. "And what would you be doing out this time of night and away from home and all now?" I asked.

"Thompson," he responded. "He and his men killed my guard and escaped, and on the eve of their hanging as well."

"Aye," I responded knowingly as I retook my seat by the fire. "We've had dealings with him recently, and we're lucky to still be alive now."

The men had gathered around the fire, many with sharpened sticks with pierced hunks of the Buffalo meat. Eight of them I counted, and none of them looked as if they were the kind to tangle with. Rugged and experienced and tired indeed they looked. One of them passed the sheriff a cup and he filled it with tea. It didn't take long for the large pot to empty and a man filled it again with water and placed it on the fire.

"You say you saw them Philander?" the sheriff finally asked.

"Aye and that we have sheriff. We've been hunting west of here and drying meat to supplement our stores for the winter now, and when I returned to our camp they had taken it over. Brody there was captured, Bill and Melvin Long were holding him. When I entered the camp, Bill pulled down on me and then the lights went out. I awoke some time later with Blake Thompson setting over me. He told me how he was going to have his revenge on me for turning them in and then the lights went out again," I told him.

"The next time I awoke they were all asleep. I worked on the ropes that bound me now until the knots came loose, crept around until I got to Brody there and untied him, and then we led them on a marry chase indeed."

"You done all that?" one of the men standing around the fire said.

"Aye, and more too," Brody put in. "We ran most of the night and about dawn Phil here decided to go back and get his gear."

"And a sight he was now, his head and neck all bloody from the blow of a rifle barrel, no shoes and no coat. He tells me to stay put and he'll return with the stock and the gear now. Aye, and he's a rounder with the wit this one is now, for he figured that they would ware out their horses trailing us, and Thompson's rage would leave the camp unguarded." Brody stopped speaking for a moment, and I could not tell whether it was for the suspense to build amongst the men he was talking to, or if he really wanted another drink of the tea in his cup.

"Well," one of the men said.

"Aye," Brody continued, a smile on his face. "We made it back to camp, set in the brush to look things over, and then Philander just stood and walked right in. We packed our gear and pushed these last hours until you found us camped here on this very spot now," he said.

The sheriff looked a bit puzzled. "And what caused you to think it safe to enter the camp lad."

I started to clear my throat to speak, and Brody beat me to it.

"Sure and this is the best part now. Phil here had shot a Buffalo before he came back to camp. The meat was packed on the horses when he arrived, and the

Long boys dumped it all on the hide in the middle of the camp now. Phil here had heard a big cat prowling around the camp when he was working with the ropes that bound him don't you know, and when we got back to the camp he saw where that cat had returned and pulled off a piece of that meat."

"So?" one of the men asked, "why would he think the camp safe then?"

"Cougar's don't like the man smell. He stalked our camp for two nights trying for a free meal now. If he entered the camp, it was only because the man smell was gone don't you know," Brody said proudly.

"Man, that there's slicker than snot on a doorknob," a rough looking deputy said. "Took some guts to escape Thompson and injun out'a camp like that, and even more to go back unarmed and all."

"Sure and it wasn't bravery at all now," I said. "I was scared to death that he would kill us both. It wasn't hard to figure that a rawhide outfit like his would leave the camp unguarded and all, and I needed my stock and my gear now. My future and the future of my wife depends on this stock,"

The rough looking deputy saw the logic in my words and shook his head, satisfied with my response, although I believe it disappointed Brody some for he had them going now.

"You reckon they're after you Philander," the sheriff asked.

"Sure and if the night follows the day, they'll be on our trail now. Thompson is a vengeful man, and wicked to the core," I responded. "They'll be along as soon as they're horses are able now. Aye and of this I am sure."

The sheriff was deep in thought for a moment, and then asked; "How far behind do you reckon they are son?"

I thought for a moment before I responded.

"And if I am any judge of character now, I'd say they'll be here by dawn, and maybe a little before."

"Hmmm," the sheriff said as he rubbed his chin with his left hand. "Boys, are you up to helpin' us set a trap for them?"

"Aye, and that we are," Brody put in quickly.

"Sam, Ed, you boys set up a proper camp here. Unload that stock and hang the meat in the trees. Philander, would you and Brody make your pallets next to the fire? Keep it burning bright all night now and get some rest. We'll be out in the woods yonder waitin' for them," he continued.

▪▪

Chapter 26

Sam and Ed unpacked our gear making a proper camp of it, while we continued our discussion with the sheriff. His plan seemed a good one, but it would place Brody and I in a bit of danger now, but we had faced worse odds and recently.

They all ate and drank up three more pots of tea before the sheriff said this was enough, and disbursed the men strategically around the camp. He instructed each and every one of them as to what he wanted from them and how he wanted it done. When the men were stationed, he came back in to talk to us.

"Gentlemen, I regret having to ask this of you, but I truly appreciate your willingness," he started. "Blake Thompson and them Long boys must be captured, and you boys seem the logical bait."

"And it's nothing of us that you have asked now sheriff," I stated. "We're in much less danger now here with you and your men now than we would be alone, and Thompson would still be after us."

He reached over and placed a hand on my shoulder. "You should'a seen this gent when he walked back into town after Thompson nearly beat him to death Brody. Couldn't keep him in bed, he insisted on goin' after him and getting his bosses property back."

"Aye," Brody stated. "He's a fine lad now, and I'm proud that he married my daughter. I'll never have to worry over her safety as long as Phil is around now."

The sheriff shook his head knowingly, and then said, "you boys had best get set. It may be hours 'afore they come, or it could be minutes, so make yourselves as comfortable as possible. Be careful an' remember we're just out'a sight yonder, an' we'll have the drop on 'em as soon as they show."

"Sure and we'll be all right now sheriff, you do what you must and we'll be fine now," Brody replied.

We made our pallets next to the fire and then added wood to it, enough so it would burn for hours and brightly. It wasn't in my nature to have such a fire, for Patrick had always taught me to keep the fire small and unnoticeable as possible. To pick the spot for my fire under a leafy tree or an evergreen to dissipate the smoke, and to use only dry wood that would smoke little. The Cherokee that I had been raised with used these methods as well. Much of the time out here on the frontier, one was trained in ways of self preservation, and it became a way of life to them, to take the precautions that would bring no identification to your presence, no trail that was easily distinguishable.

I put the shotgun under the blanket with me when I lay down, for one never knew how events could turn, and I saw Brody do a similar thing.

I had no idea of how tired I was from the stress and the work of these past few days, for as soon as my head hit the ground I was fighting sleep. My eyes wanted to close in peaceful rest and my body ached from the running we'd done to escape Thompson and his men. Determined within myself to stay awake, it was just a moment before my body overruled my good senses and I drifted into the oblivion of sleep.

It seemed only a moment that my eyes had been closed when I heard the chinking of metal upon metal as a hammer being drawn back on a rifle, and snapped to full consciousness. My hand felt for the shotgun I had lain beside me under the blankets, and I was comforted to feel the cold steel of the barrel. I lay perfectly still now, for I did not want them to know I was awake, and through slits in my eyelids, I looked around without moving my head. The problem was that I was lying on my side and facing away from the direction I had heard the sound from. I was facing Brody Shaw who lay on the other side of the fire from me, and I could see that he too had been awakened by the sound.

He noticed that I was awake, and tried to direct me with his eyes a warning that someone was behind me. Aye and this was something that I already knew, but I appreciated his efforts of warning me anyway.

The fire was well down, so I knew immediately that we had slept for hours, and then I heard a light footfall on the soft earth, and then another. Someone was trying to sneak up on us without warning, and I could be sure that it would be Thompson and the Long boys.

"Hold where you are Thompson, and drop them guns," I heard a voice say firmly from the woods.

Grasping the shotgun and bringing it up with me, I came to a setting position. All three of them were there, and were turning to look into the woods.

"That you sheriff," Thompson said in a not too friendly tone.

"Me and a good sized posse Blake. Drop them guns now or we'll open fire on you."

Blake Thompson had insolence in his voice when he spoke again. His lip was curled on his demented and unshaved face as he responded; "you go right ahead now sheriff. We done been sentenced to be hung, an' I'd rather die from a bullet as a rope any day. Besides that, we done got us two hostages in here, an' if'n you don't want to get them killed, you'll back off and do it now."

When he finished speaking, I pulled back the hammers on that shotgun, and the chink of the metal from behind them was unnaturally loud in the quiet of the predawn morning. I could see Thompson's body cringe from the sound of it and he slowly turned around to look at us.

"Sure now Blake Thompson, and I would not say that you held hostages in this camp now," I said calmly.

I could hear the cocking of Brody's gun as I spoke and knew he too was prepared should they open things up on us.

"And if it's coffee that you have come for in this camp now Mr. Thompson, you'll pardon me while I get some on now," Brody said in almost a mocking tone.

Thompson stood stark still, his eyes burning with the evil that was behind them. This was not the way he had planned things, not at all, and he searched his mind desperately for a way out.

Melvin Long looked desperately from the woods and then toward us, then back to the woods again. Bill had clearly given up, dropping the muzzle of his rifle toward the ground and holding the rifle loosely in his right hand.

A stream of obscenities began to roll from the foul mouth of Blake Thompson, and for a moment I thought that he would fight us anyway. His hate was so intense and his eyes burned with the contempt he felt for all of us.

"I said drop it Blake. You haven't a chance and I got eight guns on you out here," the sheriff stated dogmatically.

His eyes came to my own and I could feel the intensity of the hate that swelled in him. He had come to seek his revenge upon me. Revenge for not dying when he had beaten and buried me. Revenge for not allowing him to keep the property that he had stolen from me. Revenge for putting him horse less and boot less to walk back into his camp humiliated in front of his men. Revenge for taking him and his men captive through a bluff that he now knew I could never fulfill, and revenge finally for collecting a reward while he was sentenced to be hung for all of the senseless crimes and killings he had committed over the past few years.

Aye and bitter the man was. Sure and if a look could have killed, they would have to bury me before first light now, for the hatred within him was an ugly thing that demanded to be fed. His lips opened in a snarl of anger and meanness, a mad look in his eyes that was plainly visible even in the dim light of early morning. He wanted to lift the rifle, wanted to take the life out of my body and he knew that he had but a little time left, for if he survived this morning he would surely hang before the week was out.

The sheriff walked into the clearing of the camp. He could read the thoughts going through Blake's mind and see the ugly look upon his face. Three more walked into the clearing and Bill dropped his rifle to the ground raising his hands shoulder high as they appeared.

Blake's stare continued, our eyes locked in a battle to see which one would brake. My shotgun was cocked and in my hands but I doubted I could use it. The air was cold, yet so thick with the intensity of the moment that you could cut it with a knife.

His look continued to harden and you could see the insanity as it was displayed on his face and in his mannerisms. The rifle started up slowly, ever so slightly and the sheriff stopped his advance into the clearing.

"Blake, now you drop that there gun and do it now," he said. "There ain't no use in it. You're caught for sure and there ain't no escape at all."

"What are you going to do sheriff?" Blake said with a snarl, his gaze still intently placed upon my eyes. "That there boy ain't a goin' to do nothin', and you can't hang me twice," he continued.

"You'll be dead 'afore you get your rifle up Blake, and you know it. I got mine trained right on the back of your head and you won't get a shot off. Now drop it I say," the sheriff said gruffly.

For the first time since our eyes locked did Blake's own eyes blink, and that blink seemed to break the spell that was cast upon him. Some of the determination seemed to leave him that moment, and I could not tell if it was from the words spoken from the sheriff, or if the insanity of the moment had seemed to pass before he could act.

A split second, that was all that had passed, but enough time for one of the deputies who was alertly looking on to rush Blake and grab the rifle muzzle. The wrestling did not last long, for Blake was a big and powerful man, and he quickly cast the man aside. He again started to lift the rifle when the butt of the sheriff's rifle cracked loudly against his head and Blake went down like a felled tree.

Melvin, who had been watching the scene intently, dropped his own rifle when he saw Blake go down. He stood uncomfortably for a moment until two deputies came to him; their rifle muzzle's pointed directly at his head. He dropped to his knees with a whimper likened to that of a small child's and raised his hands above his head.

Another deputy was quick to Blake Thompson, straddling him and tying his hands behind him with a pigging string, and suddenly the camp was full of men as they subdued the would be murderers. Sure and I was an open nerve by this time. I had looked death straight in the eye and even though able to defend myself, I once again found that it was not in me to shoot another human being. My nerves were rattled and the shakes had hit me like when one is too cold. Carefully now, I placed my thumb on the hammers of the shotgun and pulled the trigger to let them rest softly and un-cocked, for the nightmare seemed to be over again.

When they had Thompson and the Long brothers completely subdued and tied, they set them over to the side of the camp and a guard assigned with a double-barreled shotgun in his hands to watch them. Brody was up and fixing coffee, and another of the deputies had retrieved his pot and was about fixing coffee as well. I still set on the pallet that I had been sleeping in, and the sheriff came over and set on a log adjacent to me. Thompson was awake now and spouting a constant stream of obscenities toward the Long brothers as the guard protested his language and ordered him quiet.

"You know Philander, there's not a man among us who would've blamed you if you'd dropped a cap on Thompson, not one man," he said to me.

I looked over at the sheriff and responded, " Sure and I could not shoot him now sheriff. He's a vile and an evil man, but still a man, and I have not the power of life and death given to me. I thank God that it ended this way, for my wife would surly be a widow now if it had not."

"You mean you'd of just set there and let him kill you?" the deputy making coffee at the fire asked incredulously.

"Sure and different men were made with different capabilities now," Brody responded for me. "Some like the sheriff there, who've been empowered to uphold the laws of the land. Some as yourself, who are men that are good, and hard working, and men who would fight for the freedom the liberty and the safety of others. The gift that God has given you all differs now. Although it would bother you to take another's life to uphold these rights, you've been given the capability to uphold them. "

"Philander now, he's been made a little special as I see it. He's been called to save lives and to preach God's gospel to this lost world now," he continued. "His bravery is the same as your own now, but different as well, for he would not be able to reach men with the Lord's comfort if he had bloody hands. Aye, and I've known the lad his life long now, and if it had been one of you under the gun he'd have somehow found the means to keep you safe, whether it be to fight or to shoot. But for himself he would never fire."

Chapter 27

"Sam, Ed and Lute, I want you boys to bring in our stock. We'll catch a few hours of shut eye before we head back to Knoxville," the sheriff told them.

"Mike, you and Rudy find the horses Thompson and his men rode in on and bring 'em in."

The men got up and left the camp immediately. It was plain to see who was boss here, and the sheriff was a no nonsense type of man. Gentle and kind he was, but in command at all times.

"This is my last outing," he turned and said to me. "I'm turnin' in this badge as soon as I see to it that Thompson is hung proper. I've had enough of this rough life and I want a place of my own. Maybe find some nice widow to marry and raise some children and a few crops."

"Sure and there's nothing wrong with that now sheriff," I responded to him. "And do you have the place picked out now?"

"Yea, well, at least the area," he responded. "You got me to thinkin' after you left Knoxville boy. Got me thinkin' 'bout what I want out of life, and I saw little future wearing this here star. Got me to thinkin' on that there Bankhead country we talked 'bout. I've made up my mind and no one's going to talk me out'a it this time," he said.

"Bein' the law now, it weren't no bad life when I was younger, but I want more from life than what I've had up 'till now. My nerves ain't what they used to be, and there's a chance every day that I face it may be my last. I been thinkin' hard on it ever since we talked 'afore you left," he said. "You know just what you want out'a life son, and it's those things that I want too."

"Aye and the Bankhead it is now?" I asked. "I remember what you told me about it now. Sounds like a beautiful place. I've had it on my mind ever since you mentioned it to me."

"There's land there for the taking son. Rich land that will raise good crops and fine children," he continued. "It's a dream, and it's been mine for some time. I passed through there a few years ago when I had to go after a man who had skipped on me, and I've never forgotten the sight of it."

"Yup, that's what I'll do, and as soon as I see this scum taken care of."

The boys came back into camp leading their stock, and the sheriff threw the dregs from his cup into the fire, and stood.

"Lute and Rudy, you boys take the first watch on Thompson and them. Mike and Clem will relieve you in a few hours," he said as he took the roll from the back of his saddle. "Get some sleep the rest of you. It's goin' to be a long day, and I want to get them back to Knoxville before it's over."

"Sheriff," Brody stated to him. "Philander and I will take a turn at guard, and that will save your men some now."

"Say," he said turning toward him. "That's a good idea. If you won't mind too much, we'll just get us three or four hours an' then be on our way."

"Sure and it would be our pleasure now," I responded, and got up from the pallet where I had been seated. "And would you want us to wake you now, when a few hours have past I mean."

"That would be fine son," he responded. He looked over toward Thompson and quickly pointed to him with his head. "They give you any trouble, you wake me right away."

"And there's no trouble they'll be giving us now sheriff," Brody responded. "You get some rest, and we'll wake you when it's time."

I picked up my shotgun again and relieved the men on guard duty. They quickly went to the fire, one for coffee, and one to lay down on his pallet. Thompson gave me a mean look when I set down there, a look that would have chilled a braver man than I had ever been. Obscenities started pouring from his lips, cursing me and my family and all the men holding him.

'And if I were you sir," I finally told him, "I believe that I would start thinking of the next life now, and make my preparation before the hangman's noose is lain around my neck now. There's much to repent for, and a heavy load you'll be facing him with."

He looked at me then, a wicked look that showed the hate and resentment in the depths of his heart and his soul.

"I don't need no cowardly Bible thumper tellin' me what to do," and he cursed violently again. "You let my hands free and I'll show you what." Again he cursed and the sheriff came off his pallet toward him.

"Thompson, you may not make it back to Knoxville if'n you don't hush up," he told him angrily. "We could save the taxpayers some money and just take care of you here and now."

"Sure and let him have his say now sheriff," I said. "Maybe he'll hear something from his mouth that will shock him so badly he might think of his life now, and make a change before his sentence is carried out. I hate to see any man face the fate that awaits him if he does not repent."

The sheriff nodded his head and went to lay back down. Thompson quieted down in deep sullen thought. I hoped that he was reflecting on his ill-spent life, and upon the misery he had caused others over the years, but with him it was hard to tell. If he didn't change his life in the next few hours, he'd be lost eternally and no man should have that to look forward to.

I had no idea if Thompson believed in God, although I could not see any man not believe. The evidence of God's existence is all around us now. He's in the birds that sing, the trees themselves, in all of nature and in all of life. Who could not acknowledge God's existence? Who could deny his power and his excellence? It is impossible for one to stop for a moment and reflect on life, on nature, without seeing the evidence of what he has created. I wished no harm on any man, for the love of God was in my heart. And to think that a man so close to death without any hope, well, it just made me more eager to show his love all the more. Yet I knew there was no tolerance in Thompson for me. To him, I was the cause of his problems, his current predicament that would soon take his life. I also knew that there was nothing else I could say or do, that would be interpreted the right way by him.

I was lost in my thoughts for a long time before I came out of them, and then I noticed that many hours had past since the sheriff and his men had laid down for their sleep. Soon it would be time to awaken them, and soon it would be time for them to leave for Knoxville.

"Sure and we'd best fix some breakfast for them," I said to Brody. "If you will keep the guard then I will prepare them a meal."

"Aye lad," Brody responded.

It was mid morning when we awoke the party. There were biscuits and broiled meat and coffee, and the men soon made short work of the fare. When a couple of the men had finished eating, the sheriff ordered them to unbind Thompson and the Long boys hands so they could eat, posting a heavy guard over them. They behaved themselves and went for the food eagerly.

"Say you been thinkin' on that there Bankhead country Philander?" the sheriff asked me.

"Aye sheriff, it's been on my mind now," I responded. "Sure and it sounds a beautiful country now. A place where a man could build and a country that could support a family now."

"You ought to consider commin' down there with me boy. It's folk like you that can build this country," he said.

"And it will be a few years before I am able," I responded. "I have my papers, and some stock now, but my wife has a spell to go on her contract, and I intend to work it out for her."

"It'll still be there when you're ready," he said rising from his seat. "I'll be watchin' for you."

"We'll be there sheriff," I said rising with him.

"All right men," he said loudly. "Pack up, we're heading out."

Dozing in the sun and trying to regain our strength after the last few days Brody and I rested after they pulled out. It bothered me that Thompson and the Long brothers would be executed, but the law must stand. If one breaks the law, they must be prepared to pay for their crimes, and Thompson had much to pay for. I hoped that something that was said would make him stop and think, would drive him to his knee's before it was to late, and I prayed for all three of the men.

I desperately wanted to see Caroline, yet our business was not done. We had little meat; only half of what we needed and we could hardly go back until we had all that we came for. They were depending on us, and the worst of winter was still ahead of us.

That night was a cold one, but we slept well indeed. Both of us were dead tired and it was too little sleep we had over the past few days. It started snowing lightly before dawn and continued as we arose and made our breakfast.

"And we'd best be moving back to our original camp this day," Brody told me over a cup of tea. "We'll not find the game we need here."

"Aye," I responded. "We'll finish our meal and move back then. I'd like to be done with this business and be back home now."

"Sure and me too lad, me too," Brody responded. "I'm getting too old and too lazy to be spending my time like this now. It's been a hard trip so far, and I can't see where it will get any easier."

"Aye, and there's a bit of work that we must do yet," I responded. "A bit of work indeed."

We pulled out as soon as be had broken fast. The stock was eager to go, for there was little for them to graze on here, and the snow was making them nervous. Mules and horses are smarter than most people think. They have a sense for the weather, and are protective over their feed and all. Ours wanted their warm stable, the stacks of hay we had prepared for them, and the comforts of the other stock around them. They were eager to be moving, but it took an effort on our part to keep them heading the direction we needed to go. They wanted home, and would turn as soon as our guard was down.

It took us most of the day to get back to our original camp, and we found it before dark and had time to reset it before night fell.

"We'll go early," I told Brody before we bedded down. "The stock knows that we're in for it from the weather, and the game will be feeding early if the snow holds off. As cold as it is now, we can probably dress the meat out and not dry it until we get home. It sure won't ruin in this weather."

Brody's eyes lit up. "Aye lad, and that's an idea. We could take the meat home and cure it from the comfort of our family now. Sure and I like it lad, I like the idea indeed."

It was an hour before dawn when I awoke Brody. We had some tea warmed over the fire and some cold biscuits before we headed for the hunting grounds, the field that lay beyond the edge of the woods. It was still spitting snow lightly with sporadic periods of calm. The wind was picking up on occasion, and it would cut right through you with the cold.

We stayed together this time, edging on the field from the woods, and when first light appeared, we could see the forms of Buffalo in the field. A small herd of maybe a dozen, and not too far off. We edged the woods to gain position on the beast, and when we had our position, Brody suggested that I pick a target, and he would pick another. We would fire almost at the same time and take two of them. It would be enough meat to get us by until spring, and we could have it dressed out and be on our way before noon.

It was a good idea, and I picked a big cow, while Brody aimed down on the bull. Our fire was almost simultaneous, sounding as one shot rather than two, and we saw our targets go down. The rest of the herd brought their heads up from the ground where they were grazing, and slowly moved off, not liking the smell of blood.

"Aye and that's a fine shot lad, a fine shot indeed," Brody told me. "If you will get some of the stock, I will start with the dressing of the meat now."

"Aye Mr. Shaw," I responded lowering my rifle. "I'll be back as quickly as I can now."

Chapter 28

"There, there now lass," I told Caroline as she shivered in my arms. "Sure and it will be all right now darlin'. The sheriff has Thompson and the Long boys, and they'll not bother us again."

She sniffed and cried for a moment longer, clutching me tightly in her arms.

"Philander," she said sniffing," he had them once before and they escaped to come after you again. I couldn't bare it if something happened to you now," she sniffed again, her head tightly held against my chest. "What if they find a way to escape again? What if they come after you?"

"And they won't now darlin'," I said reassuringly. "The sheriff has a dozen hard men with him, and they'll not let him escape again now. This I am sure, and the hangman awaits them as soon as they get back to Knoxville."

She shuddered again in tears, her breath coming in short rasps, catching as she clutched me tightly. "I, I just love you Philander," she said between sobs. "I, I just don't want you to get hurt now."

"Sure and it's hurt I'll never be in your arms now Caroline," I said strongly. "I'd surly hate to think of what you would do to them if they came for me while you were there."

She laughed then, in the midst of her sobs. Her head came up off my chest and she looked me squarely in the eyes. Her cheeks were soaked from the tears, her eyes watering and her breath coming in short catches, yet there was a smile in her eye and a laugh in the midst of all of those tears. Her lips curled in a half smile and a half cry, and my heart almost burst with the love and pride that I had in her.

"I knew something was wrong Phil," she said seriously to me. "I could just feel it. And when you and Pa came back with the account of what you've been through, I knew my intuition was right."

"Aye, and it's a bonny lass that you are now darlin," I told her. "You're father and I can take care of ourselves now."

Again her head came to my chest, her grasp tightened around me. "And I knew all along that I should have gone with you now."

Her head came off of my chest again quickly, and her eyes met mine. "And you can take care of yourself is it?" she responded. "You would have just set there, a shotgun cocked and in your hands, and would have let him kill you now. That's what Pa said, you would have let him shoot you and never have done a thing to protect yourself from him."

"Caroline, you know it's not in me to kill another man," I responded.

"Not even in defense of your own life?" she responded.

"No, not for my life Caroline," I said. "If it had been another who was under the gun, I would have done something."

"But why not for yourself Philander?" she asked incredulously.

"Because I am the only one who knows about my own salvation now darlin'. That man, if I would have shot him, would surely have spent eternity in hell now," I responded. "I have the security of knowing that if this life ends, I will be in the arms of my God, where eternal peace and happiness awaits me."

"I understand that Phil," she said in a reasoning tone. "But the man is condemned to die in a few hours."

"Aye, that he is," I said. "But that few hours could mean the difference between heaven and hell for him."

She looked at me curiously for a moment, and then put her head back on my chest. Her sobbing had stopped, and her breath now was long and even.

"You're a man Philander," she said softly. "Quite a man that I married. You reasoned this out and would sacrifice your life to give a condemned man a little time to repent in." She sighed deeply. "Aye, and if you were otherwise, I wouldn't love you as I do now."

Bret Sullivan who had been setting off to the side of the room next to the fire then spoke. "Sure and I could not have picked a better man for my own son now."

"Here, here," Lem echoed.

"Aye, and you should have seen him now," Brody said. "Setting there as straight and tall as a pine tree, and not a hint of fear in his eyes now as he looked over the barrel of the rifle in Blake Thompson's hands. Sure and it would have made you proud to see him there, facing down a man that could take your life in just a heartbeat now."

"And it must have been a sight for sure," Lem responded.

"Aye, and to outsmart Thompson as he done," Brody continued. "Sneaking back into the camp after we had made a clean escape now, and just to retrieve our gear and the stock."

Caroline's head again came from my chest and she looked deeply into my eyes. "And why did you go back then? I told you when you got home from the first experience you had with Thompson that no property is worth giving your life over."

"Aye, and this property is now lass," I responded. "The stock is our future now, your future, and I'll not have your future stripped away from you."

"Philander," she said seriously. "My future is not in those beasts, or in any other animal. Don't you know that by now? My future is in you. You had no right jeopardizing my future for a few head of stock now. What do you think would happen to me if I were to loose you?"

"I don't care how rich or poor we will become, as long as we are together. That's what really matter's Philander. Why, I could be happy living in a shelter made of pine bows, like the one you built when you were snowed in."

I dropped my eyes from hers, feeling a bit ashamed. "Aye Caroline, and if I thought that there was a chance that they would have been there, I would not have gone back. I would never willingly have jeopardized your future, or our ability to be together now, except over killing another."

She again placed her head on my chest, "God help me, sure but I do love you Philander."

Mrs. Shaw came from the kitchen then with a fresh pot of coffee. "Come now, there's hot coffee and cold meat on the table. You men must be starved after your adventure."

"Aye and I'm for that now," Brody Shaw said as he arose from the overstuffed horsehide chair he was setting in. "It's been a while since I've had a descent meal."

"Sure and I like that now," I told him with a chuckle. "Next time we go hunting you can fix your own food."

Throwing a hand at me, he said; "Go on with you now. There's a difference in the food prepared over an open fire and that cooked on a stove."

"Sure and I know that now Brody," I responded. "And my mouth is watering at the thought of it now."

Caroline released her grasp on me and took my hand in hers, and we walked to the table to join the others. There was cold roast, with freshly baked bread and cheese to go along with the coffee, and some apple pies made by my own darling's gentle hands. One of the chores that Bret Sullivan had me do that first year after we arrived was to plant a grove of apple trees. They were necessary in this day, for during the long months of winter it was the only thing that kept us from getting the scurvy. We kept them in barrels in the barn, and under hay, and they were eaten fried and in pies and by themselves.

We ate without too much being said, and it was good to be home again. At least we had solved one problem; there would be enough meat to last until spring now. The second problem was the stock, and if we could support them all with the little stores of food we have.

When we finished eating, our conversation again started while we drank coffee around the table.

"And how do the fields look now Mr. Sullivan?" I asked. "Is there enough grass there to feed our herd?"

"Aye, if the snows are not too deep this year, we'll make out now, with the hay that you and Lem put up."

I sat down my cup on the table and Caroline was quick to fill it again. Coffee was one of the few luxuries that we had now, that and tea. We picked chicory in the late spring to mix with the coffee and make it last longer, and one soon developed a taste for the brew.

Caroline sat at my side as we ate and talked and she was continually touching either my arm or my hand. She had missed me I knew, and oh, how I had missed her. This was the first time we had been separated since our marriage and it was rough on us both. She was more than a wife to me now, she was my friend, my best friend, and I had learned to trust her judgement in all matters. She was always there to provide an encouraging statement when things looked the bleakest. Always there to sooth my hurts and to laugh in my successes. She never complained when things were hard on her, and was ever cheerful and always had a good word for someone. Aye, and woman she was now, more of a woman than I deserved.

We talked for a good bit about conditions, our stock and made plans for the marrow. Finally, Caroline tugged at my sleeve; "Philander, I want to go to our home," she said.

"Aye lass, and that you will do. Let me build a fire while you get your possessions together," I said and stood from the table.

When I went into the door of our cabin, it was cold. The house had been vacant for nearly a week now, and it was musty from being closed up. I left the door open as I built the fire, and opened the back door as well to allow the air to flush the house out. When the fire was going good, I put a pot on the stove for coffee or tea, whichever Caroline preferred this night, and then closed up the doors to allow the house to warm. I lighted the lamps and then walked back over to Bret Sullivan's house to retrieve Caroline.

The air was brisk and invigorating this evening. It was an hour or so before nightfall, and when I got Caroline and her things, we walked slowly down the path to the cabin. She wore a thick shall, one that held out the cold, and it seemed to adorn her beauty.

"Philander, its such a beautiful evening, let's walk a bit now and watch the sunset together," she suggested.

"Aye, and that was in my mind as well," I responded. "We'll drop your things by the cabin and then go."

We went to the cabin and I set her things by the door. We left then, walking hand in hand as the sun lowered in the eastern sky. It was cool, but the colors that God painted in the sky for our view were amazing. There were clouds in the eastern horizon, and the sky turned bright orange over them, changing almost to red near the clouds, and a deep purple behind them against the backdrop of the mountains. They turned even more brilliant as the sun lowered in the sky and we stopped our walking just to watch the spectacle. The cold could not penetrate our love, and I placed my arm around her and she snuggled against my side as we watched the scene wordlessly.

“Philander”

Aye and its moments such as these that will ever warm my heart as the years pass. The wordless moments that made us so close and bonded us to each other. No matter what may happen in the future, we always had this memory to cling to, to warm our hearts during the cold nights we may have to be apart.

It was the last twilight when we turned and walked back toward the cabin. The warmth of the fire washed over us as I opened the door, and was welcomed after spending such a long time out in the cold. Caroline went right to the kitchen and added tea to the water I had put on, taking it from the stove to allow it to brew. Tea was a warming drink on such a night as this, and one welcomed by us both.

We sat there until long up into the night talking, drinking our tea, and enjoying each other’s company. She snuggled close against me as I sat on the overstuffed couch I had made for our cabin. I placed my arm around her and she snuggled closer. Aye and it was pure heaven now, the two of us alone in our little home.

I awoke the next morning to the smell of biscuits and bacon. I was still on the couch and had slept there the night through, Caroline against me. She had risen early and was preparing me a good breakfast before the day started.

Frost covered the windows of the small cabin. Ice had formed on the inside of the windows from the sweat caused by the changing temperatures against the glass. It was still dark outside, but it was the time we normally arose. The days on the farm were long, and mostly filled with hard work.

We were to move the herd this day to another field owned by Mr. Sullivan. He had told Brody and I the night before that we should take the day off, but it wasn't in either of us to skirt the responsibilities of the work. Caroline and Ruby Shaw had been helping them while we were out on the hunt, and it was time they were relieved of this work. Women had their own things to do, and the work that should naturally fall on a man should be performed by one. No woman of mine was going to have to do work that she wasn't built to handle as long as I could help it, and tired or not, I would do my share and then some.

My children when they came would be taught so as well. To respect their sex and to perform the tasks they were built by God to endure. I would never stand for a child of mine to skirt responsibilities as I have seen other men allow to happen. They would be taught right and I'd see to that.

My own father left this world early for a man. I was just six when he expired, but the things he had taught me were deeply set into my being. At times, I could still hear his voice, feel his gentle strong hand on my shoulder, and dwell in his wisdom. A man he was, and not a rich man, nor one that the world would place much value in. But he was the kind of a man who had respect for women and for the laws of God. This influenced every fiber of my life. And a good lesson I had learned from him now, one that would endure all the days of my life.

"And it's awake you are now," Caroline said as she looked into my eyes from the fire. "And good morning to you darlin'," she said.

"Aye and it's a lovely sight that I see before me now. Such a way for all men to awake," I responded.

"Go on with you now," she said as she flushed a little red. The glow from the fire enhanced her beauty, and provided an air of mystery to her appearance.

“Philander”

Caroline poured a cup of the coffee from the pot on the stove, and brought it over to me. “Breakfast will be done in a minute now,” she said as she reached down and gave me a light kiss on the lips.

“Aye and its work we have to do this day, although I’d just as well spend my day right here watching you,” I responded.

She smiled, a lovely pert smile, and turned to finish preparing the meal. I arose from the sofa and stretched, the coffee cup in my right hand, and then moved to the kitchen table. There were only two rooms to the small cabin. The great room where we now were and a bedroom that was built off to the side. The kitchen and parlor were actually one room but we liked to call them by different names.

I set at the table as Caroline set a platter of biscuits in its middle. The bacon was crackling in the skillet on the stove. She had preserves set out on the table and I got a hot biscuit and split it, and then put some of the blackberry preserves on both halves.

“And Darlin’ now,” I said to Caroline. “Aye and its land that I want. Land with fields cleared by my own hands and a cabin of my own making. I want a herd now, one that we’ve built together and that will support us in our years, and our children when they come, and our grandchildren as well now.”

“There’s land to be had I’m told. Rich land with a fair climate and rich soil. I’m told that the game is rich and plentiful as well, and the water from the springs are clear and cold,” I continued.

Caroline stopped working at the stove and turned to me, her hands on her hips and a wooden spoon in one hand. And she looked lovely, so lovely that I could hardly believe my eyes.

"And is there something wrong with the land on which we are living now?" she asked.

"Aye and its good land too now Darlin' " I responded. "But it's not our land."

"This is Bret Sullivan's land and his life. He has family back in Ireland and the land will fall to them some day. As much as I love him, we must make our own lives now," I said to her.

"Sure and I know that's true Philander. And wherever you go will be my home now and forever," she said with a sweet smile on her lovely lips.

"Aye then, and when I've fulfilled your obligation to Bret Sullivan, and we've a small herd to support us, it's the to Bankhead in Alabama for us then," I responded.

And this is how life should be I thought to myself as I tasted the biscuit and the coffee. A man in his own house, the soft swish of a skirt, the smell of good food to fill his nostrils, the warmth of the fire from the stove. Aye and it's the simple things of life that can be the most contenting now.

THE END

"Philander"

■■

www.ingramcontent.com/pod-product-compliance
Lightning Source LLC
LaVergne TN
LVHW010541160826
845677LV00013B/2954

* 9 7 9 8 8 2 1 0 2 8 9 4 5 *